Lucan ~~smiled~~ **KT-119-691** ~~reached~~ **all the way to his beautiful fiery eyes. 'Let's get married.'**

'You can't be serious.'

'I'm completely serious. You need to save the inn. I need a wife.'

'But we've already… Lucan, we've been through this before.'

'No. It's not the same offer as before.'

Severina eyed him suspiciously. 'It's not?'

'No. I'm not offering a true marriage. This would be in name only. A business relationship between you and me to solve both our problems.'

'A business relationship? No…?'

'Business only, Severina. Without obligation to fulfil those embarrassingly intimate conjugal duties.'

Severina drew in a long breath.

'Unless you want to…'

CONQUERED AND SEDUCED

Lyn Randal

MILLS & BOON®

First published in Great Britain 2010
Harlequin Mills & Boon Limited,
Eton House, 18-24 Paradise Road, Richmond, Surrey TW9 1SR

© Lyn Randal 2010

ISBN: 978 0 263 21466 6

Harlequin Mills & Boon policy is to use papers that are natural, renewable and recyclable products and made from wood grown in sustainable forests. The logging and manufacturing process conform to the legal environmental regulations of the country of origin.

Printed and bound in Great Britain
by CPI Antony Rowe, Chippenham, Wiltshire

Lyn Randal grew up on a farm in rural Mississippi, where long, hot summers away from school and friends meant entertaining herself with books and her own imagination. Now, years later, she lives on a farm in rural Alabama, where long, hot summers mean entertaining herself with—you guessed it!—more books and an even bigger imagination. She considers herself rather fortunate that her husband, two children, two cats and one dog have all become quite accustomed to her strange writing habits, hardly noticing that she mutters odd lines of dialogue while doing household chores, or disappears to take over the computer for hours on end, sometimes even managing to avoid huge mountains of laundry in the process.

Lyn especially enjoys the research that goes into writing historical novels, and she loves hearing from her readers. Contact her by visiting her website: www.lynrandal.com

Novels by Lyn Randal:

WARRIOR OR WIFE
TEMPTED BY INNOCENCE

This book is dedicated to the readers
who wrote and asked for
Lucan and Severina's story—
I hope it exceeds all your hopes.

Chapter One

It was a fine day for a fight.

Cassia Severina's brow furrowed as her fist tightened around the hem of a skilfully woven *stola*.

A fine day for a fight, indeed, with its hint of spring and warm breezes that had drawn a crowd to this busy marketplace, and if the fierce-looking matron who held the other corner of the garment thought to intimidate her, then she, Cassia Severina, who'd faced far more formidable opponents in the Amphitheatre, who'd once killed two lionesses and a bear, who—

The sow-faced matron growled, 'Let go. It's mine. I saw it first.'

'No. I was first to lay hands on it. You were still halfway across the market when I took it up.'

The woman whose wares were flung across the table stepped forwards. 'It'll belong to whoever pays me the coin for it first. Rip it, and you'll lay out the full price!'

'Let go,' threatened the sow.

'I will *not*,' Severina said, equally adamant. 'I mean to have it. It's to be a wedding garment.'

Ariadne stepped forwards in a graceful motion and placed a gentle hand on Severina's fist. 'It's all right, mistress,' she murmured. 'There are other lovely gowns here. Any will suit.'

Severina hesitated. 'I want this one for you, Ariadne. The material is fine and the embroidery's exquisite. Besides, it's the only one with the extra length you need.'

Ariadne smiled and Severina was, as always, startled by the perfection of her slave girl's appearance. Ariadne was truly a beauty. And for her coming union with the man she loved, Ariadne *deserved* the loveliest *stola* in all of Rome.

'Leave the gown,' Ariadne murmured again, her slim fingers pulling at Severina's to loosen her grip. 'I'll be happy with any other, or even with those I already own.' Her eyes met those of her mistress, her expression soft and happy. 'Am I not soon to be wife to Orthrus? And is he not the most extraordinary of men?'

She lowered her voice. 'As much as I appreciate your kindness to me, mistress, I can't help but fear for that poor matron. She has no idea of your skill at combat or how easily she'd be overcome. It wouldn't be fair.'

The sow didn't quite hear the whispered exchange, but her eyes narrowed in approval when Severina reluctantly released the garment.

'Glad you've seen some sense, girl,' the heavy woman said with a smirk. 'I *did* see it first.'

Severina stared at her adversary, feeling the hot blood surge as it had done in the past when she'd stood, a fearless gladiatrix, before the crowds cheering in the Flavian Amphitheatre. Almost she could feel the hilt of a *gladius* against her palm. Almost she wished for the sharp, metallic clang of blade against blade.

Too bad those days were behind her.

Severina had little doubt that if the arrogant woman facing her across the swath of fabric could see her arrayed in battle gear, poised for combat, she'd not be so smug.

Severina spun around and moved away before she could act on her baser urges. She was, she reminded herself, no longer fighting in the Amphitheatre.

She owned her own business now. Her image was that of a cultured gentlewoman. She must consider her inn and the affluent clients who chose it for its quiet refinement.

It would hardly do for her to welcome them at the door nursing a black eye and bruised lip.

'Well done,' Ariadne said when they'd moved out of earshot. 'Your restraint shows what a well-bred lady you truly are.'

'Hardly. For long moments there, I wished heartily for a weapon in my hand.'

The younger woman laughed. 'Well, forget about it. Just look around, stretching before us—table after table of exotic things! Wares from Germania and Egypt and Britannia and Gaul...' Ariadne made a happy sound. 'Doesn't it fill you with wonder?'

In truth, it did. Every time Severina entered the three massive stone arches that marked the entrance to the marketplace, the wonder seized her.

'Some day I'll come here and buy whatever I want,' Ariadne said wistfully. 'Maybe I'll even buy *your* wedding garment, mistress.'

Severina's laughter was a little too bright. 'You'll probably earn your freedom long before I'll need one of those.'

'Then it really is over between you and Master Lucan?'

'It is.'

Ariadne sighed. 'That's too bad. He's a fine-looking man, and a kind one. I thought he loved you very much. When he bought Orthrus and Juvenal and me to serve you, he told us you were a special woman. And his eyes shone with such feeling, I knew he was in love with you.'

Severina looked away. If she thought too deeply about Lucan, her eyes might fill with tears. She'd been the one to end their relationship, but that didn't mean she didn't sometimes regret the loss. No wonder Ariadne didn't understand; sometimes she didn't, either.

She hadn't been prepared for a man like Lucan. As handsome as a god with golden skin, sun-streaked tawny hair and curiously slanted green-gold eyes, Lucan could walk past women and make them sigh. He'd certainly snatched her own breath away the moment she'd first seen him, swinging with sensual grace out of the door of the granary on Donatus's farm. His lean, muscular body had whispered promises that made her pulse beat faster. Those beautiful, perfectly shaped lips curved into a smile that showed white teeth and deepened the dimple in his left cheek. And his eyes had lit with hot, male interest.

She'd been captivated.

Normally wary of men, she'd been drawn to him. And Lucan had closed in, an experienced male hunter with the unerring ability to sense a woman's longing.

But he'd been gentle with her, and that was her undoing. Their time had been a dream of sweetness and yearning. With tenderness he had edged past her fears. With patience he had slipped through her defences. She loved him before she knew.

The dream ended when he had asked her to marry him. But sometimes, like now, the loss of him still hurt.

Ariadne didn't notice Severina's distress. 'It's too bad you couldn't work things out with Master Lucan,' the slave said. 'I'd give *anything* if you could find the same happiness I've found with Orthrus.'

A commotion captured their attention before Severina could reply. Juvenal was hurrying their way, red-faced, heedless of the annoyance he caused as shoppers were jostled and pushed aside before him. 'Mistress!' he called when he saw her. 'Hold up!'

He breathed hard by the time he reached her.

'Orthrus says you must come home right now,' he gasped, already pulling her towards the grand arches at the entrance. 'Come, mistress. Come *now*.'

'Why? What's wrong?'

'I don't know, but Orthrus said to hurry.'

Severina felt Ariadne's anxious glance.

'All right,' Severina said. 'Lead the way.'

The censor Marcus Terentius sipped fruited wine and smiled at Severina. 'Nice,' he said, nodding. 'Good wine. Glassware from… hmmm…Alexandria, I believe.' He traced a finger over the rim. 'You have excellent taste, for a woman.'

Severina's eyes narrowed.

He glanced around the room. 'Not just in wine, either. The furnishings here are equally tasteful. Silk pillows from the East. Fur blankets from…Britannia, maybe? Cedar from Lebanon. All luxurious, beautiful…and expensive.' He eyed her with grudging respect. 'You chose these things yourself?'

Severina had indeed shopped carefully to get the finest items for the least cost, but she wasn't impressed now with the man's flattery. He was here for something and her instincts screamed that she be wary.

'I made the purchases,' she said. 'Livius Lucan owns the inn, of course, but he allows me great liberty in the daily operation of it. I buy the furnishings. He pays for them.'

The censor's wheeze of laughter seemed out of place. 'Of course. And why not, when you have such a fine eye?'

There seemed more than a hint of sarcasm in the words. Severina searched his thin face. 'I do my best.'

'Your best hasn't been sufficient, however. Not in every respect.' The censor took a long, slow sip of his drink, taking obvious delight in drawing out the tension while she puzzled over his words.

He finally met her gaze. 'A person doing business in Rome should be aware of the laws pertinent to that business, wouldn't you say?'

'Of course.'

'Then you're aware that no young, unmarried woman such as yourself is allowed to possess property of her own. Despite your claims that you're not the owner of this establishment, there are others, quite a few others, who say differently. And it's odd, you know, that I can't find any paperwork to substantiate Livius Lucan's ownership.'

Severina fought to remain calm. 'Then you must look again. The information was quite properly submitted. Emperor Trajan gave the property to Senator Flavius Donatus in return for his loyal service in the Dacian war. And he—'

'Oh, I know that much. Those who requested the investigation into your ownership of this property didn't deny any of *that*.'

Somebody had requested an investigation of her? *Who?*

She lifted her chin. 'Then you should also know that Flavius Donatus sold it Livius Lucan. They served together in Dacia and are close friends.'

'This information is not what I was told. I was told *you* received the property from Flavius Donatus. That you're his wife's bosom friend and the senator gifted you with this property at his wife's request.'

Severina didn't answer.

'If Livius Lucan is indeed the owner, there's no record of it,' the censor went on. 'Further, all witnesses questioned so far have been amazingly consistent. They all say you're the owner and that Livius Lucan is nowhere to be seen.'

Lucan was nowhere to be seen because it hurt too much.

'Perhaps you should look through the records again,' she said cooly.

'My search was quite thorough.'

Severina didn't answer.

The censor set down his wine glass with a slight thump. 'I'll find out the truth, Cassia Severina. If you're breaking the law, I *will* see this property wrested from you. You'll be prosecuted to the fullest extent possible.'

'Life as a bureaucrat must have little entertainment, if this is all you do with your time.'

'It's a matter of principle.' His eyes narrowed sharply. 'I'm a proud Roman and good at my job. I uphold the laws and put the interests of her citizens first.'

Her *male* citizens, Severina thought.

'It angers me that women like you flout our laws. Their profits rightfully belong to fathers and husbands, to men of skill and intelligence.'

Those who don't spend it on drink and prostitutes.

'Women with money are too independent. They don't need marriage. They don't want husbands and children. They scorn the virtues that lend a woman worth.'

Severina put a hand to her lips to hold in the hot words. She was only too familiar with the ideal of womanhood that most Roman men cherished, someone fertile and docile. A meek child bride who allowed herself to be used hard in the marriage bed and birthed a child every year. One who admired her husband's accomplishments, but had few of her own.

'You're being very quiet,' the censor said with a smug expression. 'You've nothing to say in your defence?'

'Only what I said before. Livius Lucan owns this inn.'

'Then I hope, for your sake, that he'll be able to substantiate that claim. For if he cannot, I will make an example out of you.'

'Is that a threat?'

'It's a promise.' The censor's lips twisted cruelly. 'There'll be a hearing, of course, and witnesses will testify. If you're telling the truth, you've nothing to fear. But if you've lied, I will take you down.'

He glanced around the room. 'This really is a lovely place, you know. If you lose it, it won't be hard to find a man interested in it.'

Severina sucked in a hard breath. So *that* was the game? He'd confiscate her inn and sell it for his own gain?

'You're despicable.'

The man's laughter was not pleasant. 'You've no idea.'

It was a nightmare. Surely. Just a bad dream.

But it wasn't. The censor still stood before her, looking around the room as if he owned it already.

'The hearing's in three weeks,' he said, handing her a parchment bearing the details and a large, official-looking seal. 'Do be on time. I'm a busy man. I don't like to be kept waiting.'

Of course you wouldn't, you greasy fat cat, Severina thought as she watched him leave. *You want to crush as many poor, struggling women as you can before the day's done.*

She stood for a moment in rank confusion, unsure of her next move. Was this a simple misunderstanding or was there something—someone—far more insidious involved? Severina chewed her lip and considered. Had her past caught up with her? Was it time to leave Rome and move on?

Five years. She'd run for five years, but her old enemy hadn't caught her yet. She'd begun to feel safe, to build a new life, to imagine a settled existence.

True, she'd had a few twinges of doubt when Donatus had given her the inn. To work in the public made her uneasy, but she'd needed the income and owning a business of her own had been the fulfilment of her dreams.

The chances of being discovered had seemed small. She'd changed drastically from the thin, pale-faced girl she'd been when she'd left her past behind at age fifteen, and Rome was a vast city with a population of millions. But had her luck now played out? She couldn't be sure.

Severina pivoted sharply, calling for Ariadne. 'My *palla*,' she said in response to the younger woman's anxious question. 'And please find Orthrus to accompany me. I must go to Lucan.'

Chapter Two

'I should warn you,' Orthrus said, slanting his dark gaze towards Severina as they neared Lucan's apartment. 'Master Lucan's changed. He's not the same as before.'

Severina heard the slight censure in her slave's voice, but ignored it. Her slaves remained on good terms with Lucan, and Orthrus visited him often.

'How is he different?'

'You know how much his faith meant to him? How he'd become a leader among the Christians here in Rome? He's turned away from that now. He doesn't attend their meetings. He doesn't talk about their God. I don't think he even prays.'

Severina halted in the street. 'Lucan's no longer a Christian? But he was…'

'So faithful? Yes. But in losing you, he lost that, too.'

This news shook Severina. Lucan's faith had mattered to him. It had been the bedrock of his life even before they'd met. It had once rescued him from a dissolute life, leading him away from strong drink and women, leading him towards peace and purpose.

Lucan's Christian faith had mattered to her, too. Because of it, he'd cared for her differently from all the women of his past, building their love on a foundation of trust rather than desire.

But Lucan no longer believed? How could that be?

'You're blaming me, Orthrus?'

'No, mistress,' he said. 'I'm saying only that a lot of things changed for him after you left.'

Orthrus *did* blame her. She could see it in his eyes. Or perhaps her imagination played tricks, making her feel guilty—again.

She pushed the feeling aside. She didn't have time to consider all her reasons for ending the relationship with Lucan.

It hadn't been her fault that love had caught her by surprise. She'd never meant to lose herself to those fierce, sweet emotions. She shouldn't have ignored the risks, but she'd foolishly wanted to be happy for just a little while.

And Lucan had made her happy. As sunny in personality as in appearance, he found humour everywhere and made her laugh. He cherished her, listened to her, valued her opinions and forced her to question her distrust of strong men, teaching her by his example that true strength in a man was sometimes very gentle.

But he'd wanted to marry her. He loved her. He was serious about it. He'd never offered marriage to any other woman.

He meant to hold her for ever, and Severina had been forced to face reality. Anxiety choked her happiness. All her memories, all her old fears found life again.

She'd fought hard for her independence, but a husband would *own* her. In the eyes of society and the law, Lucan could demand her complete obedience, and that thought filled her with unreasonable panic.

There were other reasons, too. Reasons that clawed at her from the past, reminding her that she must be careful of men and especially those who valued religion too much. Even something as valuable as faith could be a weapon in the wrong hands.

'Master Lucan hasn't completely returned to his old ways,' Orthrus said. 'He's been seeing women socially, but I don't think he's been intimate with any of them. Maybe he'd like to, but…' Orthrus glanced at his mistress '…his heart's not ready and so it hasn't worked out.'

'Orthrus, please…' Severina began walking again, as if to lead Orthrus away from the topic. To think of Lucan still hurt. To think of him with other women hurt more.

'He hasn't been drinking much, though,' Orthrus said, quickly falling into pace beside her. 'He got drunk only once, the same night you…but that was understandable.'

'Let's not discuss this.'

Orthrus ignored her. 'Instead, he's working all the time. Like a madman. He sleeps little, doesn't eat well…he's driving himself into the ground.'

Severina looked away. 'Which apartment?' she asked, indicating the long row before them with a slight jerk of her head.

During her time with Lucan, he'd lived with their mutual friends Donatus and Lelia, but he'd moved out after Severina ended the relationship. She'd been relieved at the time, unwilling to see him. And now…?

'This way,' Orthrus said. 'Follow me.'

Nobody answered their repeated knocking at Lucan's door. Orthrus swore softly. They'd walked a long distance, but Lucan wasn't home.

'It's all right,' Severina said. 'We'll come back tomorrow.'

'Wait. Maybe I know where to find him. He's bought a run-down property nearby. He's probably there, directing the labourers who are restoring it.'

Severina's eyebrows rose. 'Lucan's doing that?'

Orthrus smiled. 'He's shown a talent for it. Come, I'll show you.'

He led Severina back the way they'd come, steering her left and through a maze of streets until they approached a dwelling that had once been a ramshackle building, its yard overgrown with weeds and covered with debris. Severina now gaped at the change in the property. In place of the ugly old building stood an attractive new one. The cluttered and weed-strewn lot had been replaced by a paved courtyard, complete with a fountain and lush plantings. Even now workmen were setting out trees and shrubs, sweating in the growing heat.

Her gaze immediately found the one labourer whose muscular back she recognised, and whose familiar lean hips and legs worked powerfully as he and another man struggled to lower a tree into a hole in the ground.

Lucan.

'More to the left,' she heard him say. 'Centre it, Maro. That's it. Now set it down. We'll let Catulus cover the root ball. He's got the shovel.'

Severina watched in abject fascination as Lucan straightened and grinned happily at Maro, his smile dazzling. And then, as if he sensed her presence like she'd sensed his, his eyes found her.

Their gazes locked.

For a moment, neither could move or speak. The entire universe narrowed to the short distance between them.

Lucan was the first to break the gaze. 'Excuse me,' he said to Maro, gesturing towards Orthrus and Severina. 'It looks like I'm being summoned away. Buteo will help you.'

The other man nodded. Lucan turned, hesitating almost imperceptibly before he came towards her.

Like one in a dream, she noticed that he wiped dirt from his large hands against his coarse tunic, that there was a faint rasp of his callused skin as he shook hands with Orthrus.

She marvelled that Lucan showed respect to the slave, but it was like him to do that. Just as he was one of the few Romans who'd be out here sweating alongside his hired labourers.

'Severina,' he said.

The one word, softly spoken, almost a sigh.

He clasped her shoulders in both hands before giving her the customary greeting of friendship, a light, quick kiss to first one cheek and then the other. 'Why have you come?'

She had trouble finding words with his heat so close, with his hand still firm on her shoulder, searing her skin even through the cloth of her *palla*. She was devastated by his nearness, by the masculine scent that enveloped her, by the startling golden light in his eyes and the shimmer of sunlight in the blond streaks of his shoulder-length, honey-coloured hair.

'I need you.' The words rushed out before she thought.

Amusement made him unbearably attractive. His grin flashed, deepening the dimple in his cheek. He pressed his palm to his chest, drawing her attention down to the lean, tanned fingers splayed against hard muscle and bone there. 'Be still, my heart,' he groaned, winking at Orthrus. 'For I can hardly assuage a lady's passion here in this public place.'

Severina's face flamed at Orthrus's laughter, low and undeniably male. '*That* is not my need,' she said in her haughtiest tone.

'My apologies, then,' Lucan said, sketching a slight bow. 'But a man can always hope, can't he?'

And there *was* hope in his gaze, flickering to life within the golden-flecked light.

No, no! Don't do this to me, Lucan. I can hardly bear it.

'A censor came to the inn this morning,' she said. 'He's investigating the ownership of the inn.'

Lucan shrugged. 'So? Let him investigate. *I* own the inn; he'll discover that soon enough.'

'But that's the problem. He says there's nothing to substantiate your claim. No paperwork to prove you're the titular owner, and…' she drew in a deep breath '…many witnesses who'll testify that I am. He's threatening to make an example of me.'

Lucan's eyes narrowed. 'Who is this censor? What's his name?'

'Marcus Terentius.'

'Not good.'

Orthrus frowned. 'Why?'

'He's formidable. The most corrupt official in all of Rome, known for ruthlessness, vicious to anyone who stands in his way.'

Severina began to fear. 'But we can defeat him, can't we, Lucan? You have the documentation to prove your legal claim to the inn, don't you?'

She breathed again when he nodded.

'It's back at my apartment.' Lucan glanced towards the men working behind him. 'Let me tell these others to break for lunch while we walk there together.'

Severina was afraid. Lucan knew it.

He studied her now as she walked between him and Orthrus, worry evident in her eyes and in the tight, anxious line of her body.

He'd long made a study of her. It was habitual, once his favoured pastime. Since his religious beliefs had denied him the intimacy of her body until marriage, he'd focused instead on knowing every other thing about her. He had memorised the lilt and cadence of her speech, the way sunlight brought fire to her chestnut hair, the sultry lowering of her dark eyelashes when desire coursed through her cool grey eyes.

Such intimacy with a woman had been a new experience for one who'd made a careless sport of sex in his pre-Christian days. Chastity had been the most demanding challenge of his lifetime, but with Severina, he'd deliberately chosen it. She would not be like the others.

Slowly he'd come to understand the reasons why the God of his faith demanded it. Sexual intimacy was fairly easy, but often deceptive. It was in the *waiting* that one began to truly know a lover, without the interference of carnal desire. It fostered deep emotional intimacy, the only foundation strong enough for the mating bond of a lifetime.

To his great sorrow, Lucan hadn't achieved that lifetime bond. But he'd learned Severina and knew her. Walking at her side now and feeling her tension, he was keenly aware of her fear and desperate to ease it.

'Thank you for your help,' she said quietly. 'I was worried you wouldn't be willing.'

He stopped in the street. He lifted his hand to cradle her jaw, holding her in place with a gentle, familiar touch. Surprise came into her eyes. Her lips parted; she struggled to breathe. She tried to look away, but Lucan held her gaze. He wondered if she could see in his expression how much he wanted to kiss her.

'Of course I'll help you,' he said in a low voice. 'The inn is our joint responsibility, one I willingly agreed to shoulder with you. I'll always be here if you need me.'

My love.

He almost added the words by habit. Were they still true? He wasn't sure. Pain and hurt had confused him. He was pleased that he'd caught the words in time, but he couldn't halt the surge of emotion that accompanied them.

There was a long moment of silence.

'Trust me,' he said, dropping the hand that ached to caress her skin. 'No matter what's passed between us, I'll never let that censor take the inn from you.'

She swallowed hard. 'Thank you. I do trust you, Lucan.'

'Do you?' His eyes searched her face. They both knew he spoke of more than the inn and the urgency of the moment. Confusion came into her eyes and in that confusion, Lucan understood how little their relationship had changed. There was still something deep within her that he didn't understand, something holding her back. Maybe Severina had come *to* him, but she hadn't come *for* him.

Angry at his own eager dreams, Lucan stepped away, putting distance between them before he made a fool of himself.

'Come,' he said. 'The sooner we find those documents, the sooner the censor's plans are overturned.'

They reached his apartment and went inside. Severina sat quietly beside Orthrus while Lucan searched through every record he owned. He was methodical to a fault; in his business dealings, he was unfailingly careful and organised, with everything catalogued neatly and in strict chronological order. The documentation for every other piece of property he owned, all were in their proper places, everything except for the one vital piece of documentation Severina needed. Only that one thing was missing.

Chapter Three

By the time Donatus and Lucan left the censor's office the following day, the sun was high and blazed hot. They talked little as they headed to a nearby *popina* for a cool drink and food.

'You want wine?' Donatus asked as they made their way towards the counter where delicious smells wafted from clay jars set into the stone surface. 'They have good wine here, laced with honey and herbs for a flavour different from most.'

Lucan rubbed tension from the back of his neck. 'No, not wine. Ask if they have beer. I need something more robust.'

Donatus nodded and Lucan moved away to find a table. It was well past mid-day so the place wasn't crowded. Even so, he hardly noticed the few people who came and went. His mind was restless and disturbed after the interview they'd just had with the censor.

Donatus returned with food and drink. He set it before Lucan and watched as his friend bit into his bread.

'What's this?' he asked. 'Not going to thank your god before you eat it?'

'No.'

'But you always do that.'

'I don't do it now.'

Donatus shrugged, hearing the low growl of warning in his friend's voice. 'All right. Whatever you say.'

He took up his own small circular loaf, pinched off a generous portion and dipped it into warm broth. 'That censor made you angry, didn't he?'

'Furious.'

'I thought for a moment there you might slam your fist into his face.'

'I considered that. Among other things.'

'Yes. As did I.'

'He's after her, Donatus. And we can't prove anything, not with both our copies of the transaction completely gone—stolen, no doubt. But why Severina? Why her inn of all those in this city?'

'He's a predator. He goes after properties owned by poor Romans who can't afford a legal defence, or foreigners, or women. But I thought he'd give up once we took up for her and he realised he'd have a fight on his hands.'

'I'd hoped so, too.'

'That part doesn't make sense. I know he's in good with the Emperor because he contributes much to Trajan's coffers. But I'm a senator with powerful friends, and I'm also privy to the Emperor. Trajan was the one who gave me the inn to begin with, and I can call witnesses who'll swear that I sold it to you. So why is Terentius pursuing Severina? I have a hard time believing he hates the thought of a successful woman so much.'

'Maybe it was the amount of the sale that made him suspicious. Two *sesterces*? Maybe you shouldn't have sold it to me for so little.'

'It was mine to sell for any amount I chose. The price was a fair one since you'd risked your life to help protect my wife and find my son.'

'Not to mention that the inn was a fairly sordid place when I took ownership. Don't forget that.'

Donatus grimaced. 'How could I? I got the dubious honour of painting over that disgusting mural on the atrium wall.'

Lucan laughed. 'Can you imagine if Lelia had seen that? Or Severina, who once told me her skin crawled just knowing the place had once been a brothel? She might have refused to take it at all if she'd seen that mural and its lurid contents. But wouldn't it be nice if all men were as well endowed as those in the paintings?'

'Yes, and all women as well.' Donatus laughed softly. He took another bite of his food. 'The place looks vastly different now.'

'Yes, it's stunning. Few inns can match it in either opulence or comfort. Severina has a rare gift.'

'No wonder the censor wants it.'

'I'm not totally convinced *he* wants it,' Lucan said quietly. 'But he knows the one who does. So maybe he's doing the dirty work in a way that won't be questioned for somebody who's paying him under the table. But who? It could be anybody.'

Both men were silent for a while, chewing their food and washing it down with beer. 'So what are we going to do?' Donatus said finally. 'The inn's not lost yet. We have some options. No good ones, but options none the less.'

Lucan drew in a deep breath.

He'd thought of one option that *was* a good one. One way that would absolutely work, without question, without challenge.

'I'll give you money,' Donatus said. 'There'll be lawyers to pay for, and they cost—'

'No.'

'Look, I know you've got your pride. But if you can buy off that greedy bastard to give Severina a chance at a decent future, then—'

'I don't need your money, Donatus. I have my own. And besides that, there's an even better way.'

Donatus eyed him suspiciously. 'You won't do something foolish, will you? The man does surely deserve a dire fate, but I don't want to see you in gaol because of garbage like him.'

Lucan pushed away his now-empty plate. 'I'm not going to gaol. I'm going to marry Severina.'

Donatus stared at Lucan incredulously for a moment, then laughed. 'That's perfect,' he said. 'The censor couldn't do anything to either of you then. Not one damned thing.'

'No.'

'But sweet gods above… How are you going to talk Severina into that?'

Lucan met his friend's half-amused, half-worried gaze. 'That's the part I haven't worked out yet.'

Donatus looked up at the ceiling, studying its dark beams for a moment with a curiously gentle smile on his lips. He shook his head as he took up his beer. 'Lucan, I've been your friend for a long time. I've ridden with you and wielded a sword with you and suffered through fevers with you. I'd probably even march through the land of the dead with you. But if you're truly serious about marrying Severina, then...' he gulped down a big swallow and set his goblet down with a thump '...this time, you're on your own.'

Lucan nodded, knowing he'd never faced a more serious challenge. He'd never been more likely to come out wounded and battered. But...*hell*. The risk would be worth it if he succeeded.

And Lucan fully intended to succeed.

The afternoon shadows were lengthening by the time Lucan made his way home through a city bustling with life. He wended through the vendors of the Forum Holitorium, only half-aware of the chaos all around him because of the chaos within.

He'd made a hasty decision and spoken it aloud to Donatus before he'd thought.

It seemed the right thing at the time; Lucan was rarely ambivalent. He'd learned in battle to follow his instincts to clear, decisive action. Warriors who were too careful often missed the advantage of the moment, and losing an advantage meant losing lives.

But Lucan was no longer on a battlefield where men with weapons faced others in a straightforward and fair fight.

Love was anything but a straightforward and fair fight, and he now questioned whether he'd been momentarily insane to consider marriage with Severina.

Did he still love her, then?

No. Her rejection had gone bone-deep.

His love had not been shallow or self-serving. At the time, he'd believed it strong enough to withstand a lifetime of challenges, changes, joys and griefs.

But deep hurt seared emotion like a heated brand seared nerves and flesh, and so it had been for him. He was no longer angry. He didn't want to retaliate or hurt Severina in return.

He'd like to say that he felt nothing, but that wasn't true. He felt sadness. A lingering, bittersweet melancholy, as when summer gave way to autumn or a brave adversary fell in battle.

Yes, he felt sadness. Even in his dreams, he sometimes still mourned Severina's loss.

Surprisingly, he'd dreamed of her often in recent weeks, usually following an evening in another woman's company. That had startled him, made him uneasy, pierced him with guilt.

Until he admitted the truth. His desire for Severina still lived, perhaps the one emotion untouched by everything painful between them.

The lust didn't actually surprise him. In another time, lust had been his most practised, most cherished sin.

To think of Severina without desire was impossible. He'd loved her and he'd wanted her. The two emotions had naturally gone together. He hadn't consummated the desire for reasons he deemed important at the time, but the urge had been intense just the same.

Now maybe love had died, but the lust remained, as strong and pure as ever, mocking him with what he'd never taken, tormenting him with questions he couldn't answer. What would it have been like to sheath himself in Severina? What was her most intimate smell…her taste? How would she have sounded at the pinnacle of passion, her cries mingling with his own rasping breath?

If he married her, he might yet know those answers. But lust by itself wasn't a good reason to marry someone.

As for himself, he was now thirty years old. It was time he settled down, became domestic, sired children. But even now he couldn't imagine himself in such a life with anyone but Severina.

He'd prefer that his wife love him, but marriage without love happened all the time to men of his class. His father, bearing down on him with all the authority of the *pater familias*, had mentioned several times the possibility of an arranged marriage in Lucan's near future.

By marrying Severina, perhaps he'd satisfy everyone. He'd make his parents happy with heirs to secure his family's holdings. He'd have a wife of his own choosing.

All afternoon long he waited for the cool of evening to descend on the bustling city, deep thoughts churning within him. At long length the disquiet abated; resignation took over.

He could do it.

He could take Severina's hand and pledge a lifetime of fidelity and kindness. He needed heirs. She needed her business. It was the only way.

But would she agree?

He'd have to put the facts plainly before her. Marriage was the most certain way to protect her claim. No man—not the censor, not even the Emperor himself—could debate Lucan's ownership then. Roman law made the husband responsible for all: wife, children, property. He'd be undisputed lord and master in the eyes of any jury who judged.

Lord and master.

Those words rang hollow, though, when he thought of Severina. She wasn't docile. She was stubborn and intelligent, no man's lapdog. She'd be led only if she chose to be led, and about that Lucan had no illusions.

Independence was important to her. She held on to it as to a lifeline. She'd refused to give it up even for love, and he'd never been sure why.

His first proposal of marriage had ended their relationship.

He still wondered at her reasons, and he still had no answers.

Too late now. The past was done, water under a bridge and gone on to the sea, but he'd learned from his mistakes.

He'd be far more careful with Severina this time around. He'd not make any outright assault on her cherished independence. He'd let the idea of marriage sink in slowly, a sneak-thief who captured her inch by inch.

And he'd be far more careful with his own heart. He'd wed her, but he'd not be twice the fool.

Chapter Four

He had three weeks. The date of the hearing had already been set. Only three weeks.

Lucan tried to avoid feeling urgency as he made his way through the darkness to Severina's inn, but that deadline sounded a subliminal, ominous note through his every thought.

Or maybe it was the wine. He'd had several large goblets. He wasn't drunk, but he was definitely feeling the effects of the alcohol.

Maybe he shouldn't be trying to think through his situation while in this unsteady state, but he'd decided on a plan of action. It was unusual, as daring as some of the cavalry manoeuvres for which he and Donatus had been known. Simple. Decisive. A punitive strike at the enemy censor while capturing the female prize so dearly held and closely guarded.

The thought of it made Lucan's pulse quicken. He liked a challenge. He thrived on momentum—life or death, winner takes all.

He could win the inn for Severina, and Severina for himself. He would exploit his strengths.

It wasn't vanity to acknowledge that he knew how to use his good looks and charm to woo her. It was the simple truth. Other men teased him about his skill with women. Some openly envied what Lucan merely accepted. To captivate females came easily to him. With little or no effort on his part, women of all ages watched him, smiled at him, gravitated towards him. Some immediately offered themselves. Those who didn't could usually be persuaded. His was a magnetic, almost bewitching power.

He'd not always used it responsibly, but he'd always used it well. And if he'd been selfish, well…he'd also left a satisfied woman behind when the tide of passion receded.

The only woman with whom he'd shown any noble restraint had been Severina. By the time he met her, his Christian faith had changed him. Severina would be his chosen mate for life, not a plaything for a season. But the result hadn't been satisfactory.

So now he'd resort to the tried and true. For him, it would be familiar ground; for Severina, it would be a surprise attack at night. Uncharted territory.

Lucan smiled into the darkness as he made his way through the almost-empty streets towards Severina's neighbourhood. She'd long ago given him his own key to the building, and now he wanted to talk to her.

He'd wake her if she slept. To find her groggy with sleep and unguarded might suit nicely, and he was surprisingly eager to begin the game. The thought stirred his blood. Even addled as he was, he didn't doubt he could hold his own.

What small sound alerted her, Severina wasn't sure. She'd been dozing lightly, caught in sleep somewhere between the anxieties of her day and the desperate need to rest. But the moment she awoke, she knew something was wrong.

The house was quiet in an odd, abnormal way, all except for the fountain in the colonnaded atrium. It sang softly as always, its stone-faced Grecian woman pouring water from an amphora in an eternal attempt to fill the larger pool.

Severina lay still, listening intently. Did she imagine stealthy movements? Deliberate footsteps? Should she scream and wake her slaves? Should she hide?

Her heart pounded. She seemed unable to breathe. In the void of air, she heard a noise. The bump of a leather shoe against a table leg, followed by muffled sound as the intruder bit back a curse.

A stranger was in her home, not far from her bedroom. Anger surged through her, accompanied by a strong impulse to act. It occurred to her that this intrusion might be related to the censor's visit. Somebody somewhere wanted this inn badly enough to frighten her. Or worse.

The moon was a mere sliver outside her window, giving scant light. It was difficult to see the objects in the room. She mentally scanned each wall, every corner, the tabletop on the other side of the room, the cupboard above it.

The cupboard. The household gods were inside it. Made of silver and bronze, they were heavy. She'd need something substantial to lay a man out cold, but any of those statuettes could do that, given her strength and training as a gladiatrix. She knew where to strike to kill.

She eased across the room, her bare feet twitching against the cold, smooth stone. The cupboard creaked open. It sounded loud, but so did her own heartbeat.

She had little time to choose and so was relieved when her hand closed around an idol of the perfect size and weight. She grabbed it and retreated soundlessly to a protected area behind the door to await the intruder.

As if summoned by her thoughts alone, the door to her bedroom pushed open and a man materialised, tall and muscular and garbed in a dark cloak.

He didn't see her. His attention was focused on the bed. In another moment, he'd move closer to it and realise that no one lay there. She hefted her weapon and rushed forwards to crush his skull.

The man caught movement from the corner of his eye, gave a shout and threw up one hand. Severina realised who the attacker was the moment the bronze statuette in her hand fell forwards.

She couldn't alter gravity, but she managed to twist, jerking her hand backwards enough to avoid killing Lucan. Or at least, she hoped she had.

He dropped hard and fast, blood spurting from the gash on his head. Her gorge rose in Severina's throat at the thought of what she'd done.

'Gods, be merciful,' she prayed. She looked down at the idol she held, feeling strangely betrayed. She tossed it to the bed with a shudder, then hurried to light a lamp with shaking hands. She knelt beside Lucan, biting her lip as she tested the rapidly swelling lump on his skull. She bent and put her ear to his face. He was breathing.

'What were you *doing*, sneaking into my bedroom like this?' she murmured. 'And you smell like wine! Are you *drunk*?'

The prone figure didn't respond. She jumped up and ran out, across the atrium and up a stairway to the small room Ariadne shared with the cook.

By the time she and Ariadne returned with cool compresses, Lucan was beginning to stir and to groan.

She ran to him in utter relief. 'Oh, Lucan. Oh, Lucan.' She kept saying the words, making little sense and not caring that she didn't.

'Severina,' he breathed. 'You *hit* me?'

'I thought you were an intruder.'

He made a sound somewhere between a laugh and a groan. 'Just help me to a bed, will you? My head hurts like hell.'

Ariadne caught Severina's hand. 'He mustn't go to sleep. I'm no physician, but I know that much. A head injury like this…he shouldn't sleep.'

'Don't go to sleep, Lucan,' Severina said. She helped him move to the bed.

He fell heavily on to the mattress. 'Only if you'll stay and talk to me.' His lids half-lowered, his gaze slid to the slave. 'None will accuse me of compromising your virtue, will they?'

'Of course not,' Ariadne said, tucking a pillow beneath his head. She didn't seem to question Lucan's presence in the room in the first place.

'Then stay, Severina. Please.'

Severina nodded, suddenly aware that she stood barefoot in her thin nightclothes in a dimly lit room, with Lucan's long body in the bed a few short feet away.

Ariadne placed the compress on Lucan's brow. He winced at the slight pressure.

'Don't get up for a while,' Ariadne ordered. 'Don't exert yourself, but don't go to sleep, either. I'll be back shortly with something for the pain.'

Lucan muttered assent. Severina stood rooted in place, suddenly unsure as Ariadne departed. Lucan lay against her pillows with his eyes closed, the wet compress plastered against his hair. He looked slightly pale, his hair damp, but otherwise he seemed strong and manly. Utterly attractive. She swallowed hard.

As if he sensed her indecision, he lifted a hand and beckoned her closer.

She stepped forwards. He opened his eyes. 'I need to talk to you,' he said. 'That's why I came. I couldn't sleep and hoped maybe you'd still be awake.'

'I was. That's how I heard you. You'd be a terrible thief, you know that? You bumped around and made enough noise to wake the dead.'

Lucan's low laughter warmed her. She realised suddenly how much she'd missed his wicked sense of humour.

'I'd have been quieter if I'd known what lay in wait for me. God help me, I keep forgetting you were a gladiatrix. What did you hit me with, anyway?'

She picked up the bronze statuette and handed it to him. He studied it, fingering the distinctive diadem on the head of the idol, with its full sun hung between two tall horns of a cow.

'Isis. I should've guessed. Protector of women. The irony does not escape me.'

His eyes found Severina's again. 'I didn't know you worshipped the Egyptian goddess.'

'I don't. She was already in the house when I took—I mean, when *you* took —possession of it.'

'This property is yours and you know it.'

'But one slip like that in front of the wrong person and I'll lose it for both of us, won't I?' Severina's voice held a sharp edge.

Lucan struggled to sit up. 'That's what I came to talk to you about.'

He settled himself into a comfortable position higher against the pillows. 'The hearing's in three weeks, but I think we can do something in the meantime to strengthen our case.'

He smiled, and the smile reached all the way to his beautiful, fiery eyes. 'Let's get married.'

'You can't be serious.'

'I'm completely serious. You need to save the inn. I need a wife before my father chooses one for me.'

'But we've already… Lucan, we've been through this before.'

'No. It's not the same offer as before.'

Severina eyed him suspiciously. 'It's not?'

'No. I'm not offering a true marriage. This would be in name only. A business relationship between you and me to solve both our problems.'

'A *business* relationship. No…?'

'Business only, Severina. Without obligation to fulfil those embarrassingly intimate conjugal duties.'

Severina drew in a long breath.

'Unless you want to,' he added hopefully.

Severina snorted and crossed her arms. Lucan grinned at her. That grin made her stomach flutter.

Dear gods. She could hardly control her physical response to him. She certainly shouldn't be considering marriage to him, even one made for convenience. But desperation did strange things to people, and she was desperate.

'In name only. And only for a short time?'

'Till divorce do us part.'

Severina's frown deepened. She wanted to trust Lucan, but there was much to consider. And here alone with him in a dimly lit room, with his tall body stretched out in her bed, was hardly the time or place to consider all the implications.

'I'll give you your freedom the minute you ask for it,' he said quietly. 'When you want to leave, I'll let go. But who can know the future? Maybe you'll be happy with me. Maybe you'll never ask to go. Maybe we'll fall in love and make a dozen pretty little babies.'

Without thinking, Severina uttered a word she'd not even heard since her days in gladiatorial training. It was something no gently bred woman should have said.

Lucan's laughter was genuine, and it held a quality that was almost sensual. Her body clenched at the sound, hot and burning. For a moment, Severina could only stare at him. He was washed in warm, golden lamplight that turned his tawny hair to a richer hue and softened the chiselled planes of his face. His pulse beat strong at the base of his neck and she suddenly wanted to feel its throb against her lips, mingling with the taste of his skin.

She knew in that moment there was no way she could marry him as a business arrangement, no way she could be near him and not want him as she wanted him now.

He didn't seem to notice that she couldn't breathe.

'Let me sweeten the pot a little more,' he said, his gaze becoming intent. 'You know those improvements you've been wanting to make to the inn?'

She nodded.

'Marry me, and I'll see them done. My wedding gift to you.'

'No.' Severina shook her head. 'No.'

'Why not? This is a business arrangement…with very agreeable terms.'

'It feels more like a bribe.'

Lucan spread his hands in supplication. 'Maybe it *is* a bribe, but I need a wife and I don't want anyone but you.'

'Lucan—'

'Severina, be logical. The censor can't take your inn if we're married. And those improvements would still be there for you long after I'm gone. Divorce me whenever you want, but keep the new and improved inn. You gain much and lose nothing. Think of that.'

Damn him. He'd known exactly which lure to dangle before her.

Silence stretched between them, tension mounting as each second ticked by.

Lucan stood and came to her. He raised a hand, but stopped just short of touching her as if he, too, sensed the power that would be unleashed with the contact. 'Severina…' he whispered into the hushed air.

'Don't touch me,' she murmured, licking dry lips. She closed her eyes against the hard pulse of her drumming blood.

'I can't help wanting you,' he whispered, his breath fanning warmth against the moisture her tongue had left on her lips. 'I always have. I still do.'

He waited for her to respond, to open her eyes and look at him, but she didn't dare. She knew what she'd see—Lucan, his eyes dark and intent, hunger in his lean, bronzed face. He would be as beautiful as sin, tempting her towards all the dark glories a man like him could give.

She did not look. Her eyes remained closed, but her other senses heightened, expanding to fill the void. She felt his heat as his body came nearer and heard the whisper of his clothing as he moved. He slid one large, callused hand underneath the fall of her hair to caress the back of her neck. She was aware of the pad of every individual fingertip against her sensitive nape, the elegant curve of his hand as he held her there with the lightest of pressures. His clean scent twined around her, an essence of sunshine and fresh air, of warm and sensual man.

And then his lips came down on hers, gently at first, as if he teased her with softness.

Her answering whimper spoke of hunger as her hands clutched and held in the folds of his cloak, and his kiss deepened to satisfy the subtle urging that he somehow understood.

His mouth was hot and flavoured with wine; Severina's heart hurt with yearning for the sweet familiarity of him. His tongue licked across the seam of her lips and she opened herself to him, rejoicing in his harsh groan as he took her and filled her with his taste.

It had been too long. She'd missed this, missed *him*. Her hands moved restlessly over his rough clothing, exulting in the feel of his muscled back beneath her palms, in the powerful strength of his arms and the silk of his tousled hair. His body was lean and hard and towered over her, enveloping her, heating her.

She was glad he'd missed her, too, glad for the powerful hands that moulded her buttocks and lifted her up and against him, glad for the startling friction of his hardened ridge against her core. She couldn't breathe beneath such an onslaught of sensation.

When she thought she might die in the void of air, his mouth left hers and moved lower, burning a path of wet fire through the hollows of her neck, behind her ear, across her collarbone. He moved slowly, tantalising, tempting, teasing her into gasps and moans.

She was restless now, and needy. Her breasts ached with an unfamiliar heaviness, the peaks hard and thrusting forwards, beseeching his touch, begging for his lips.

The silver *fibula* that held her *stola* at the shoulder dropped to the floor near her feet. She barely noted its fall; Lucan's hand closed around her breast and his mouth found the soft pink pebble of her bare nipple, shocking her with the intense, sweet pull into pleasure.

'Oh!' she gasped. 'Oh, Lucan!'

Her hands left his shoulders and speared into his hair, clenching in the softness, holding him fettered so he couldn't leave her and stop the laving that made her senseless, mindless, crazed with need.

'I'm here,' he murmured against her skin. 'I won't leave you.'

She whimpered and mewled, twisting in his arms until he lifted her and carried her the few feet to the bed. He placed her gently against the pillows and covered her with his weight and heat. The sheets were cool against her naked back, and Lucan's mouth was like flowing lava across the swell and heave of her bosom.

'You taste good,' he whispered. 'So sweet.' And he circled his tongue around her areola and drew her aching nipple into his mouth again.

She writhed beneath him, her hips jerking and thrusting, her pubis pulsing hard against his. Need ravaged her. It made her wild, eager, beside herself with desire, not caring if he thought her shameless.

She gloried in sheer physical splendour, dizzy with longing, unable to find reason in the deluge of wanting. Her limbs trembled; her womb clenched with strange urgency and wept for more. Because it was Lucan. Because she'd missed him so…

A sound at the door caused Lucan to jerk away from her, flinging himself partially upright with a growled oath. He threw the bed-clothes over Severina's exposed breasts and shook his head when, still befuddled and confused, she tried to rise.

Ariadne coughed again, delicately, and rapped on the door frame before tentatively peering inside. 'I brought an elixir for your pain, Master Lucan,' she said. 'It tastes awful, but works wonders for the headache. And here's wine to follow it.'

'Thank you,' Lucan said, his voice amazingly steady. 'Put it on the table. I'll get to it in a minute.'

Ariadne slipped in and hurriedly did as directed, studiously keeping her eyes away from Lucan and from Severina, who lay rigid in the bed. Lucan kept his back to the slave, not wanting to shock her with his arousal. He raked one hand through his hair and rubbed tension from the back of his neck.

He exhaled deeply when Ariadne pulled the door closed behind her.

Severina left the bed immediately, retrieving her silver *fibula* from the floor so she could cover her nakedness.

'Severina…' Lucan's voice was soft.

'No,' she said. 'Don't apologise. Just…forget it.'

She felt his eyes on her as she tried to pin her garment together with hands that were shaking.

'Here,' he said, taking the *fibula* from her, pushing her nervous hands aside. 'Let me do that.'

It made her angry that he could speak and act so calmly while she felt she'd been blown through a tempest. It made her angry that her breasts still tingled and that he seemed to know it, the back and side of his hands torturing her aching flesh as he pinned her garment into place. She made an exasperated sound and looked up to the ceiling until he finished.

She wasn't angry with Lucan; she was angry with herself. What had she been thinking, to let desire carry her away like that? If they hadn't been interrupted, she'd have given herself to him, and that would have been a disaster too deep for words.

If they hadn't been interrupted, Severina would have given herself to him, and that would have been a triumph too perfect for words.

As it was, Lucan wanted to grin and crow with success; his first assault had gone better than expected. She remembered now how hot the fire had once blazed between them. Her guard lowered long enough to taste her hungers and that was good, one more reason to wed him. Desire wasn't the best foundation for a lifetime, but it would do.

'Aren't you going to take your medicine?' she said, gesturing towards the table. 'Your head's probably hurting.'

Ah, the old distraction trick…too simple, something he'd encountered enough times to recognise it right away. He held back a smile.

'I'm hurting, all right. But my head's the least of my worries.'

She glanced down at his arousal and flushed scarlet. She worried her lower lip with her teeth, a nervous gesture that suddenly had him imagining a pleasingly wicked scenario.

'I didn't mean for that to happen,' she said, looking away. 'It can't happen again. Not if our marriage is to be for business only, without conjugal obligations.'

'Then you're agreeing to marry me?'

Her frown was fierce, but her hesitation was good news for him. At least she wasn't rejecting his proposal outright.

'I'm agreeing to think about it,' she said finally. 'I won't be rushed into anything so important.'

'I'm not rushing you. But the hearing's in three weeks.'

'I know that. You'll have an answer before then.'

'I'd rather have *you* before then.'

She glanced up sharply. She'd caught the undercurrent of sensual meaning, but he wouldn't recant.

'Can I trust you?' she asked suddenly, her eyes narrowing in appraisal. 'We're to have a business arrangement, but then you kiss me?'

'You did not protest.'

She had the grace to blush.

He moved closer and took her gently into his arms. 'I wish to understand you,' he said quietly. 'Tell me your fears, Severina, and I will fight them for you.'

He felt her slight shudder. 'You can't fight them, Lucan. I have to work them out for myself.'

He was silent for a moment, considering. 'At least let me fight the censor for you.'

'Of course. I can't do that without you.'

'Then trust me. Let me move into the inn and pretend I'm the owner. Let me escort you to the architect tomorrow so we can draft building plans. Let us do that much, only that much. You can decide the rest later.'

She turned her face up to him and for a moment he almost stopped breathing, struck by her beauty and the fear in her eyes. He wanted to touch her, to caress the soft skin of her cheek, to smooth the furrow from her brow, to kiss those gently parted lips…

'Do you really think doing those things will help?'

'We can't let Marcus Terentius take it without a fight.'

'No,' she said. 'We can't.'

Their gazes locked. Lucan's chest tightened painfully. And then because he couldn't help himself, he lowered his head and gave in to the temptation to kiss her again—lightly, sweetly, a mere whisper of desire.

'I'll return for you in the morning. We'll take your construction ideas to an architect friend of mine and get an estimate of the cost,' he said. 'You'll agree to that, won't you? No harm in knowing all you can before making a decision, right?'

He knew he had her there. Nobody admired ignorance.

'Yes, I'll do that much,' she said. 'It can't hurt.'

Lucan smiled and moved to the door. 'Sleep sweetly, Severina.'

But he knew, from the flare of desire in her eyes as he pulled away, that Severina would have as hard a time resting as he, and that her biggest fear would be for her heart, not her inn.

Chapter Five

When Severina awoke, the sun illuminated the sky outside her window with soft peach light. She rose and washed quickly, wincing at her stiffness as she shrugged into a tunic of pale blue linen. She'd slept little and was tired.

But the work of the inn wouldn't wait and it couldn't all be done by her few slaves, even if it was hard not to eye her mattress and cool sheets without regret. Her bed was comfortable, the most sumptuous in the inn. Its stout ebony frame was carved with Egyptian motifs that reminded her of her childhood.

Its mattress was thick and soft, but during the night she'd have sworn someone had replaced the cotton with boulders. She'd tossed for hours, unable to quiet the anxious whirl of thought. The few times her weariness had overcome her, she'd been jerked back to wakefulness by strange things. The memory of a man's green-gold eyes. The scent of Lucan on her pillow. And once, she thought she heard his laughter in another part of the house.

She'd foolishly thought herself prepared to meet him again. She'd bolstered herself for it. In a city as large as Rome, they must inevitably meet. They shared friends. They shopped the same markets and enjoyed the same entertainments. She'd always known the day would come when she'd feel someone's gaze and suddenly look up into dark-fringed, oddly slanted tiger eyes. She'd practised the smile, prepared the words. *Lucan. How nice to see you again. You're looking very well...*

But the moment had gone nothing like she'd planned.

And then he'd appeared in her bedroom and she'd smashed a bronze figurine into his skull. He'd proposed something outrageous and she'd almost agreed, just before she'd made a fool of herself because the old feelings had still been there. Oh, how they'd been there.

It seemed unreal now, like something out of a dream. But it wasn't. The statuette remained there on a nearby table, mute evidence that she hadn't imagined everything.

And besides that, one had to have actually *slept* in order to dream.

The only good thing about the restless night was that she'd decided on several improvements to the inn. She wasn't sure she could marry Lucan, but it wouldn't hurt to consider his proposition.

He'd told her to spare no expense, that his coffers were deep and he could afford anything she needed.

She wasn't so sure. She'd never seen evidence of his wealth. He'd been a *soldier*, and everyone knew that even experienced officers like Lucan didn't command a huge salary. He'd occasionally spoken of business ventures, but none had seemed particularly lucrative.

Rich men lived in grand houses, and Lucan lived simply.

Rich men had fine garb, and Lucan dressed in ordinary clothing, letting his fair looks serve him well enough.

A simple man without great wealth, but she hadn't cared. Mostly she'd admired his integrity and his golden male beauty, not sure she was worthy of him. She usually felt plain and mousy. Her chestnut hair tended to be unruly. Her eyes were grey. *Grey.* How boring.

And yet, Lucan had thought her beautiful and wanted her. Sometimes the look in his eyes had taken her breath. She'd known with surety that he kept his body tightly reined.

Now she was pleased that he had. Physical union with Lucan would have been too wonderful to forsake. She wouldn't have been able to walk away. But more than once she'd wondered—what would it have been like to be loved by a man like that?

Last night she'd come close to knowing.

For hours afterwards she'd thought of him and foolishly yearned for what almost happened between them. To make love with him would be foolish, even dangerous, if she hoped to remain free, but her body had wanted its way.

Lucan would return soon. She'd better forget that desire and concentrate on her inn instead.

Lucan told her to make construction plans, but she'd been modest in her choices because Lucan wasn't a rich man. He had no fine mansion, no slaves. He had no gilded litter, no rich clothing, no jewelled rings. No clients waited in his atrium every morning to shower him with praise as they would for a wealthy nobleman.

Perhaps he'd saved his soldier's pay. Maybe he'd hoarded his share of the rich spoils of Dacia. But it was likely that masculine pride forced him to claim more wealth than he truly possessed.

So she kept her construction plans to a minimum. She could use a larger kitchen, but moving out one wall would provide enough space. A larger dining area could be had by the same method, allowing for several more dining couches.

There were already ample bedrooms, thanks to the inn's dubious past as a brothel. And the bathing room across the courtyard was a marvel of design. Sumptuous with pristine Carrara marble, it contained one large heated pool and a smaller unheated one. Surrounding the pools were comfortable seats for conversing.

That bath and the toileting facility beside it that had actual running water were two of the main selling points of the property, and Severina was extremely proud of them. She might add more to them in the future, but she wouldn't do it now at Lucan's expense.

She wanted to give Orthrus and Ariadne some privacy, however. The slaves' quarters were small and uncomfortable. Ariadne currently shared a room with the cook, but after the wedding, she'd share Orthrus's bed. Orthrus, however, currently slept with young Juvenal. It wouldn't be proper for Juvenal and the cook to share a room, so Severina had been fretting about what to do.

She'd planned to sacrifice one of the bedrooms usually rented to paying guests. But the disadvantages of that were obvious, given her need to make a profit.

Unless she went along with Lucan's proposal.

During the long, wakeful night she'd realised that the flat roof of the kitchen could become the floor of a small apartment built above it. The space wouldn't be luxurious, but it would be private, a perfect little nest for lovers and a quaint but serviceable home when their babies began to come.

Severina had no doubt, given the way Orthrus looked at Ariadne and the way she looked at him in return, that babies wouldn't be long in coming. Severina had once seen that same look pass between Donatus and Lelia, and now they had two beautiful sons.

Severina wondered whether the addition could possibly be completed by Ariadne's wedding day. She'd like to surprise the couple with it, clean and comfortably furnished and ready for the special glories of their wedding night.

Severina could imagine their reactions already. Ariadne would squeal and then cry. Orthrus would stand dumbfounded, his huge, work-roughened hands clenching and unclenching in the struggle for words.

But his eyes would shine, and so would Ariadne's, and it was that thought that now made Severina eager for the coming day despite her lack of sleep.

She and Lucan would fight to save the inn. Maybe she'd even consider marriage to Lucan as a business arrangement—just long enough to foil the censor, and only because people she loved were depending on her.

Severina took a deep breath and straightened her shoulders, feeling a lot like the gladiatrix of old.

Chapter Six

Lucan's blood was singing. It always hummed through his veins hard and fast whenever he faced a challenge. It was one of the few things he'd liked about being a soldier. Maybe the *only* thing.

The exhilaration hadn't compensated for the long, weary days chasing down Rome's enemies on the back of a horse. It hadn't eased the unholy memories of watching men die. But the raw excitement that was the prelude to battle had at least given him something pleasant in the chaos.

Maybe that feeling was what he'd once sought in his youthful pursuit of women. Maybe that feeling, combined with lust, explained his desire to conquer.

But he'd been younger then and too foolish to understand that sleeping with the wives of senior officers wasn't worth the excitement.

For that stupidity he'd been sent to a legion in Antioch as a punitive measure. Donatus had finally unsnarled the situation and brought Lucan back to his own cavalry, but the experience had been a humbling one for Lucan.

And a good one, too. He'd learned about consequences. And while in Antioch, he'd met men unlike any he'd known before. He admired their integrity and ultimately followed them into their Christian faith.

With that decision, he abandoned the pursuit of sin, but found he missed its fine exhilaration—until he chanced upon something that provided a similar fascination.

He'd been hosting a visiting Christian missionary and somehow the conversation at the dinner table turned to matters of money. Lucan believed, as did many others who practised his faith, that riches were a corrupting influence. Was it not the rich who exploited his fellow believers? Did not the wealthy put his brothers into chains and kill them?

'It's not that simple,' the missionary had cautioned. 'Money is amoral, neither good nor evil. It only becomes one or the other in the hands of the one who possesses it.'

The corners of the older man's eyes crinkled as he smiled gently. 'Money can be put to good use. I couldn't continue my ministry, for example, if not for the generosity of those who work hard to have funds to spare for me.'

'But that's different,' Lucan protested. 'Of course we must share the good news we've received. Didn't the Lord say so?'

'He did. But he didn't leave behind the gold for us to use, did he?' The missionary chuckled. 'That becomes our task, Lucan. To go to the world, yes. But if we can't go ourselves, then to give to those who can. The more money is in our hands to give, the more people we send and the more people we serve. With money we help the poor, relieving the plight of widows and orphans. Wealth in the hands of a man strong enough to remain uncorrupted by it can be a powerful thing.'

Lucan pondered that. It was a seed planted in fertile soil. It gave him new purpose.

To make money became his goal. To do that, he would learn about business and become good at it. He would grow the wealth he had, and he would use it for good purposes. Money would be made to serve a worthy master.

For three years now he'd pursued that goal intently, discovering latent talents within himself. He lived frugally to have a surplus of funds. He invested that surplus in carefully researched properties. Gradually he'd expanded his assets.

Strangely, the world now seemed full of opportunities. There were many open doors for a man with eyes to see them. He had a knack for making money, a golden touch. Everything he did prospered. He believed it was due to the favour of his God, who understood his heart and knew his purpose. He enjoyed giving money to needy people and good causes.

Whatever the cause, Lucan found in business the excitement he craved. Negotiating terms gave him a creative outlet for his intelligence. It even helped curb his need for physical gratification, providing a safe valve for dispersing his strong male needs.

And it had made him wealthy, although Lucan hadn't needed the money for himself until now.

It seemed a rare event that today all three of his most intense passions converged—a woman for whom he cared, a business transaction that challenged his skills, and a moral imperative to right a wrong.

No wonder he could scarcely breathe.

Yet he worried, fearing disappointment again. Hadn't he already hurt enough?

Severina needed him right now. She'd do nearly anything to protect her dream. But when the crisis passed, she'd certainly divorce him. Her independence mattered more to her than anything. More than *he* mattered.

Lucan now paced Severina's peaceful, colonnaded atrium, agitated by these thoughts as he waited. He halted and took a deep breath, seeking calm as he took in all the small details of his surroundings.

He realised with pride that Severina had done much with the place. The fountain in the middle of the open courtyard sparkled with clear, clean water. Around it were lush plantings and elegant statuary. Comfortable silk cushions in muted, earthy tones of terra cotta and olive green softened stone benches and invited her guests to enjoy cool shade and the musical splash of water.

'You're here early.' Severina's voice startled him from his reverie. He looked up to see her standing uneasily in the door of the *triclinium*, watching him.

He ignored the sudden trip-hammer of his heart. It wasn't fair that she stood illuminated in sunshine—like a dream, like a goddess, surrounded by light.

So beautiful.

He'd known other lovely women, some with features more classically beautiful than hers. But there was an amazing *something* about Severina that had captured him from the start.

She was tall for a female, though not as tall as he. She was statuesque and moved with a serene elegance. Her neck and shoulders were graceful and seemed especially so when she wore her hair braided like a crown as she did this morning. With the sun firing those chestnut strands with burnished golds and reds, he could almost imagine it as a jewelled royal diadem.

Her arms were long and sleek, smoothly muscled. Her hands were nervous today. Without meaning to, he thought of her palms sliding over his body during the night, of how urgently she'd held him. He'd always known her calm exterior hid inner fire, but he'd been startled by the heat in her kisses. She'd been hungry… Could it be that she'd missed him?

Lucan forced himself away from that particular pain.

His eyes swept down her body, which was perfectly proportioned and slender, but with curves that made him ache. He envisioned the long legs beneath her tunic and then wished he had not. Those legs had parted beneath him last night; he'd understood the invitation and moved eagerly into the place, shuddering with pleasure at the heat and moisture he'd felt even through their clothing. Another few minutes and he'd have stripped them both bare and made love to her. He'd probably be regretting that now if he had.

Or would he?

He wondered if he'd gone about everything backwards. He'd once hoped for trust before intimacy, but maybe intimacy would have helped her find trust.

He didn't know. She made him so damned confused.

He pushed the disturbing thoughts aside and focused on Severina as she stood before him. The garment she wore today enhanced her beauty perfectly. Its deep indigo colour deepened the silvery charcoal of her eyes and made her skin as smooth as polished ivory.

She watched him, too.

Together they stood, quietly observant, each tasting the familiar essence of the other as wisps of desire curled around the room. It was he who finally broke the spell.

'I'm not early,' he said. 'You're late.'

Her lips curved. 'I'm never late.'

It was a nod to the familiar. They'd practised this as a ritual during their courtship.

The mood this morning was different, not quite playful, not completely trusting, and with the memory of the night's shared passion still twisting between them. But they found comfort in sharing this familiar ground.

'Call it whatever you will.' He smiled as he extended his hand for her to come to him. 'I forgive you, Severina.'

The words came out all wrong. Somehow, his offering of a light-hearted jest transfigured itself into a bitter imp so that anger and hurt from the past spilled out instead.

He hadn't expected that and neither had she. She sensed the darkness in his tone and glanced sharply up at him.

He hurried to smooth over his misstep. 'Be late any time you want,' he said, 'if only you'll arrive looking as beautiful as now.'

She'd already taken his arm, and because she was so near he could easily see the tumble of emotion in her eyes.

She was as confused as he.

She drew in a breath and forced a smile. 'Thank you,' she said simply.

It hurt him, the pain he glimpsed in her. For a moment he was tempted to feel compassion, but he resisted that dangerous pull. This time, he'd take care to protect his heart, even if she wed him. *Especially* if she wed him.

'I've sent word ahead,' he said, leading her towards the door. 'The architect will be waiting.'

He smiled and opened the way to the street. 'Apollodorus is a busy man and an exacting one. You'll need to be specific and detailed about proposed changes, but I promise you'll not be disappointed in his work. He's a genius, the best. He is the very best.'

She'd been surveying their surroundings, but turned in sudden concern. 'Can you…can we afford him?'

Lucan chuckled. 'Yes, we can.' He took her elbow and steered her down the street. 'Stop worrying and come along. We have an inn to save.'

For a moment she looked disturbed, but then she smiled.

And Lucan, caught by the shimmer of light in her silvery eyes, knew how it felt to take an arrow straight through the heart.

Rome was a vibrant city. Even at this early hour it teemed with the energy of its masses—slave women carrying clay vessels to and from the public water fountains, men on their way to the baths or to the homes of their patrons, young boys hawking their family's wares or, if they were of wealthier parents, making their way to school.

Severina was pleased that Lucan was in the mood to talk. She'd been afraid of awkwardness between them because of the passion they'd fallen into the night before.

But Lucan must have forgot it already. Instead, he talked about the man she was soon to meet. Apollodorus had built Emperor Trajan's war bridges and siegeworks during the Dacian War, and according to Lucan, the architect was a veritable genius—part-engineer, part-builder, part-sculptor, part-artist. His designs were masterworks of quality. When the war was done, he'd returned with the Emperor to Rome and was currently engaged in a huge design project, the awe-inspiring new forum that Trajan was building as his legacy and gift to the Roman people.

It helped that Lucan was in a talkative mood, because she certainly wasn't. All she could think about as he led her through the streets was the strength of the muscled arm beneath her fingertips, the earthy scent of man which surrounded her and…sex.

Maybe that was because of the erotic dream she'd had about Lucan during her turbulent night.

The more intimate details were somewhat sketchy now. But Lucan had loved her and she'd taken him eagerly, wanting him as he came into her warmth, hungry for the slide of his flesh into hers. His body was strong and warm, and he'd murmured gentle love words against her skin—

'Did you hear me, Severina?' Lucan's voice intruded. 'I asked you a question.'

'I'm sorry,' she stammered. 'I was…elsewhere.'

There was amusement in his gaze. 'I'm boring you.'

'No, no.' *Quite the opposite. I'm fascinated by the way you move, by the heat of your hand on the small of my back, by the gold fire in your eyes…*

Gods above—what was the matter with her? Her body was so alive that even the rub of her *stola* against her nipples was an almost unbearable stimulation.

'I was saying that we're a little early yet. Do you want something to eat?'

As if she could think about food right now, when her lower body tingled with unaccustomed heat.

'I'm not hungry,' she said. 'But if you are, then please…go ahead.'

His lips curved. What beautiful lips he had. She wanted to taste them with an almost fierce longing.

'Yes, I'm hungry,' he said. 'I'm always hungry.'

Was it her imagination that there seemed deeper meaning in that simple statement? Could he be thinking the same erotic thoughts as she?

Of course not.

And she'd better stop this. It was ridiculous to want Lucan. Even when they'd been on better terms, she'd known that kind of intimacy to be off limits for him.

But that was before Lucan had left his faith.

And now? She didn't know. She could hardly ask him if he'd given up his celibacy, if he was enjoying sensual pleasures again and if he might want to enjoy them with her…. She wasn't seriously thinking of doing *that*, was she?

She was.

Her entire body sang with desire. Her breasts were full and throbbing, her lower parts twitched every time he smiled. He smiled far too often.

Thankfully, Lucan didn't notice her unusual preoccupation with lust. His conversation was common and easy, his glances no deeper than usual. And when his hand accidentally grazed too far down her backside in guiding her through the restaurant door, he'd been unaffected by the touch.

She was the one with the problem.

Severina looked around the restaurant, breathed deeply of the food-scented air, and stubbornly willed her body into submission. Time to give herself a good scolding.

It was one thing to acknowledge that she was a normal female and had physical needs. It was another thing entirely to use Lucan to appease those hungers. That would open a door she'd already closed. It would renew old feelings, quicken old hurts. It would be the *wrong* thing to do.

But then Lucan returned with a round cake of bread and a plump sausage. A long, plump sausage cased in a moist, oily skin. She watched in utter fascination as his deft fingers took up a knife, opened a small slit in the round crust of bread and slowly, so slowly slid the meat into the opening. Her lips parted as he lifted the food to his mouth.

Lucan's low groan of satisfaction started the sharp throbbing in her body all over again. 'Oh, yes,' he said. 'That's *good* bread.'

She sucked in air and tried not to notice the ecstasy of his chewing and swallowing.

'Sure you're not hungry?' Lucan's voice held a touch of amusement.

She jerked back to reality. 'Hungry?' she repeated, the word sounding an odd, husky note. She cleared her throat. 'No, I'm not…really, I'm not.'

He gestured towards the bread-wrapped sausage he'd lowered from his mouth to his plate. 'Are you sure? You're staring at my food.'

'Oh, please. I am not.'

'You were. I swear you were.' His eyes seemed to dance with laughter. 'You looked at my food like you're starving, like you've never seen a sausage, like you've never before watched a man eat.'

Severina's face suffused with heat. She *had* been staring in just that way and she knew it. But not for the reasons he thought.

It was only that she'd dreamed that dream.

'I'll be happy to buy you something.' He gestured towards his plate. 'Do you like sausage, Severina? I'll buy one for you. Or I'll share mine.'

She smothered a groan beneath her fist. She shook her head, not trusting herself to speak.

'All right, I know what we'll do.' Lucan took up his knife, cut the big roll in half and handed the larger part to her.

'No. I do not want your sausage,' she said through tight lips.

Lucan's smile surprised her. Did he mock her?

'Ah, I remember now. You prefer sweet.' He lowered the food to the plate, slid the sausage from the bread and took up a small clay jar with a spoon. 'This citrus spread should be just the thing.'

Delicately, almost lovingly, Lucan widened the slit in the bread with his knife.

'The bread's good,' Lucan said as he put down his knife and scooped up a spoon full of the citrus spread. 'But sometimes it's a little dry without the right touch. Let me see if this helps.' He filled the crevice with a generous amount of the sticky spread and closed the two halves together.

Severina watched in helpless fascination as he lifted it to his lips. His tongue…oh, gods. His tongue came out to lick the spread at the edges of the slit.

Severina realised she held her breath.

Lucan's eyes closed in brief appreciation. 'Perfect,' he said, opening them again to fix his intense gaze on her. 'I love that sweet taste. It's good. And it's all yours if you want it.'

Severina let out her breath in an unsteady puff.

He didn't notice that as he handed her the food. 'I like sharing this with you again,' he said quietly, his gaze locking with hers.

Severina wondered if she were wrong to hear subtle meaning in the words. It seemed he didn't refer to the food at all.

Their gazes held. There was a long moment of silence.

'You should enjoy life more,' he said. 'There's much beauty to be found in this world, if one only looks for it.'

'And what beauty should I seek, Lucan?' she asked breathlessly. 'Where should I look?'

His smile was slow and sensual. His gold-tipped lashes lowered to shield his gaze. 'You can find pleasure nearly anywhere,' he said, his voice a deep, low rumble. 'Sometimes it's right in front of you. But you must be willing to let go of your fear. Trust that everything will work out.'

Let go of your fear. Trust.

The words hung in the air between them. She was sure they were speaking of more than this meal or this moment.

'What are you saying?' Her voice was a whisper. 'We can't go back…can we?'

His expression softened. One hand came up to gently caress her cheek. 'No. We can't go back. Nobody ever can. But there's always tomorrow.'

She closed her eyes against the sadness. 'Sometimes I wish it could have been different for us.'

He leaned closer. She tasted him in the air she breathed. 'Do you wish that, Severina? Then speak the word and make it so.'

She wanted to. She wanted him. And she might find such pleasure in this day, this moment…if pleasure were all they sought.

But today led to tomorrow, and that was the problem. Lucan had proposed marriage. It would save her from the censor, but—what if the censor wasn't the only enemy she faced?

She dared not explain to Lucan why she couldn't yet give him an answer, or why the choice of marriage could never be a simple yes or no, not for her, not until she knew all the facts.

Did the censor work alone, motivated by nothing more than his own greed? If so, Severina would marry Lucan and do it happily.

But if the censor were in league with her old enemy, marriage to Lucan would not solve her problem. It would only compound it, bringing him into danger along with her.

Until she knew, her future would be uncertain and so would his. If Anok Khai had found her, her worst fears would be realised. And her nightmare might easily become Lucan's, too.

'You're right, Lucan,' she said, a gladiatrix going for the quick thrust, the most merciful kill. 'We can't go back. Nobody ever can.'

Lucan studied her for a long moment, the warmth in his eyes growing colder with every passing second.

He pushed away from her. 'We should move along now. Apollodorus, for all he's been a good friend to me, is not always a patient man.'

Severina rose without speaking.

'Apollodorus isn't patient,' Lucan said as he took her hand and drew her towards the door. 'But I am, Severina.'

She looked up sharply.

'Remember that. I won't rest until I get what I want.'

'And what do you want, Lucan?'

His eyes were cool and determined when they met hers. 'You,' he said. 'I want you.'

Chapter Seven

'Don't look now, but we're being followed,' Lucan said as they shouldered their way through the crowded Forum.

She turned impulsively, and he jerked her back around. 'No! I said not to look around, and what's the first thing you do?'

He rolled his eyes. 'Let's do this *my* way, shall we? In a minute I'm going to stop and put my arms around you and kiss you. And despite my outstanding abilities as a lover, you'll have to keep your head together and attend to business.'

Severina's heart clenched with abrupt, intense longing. She was half-afraid he was teasing—and totally afraid he wasn't.

He chuckled at her startled expression. 'Relax, will you? I'm not trying to seduce you. While you're in my arms, you'll look over my shoulder and tell me whether you know the man who's following us. Tell me if you've ever seen him before.'

'But you have to *kiss* me?'

'Yes. I think maybe he's merely a hopeful suitor smitten by your beauty. If so, he'll turn aside when he sees our kiss. If he doesn't, then he's either damned persistent or up to no good.'

'Smitten by my beauty? You can't be serious.'

'Don't laugh. I'm entirely serious. I once followed a beautiful woman through Ostia for an entire afternoon: to the butcher's shop, the vegetable market, the clothing vendors. I was in serious pursuit, until a man built like a gladiator joined her for an afternoon at the theatre. The minute he kissed her, I abandoned all my romantic hopes.' Lucan sighed dramatically. 'A woeful tale, but true.'

'She must've been a great beauty.'

'She was. But then, so are you.'

Severina made a sound of disbelief.

'Do you find it so hard to believe that you're beautiful?'

Severina didn't answer.

'Trust me,' he said quietly. 'You hold a sensual allure that any normal man would desperately long to explore. It's almost mystical, Severina, and very compelling.' He shook his head. 'So I don't blame that man for following you. But I do need to make sure he's not dangerous.'

He pointed up the street. 'See that small alcove there? It's perfect. I'll push you back gently against that wall and I'll kiss you. You pretend to go along, but you'll really be looking behind me for a tall, angular man with black hair and a thick beard. Not many Romans wear a beard, so look for that. It'll make him easier to spot.'

'Look for a beard,' Severina repeated.

'Yes.' Lucan glanced at her almost sympathetically. 'We're almost there. Let me know when you're ready.'

Severina drew in her breath, knowing she'd never really be ready.

At her word, Lucan halted and pulled her into his embrace, carrying her backwards with him to the stone wall and into a passion that felt far more real to her than feigned. The moment his lean body made full contact with hers, Severina gasped. 'Lucan! Oh, no.'

'Look. Look for him!' His command was hard and breathy. Then his lips came down on hers.

Severina was suddenly drowning in sensation. Thought fled away beneath the primitive power of Lucan's kiss. His hands held her, clenched tightly in the folds of her cloak. His body held her, pressed hard and tightly against his own.

His breath seared her lips.

'The man, Severina! Look for him!' Lucan's low-voiced command forced her to open her eyes. She struggled for coherence, fought the flood of sensation, but Lucan's lips were warm as they returned to her mouth, tracing a light path across the sensitive edge of her lips, a whisper of touch, barely there, teasing, making her wish for more.

Her lips parted, and her breath sighed out between them. Her hands tightened on his shoulders, fingers pressing into his muscle in an unspoken request for something deeper, firmer, something—

'Look for that man,' Lucan growled.

She resented having to look when what she really wanted was Lucan's kiss. And his hands on her body. And his—

'I see him,' she said finally, her eyes closing languidly even as she spoke. She didn't want to think about anything now but the feel of Lucan's arms around her, his powerful body holding her firmly against the wall. He felt beautiful, so mighty and so strong. A warrior and a lover, as fully man as she was fully woman.

His lips touched on her chin, her cheek, her brow, so careful with her. She didn't want such reticence. She wanted his lips to come back to her mouth, so that her stomach fluttered hard and made her ache. She wanted to taste him, to burn in deep places. To grow weak and hot and…to feel utterly wonderful.

Lucan pulled back to look down into her face. 'Sweet hell and damnation, Severina. Don't *do* this to me.'

He took a ragged breath that shuddered all the way through her. She could feel his tension and his growing desire; their bodies were indecently close.

'Pay attention to that stranger. Do you know him? Have you ever seen him before?'

'No.'

'He's still there?'

She could barely open her eyes. Her lashes rose, fluttered, fell again. 'No.'

Relief rolled through Lucan. His muscles loosened a little as he drew in a long breath. His hands released her cloak. Severina sensed his intention to pull away and suddenly she didn't want that.

'Don't go.' The words were her own, but they sounded strange.

He went immediately still.

There was a moment when everything hung in the balance, when the world stopped and even time itself slowed.

His growl of surrender gave her a fierce and immediate satisfaction. His mouth came down hard on hers, tasting of strong, raw desire. This time, he gave her no light kiss. It did not flirt or tease at the edges of her mouth.

It took her breath and demanded even more. It was hot and hungry, possessing, devouring.

Severina's knees weakened and Lucan pushed her into the wall with the hard pressure of his body. The rough stones dug into her backside, but she welcomed the brutal sensation.

She was alive, gloriously alive, wanting this man, needing him, aware of his answering desire as his lips left her neck and burned down her throat. Aware that his lower body ground hard against her skirts, pulsing against her aching core, soothing and arousing at once. She wanted to part her legs and let him slip into place between them. She wanted more, and she wanted it harder, faster, hotter.

Lucan groaned as he pulled away. 'Not here. Not now. Not like this.'

He steadied her with one hand as his supporting weight was withdrawn, leaving her limp and miserable against the cold wall, her knees trembling, her loins moist and suffused with fire.

Lucan ran an agitated hand through his hair. 'I'm sorry. I didn't mean to do that.' His eyes seemed abnormally dark, a deep green forest burning with gold fire, the pupils wide.

Long moments passed. Severina fought for control.

'Don't apologise,' she said finally. 'It wasn't your fault. I wanted it, too, and that's what frightens me.'

'It frightens you?' He made a sound of exasperation. 'Forgive me, but you hardly seemed *frightened* just now.'

'Maybe it's myself I'm afraid of. Or maybe it's the way you make me feel. So hungry, so out of control. And it's always been that way with you, never with anybody else. Just you, because…because I *want* to yield to you.'

'Then do it.'

'I can't. It tears me inside to think of submitting to a man, any man, even you.' Severina brushed tears away with the heel of her hand. 'But then there's this…this passion between us. I've denied it, fought it, hated and loved it…and still it's there. And it will be there if we marry.'

'And that would be a bad thing?'

'I don't want to lose myself to you.'

His expression grew immediately wary. She could only guess at his thoughts.

He looked away, his jaw working in agitation. 'I won't hurt you,' he said after a long moment of silence. 'I'll take nothing from you but what you willingly give me.'

'But there's the problem, don't you see? I'd willingly give you everything. Then you'd control me, Lucan. You'd *own* me.'

Lucan exhaled deeply. 'Fear. Always fear. And you'll never tell me *why*, damn it. And in the meantime, you're missing so much. We're missing so much.'

'I'm sorry, Lucan. I don't mean to hurt you.'

'You say I would own you,' he went on, 'but that's not true. No person can ever truly own another. But bodies and minds and hearts…they can be *shared*, Severina, and there is joy in that. Not pain, as you fear.'

His face softened, becoming more gentle and sad. He lifted a hand to her face and stroked warm fingertips down the smooth line of her jaw. 'Don't fear my possession, for you would own me, too. We would take from one another. We would give to one another. Marriage would make us better and stronger, never less. Only more. Trust me.'

She closed her eyes against such sweet seduction.

'Who was the man who hurt you before?' he growled. 'I would willingly sheath my dagger in his heart for you. But, Severina… know that I am not he. All men are not the same. Whatever pain you experienced in the past, whatever this hurt that makes you fear and cleave to your freedom…I swear you'll never know it again. To my dying day I'll protect and cherish you. Do you believe me?'

His gaze captured hers and she saw how sincerely he meant the words. 'Yes,' she answered truthfully. 'I do believe you.'

But she still couldn't find enough faith to yield.

Neither could she explain. There was still much she didn't understand and until she did, she'd have to endure the deep hurt in Lucan's eyes.

Unless she moved on.

The thought had come before, but she'd avoided it. She couldn't avoid it now. It probably was time to pull up stakes and leave Rome, taking on a new identity in some other place.

Maybe she'd grown too complacent. Maybe in grasping for happiness, she'd exposed both herself and Lucan to danger.

Leaving would be the most drastic solution to the questions she couldn't yet answer, and it had disadvantages. She'd leave behind people and dreams she valued. She'd hurt Lucan—again.

But leaving had even more advantages. She'd leave behind her confusion. She'd never have to decide whether to divorce Lucan or yield to her desire for him, and she'd protect both of them from the secrets of her past.

It was time to leave.

Her eyes filled with tears at the thought. She blinked them away quickly, before Lucan could see.

He took her hand and raised it to his lips, brushing a warm kiss across her knuckles. 'We'll discuss this later. Now we must go. Apollodorus will be waiting.'

Apollodorus had sent word to Lucan that he'd be at the work site of the new forum being constructed for Emperor Trajan. Lucan was glad it wasn't far from where he and Severina had just enjoyed one of the most arousing sexual episodes of his life. Her passion amazed him, even though he'd done nothing more than kiss her.

Doubtless he'd regret not doing more while lying alone in his cold bed later. She'd almost been *willing*, and he'd probably been a fool to turn away from that. But like any lucky madman who gambled for high stakes, he'd gathered his hopes into one huge pile and staked everything on the still-undetermined roll of the dice.

Maybe he could have had one long afternoon of magnificent pleasure with Severina, but he'd rather have her pledge her life to him for ever.

Yet she had admitted that she desired him, and that made him feel like a king. At least passion hadn't died. It had always been strong between them, burning white-hot from almost the first moment he'd laid eyes on her outside the granary of Donatus's farm. He'd been faithfully serving the Christ at the time, but he'd still been carnal man enough to notice Severina's well-shaped feminine attributes. He'd decided on the spot that this woman would be different from the rest. The statuesque beauty with flame in her hair and eyes of cool grey would someday become his lover and his wife.

Such noble intentions hadn't always eased the lust they'd felt, but his sincere commitment to his faith, and Severina's sincere commitment to helping him honour that, had somehow kept them from free-falling into uncontrollable desire.

Today they'd both known the barrier of his faith was gone.

Anything might happen between them now, and Lucan couldn't fault either of them for wanting to assuage the hunger that had gnawed their bones for long months now.

But truthfully, he had to claim most of the guilt for this current episode of it. That wonderful seduction in the *popina* had been one of his finest moments, and he'd enjoyed every tender nuance of it. Severina had almost combusted on the spot. But she wasn't the only one feeling that sweet, familiar tension. His manly parts had throbbed the entire time.

Delicious. And he wasn't thinking of the food.

Now his passion had cooled. Colder reason had taken its place. He was gradually putting together all the pieces of Severina's complicated puzzle, piece by delicate piece, and beginning to touch the sensitive place of her core fears.

She didn't want to lose control. She was desperate to retain her independence. She feared losing herself, even to something as wonderful as desire.

But the most worrisome part, the elusive piece he did not yet have, was *why*. As badly as he wanted her body, he wanted one other thing more—her trust. Only when she shared her past with him would he feel like he'd won her. And that, he now realised, would take more time and patience.

He was, however, no novice in the art of siege warfare. He meant to discover those secrets, and he meant to wed her. The only thing that bothered him, as he led her up the long street towards the building site on the hill of the Quirinal, was the issue of time.

Whether she married him or whether she didn't, the censor's hearing was all that kept them together. That hearing would be held in three weeks, and Lucan wasn't sure three weeks would be long enough.

But he'd gone into battle with worse odds before.

Lucan was being too quiet. It worried Severina that he'd been so talkative before, but was withdrawn now.

She shouldn't have told him how she wanted him. Their relationship was confused enough already without throwing passion into the mixture.

It couldn't happen again, no matter that Lucan was as handsome as a god, no matter that he smelled like heaven and tasted like sin and knew how to touch her in ways that spiralled her into insanity.

She'd leave some day soon and until then, she must concentrate only on doing what she could to save the inn for Lucan's sake. She owed him that. But she'd give him nothing else—no kisses, no intimacy, nothing to deepen the pain when she left. That way, she'd always remember that she'd done him good and not harm.

Small comfort, that, but life could be unfair. She'd learned long ago to take what was given and not ask for more.

She was in the middle of these unhappy thoughts when she and Lucan reached the top of the hill. He turned to her, his eyes shining like spring leaves in the sunshine. 'Look at this, Severina. It's amazing, isn't it?'

It *was* amazing. It seemed the entirety of the Quirinal was alive with activity. In places even the hill itself was being moved, cut away to provide a level building site. Elsewhere foundations were being laid. Even without walls up, Severina could see that the buildings would be massive.

Sadness struck her. If she left Rome, she'd never see them completed. By the time they were finished, she'd be in Alexandria or Athens, Corinth or Crete.

That hurt, though she knew it would be the best way to protect her heart—and possibly, Lucan's life.

She looked at him now, standing like a god on the sunlit hill, his face alive with excitement. She'd remember him as he was at this moment, a vibrant man cloaked in careless grace. A light breeze caressed and lifted the sun-streaked gold of his hair, billowing through the dark brown, coarse fabric of his *paenula* to fling it out behind him. He looked like a captain at the helm of his ship, peering out towards dark waves with excitement and longing.

She'd imagine him this way for ever. It would give her peace to remember him so happy.

He turned and held out his hand, palm up, inviting her to step into the vision with him. 'Come,' he said, and his smile was beautiful. 'We'll find Apollodorus somewhere in the midst of all this work. He'll be wherever the problems are the most aggravating, I'm sure.'

'He's good at solving problems?'

Lucan chuckled. 'After he's spent all the time he wants screaming and swearing about them.'

'That sounds ominous. I bet the workers fear him.'

Lucan laughed. 'No. They *adore* him. He could ask them to jump off a cliff and they would. It sounds contradictory, and I guess it is. He's the most vexing man you'll ever meet, but he's also one of the kindest. He's bossy as hell, and arrogant, but he's an undisputed genius in his work. He'll quarry stone and lay brick and sweat like a slave, but he dreams with all the clarity and vision of a gifted artist. You'll understand better when you meet the old goat.'

'*The old goat?*'

Lucan laughed and pulled her forwards. 'You'll love him. Everyone does.'

Lucan's descriptive expression turned out to be an apt one when she and Lucan found Apollodorus the architect. Short and squat, with long, hairy arms and a dark-eyed, saturnine face topped off by a disorderly shock of iron-grey hair, Apollodorus stood in front of a sun-bleached and tattered army tent set up in the centre of the construction, issuing orders to a variety of subordinates.

When he noticed Lucan and Severina's approach, he waved away all the men surrounding him. 'Get on with your tasks, you bunch of worrisome insects,' he said in a gruff voice so loud it carried to Severina. 'Work on your own problems so I can spend some time with Livius Lucan. And I swear I'll flog the first one who pokes his head in my door. You hear me?'

Lucan was laughing as he reached the tent. He extended his hand, shook the one offered him and suddenly found himself embraced most enthusiastically.

'Apollodorus.' Lucan grinned as the other man thumped him rhythmically on the back. 'You've not changed a bit. Not one bit.'

The old fellow scowled up into Lucan's face. 'Aye, lad. I have. I'm not half as ornery as I used to be. I'm too damn soft in my old age.'

'Yes, I can see that.'

The older fellow grinned and turned his attention to Severina. 'And who might we have here? What a wondrous, lovely creature…'

'This is Cassia Severina, my…friend.'

Apollodorus didn't miss much. Severina saw interest and amusement flicker through his dark eyes and knew he'd noticed Lucan's slight hesitation.

Lucan drew her forwards. 'Severina, meet my old friend, Apollodorus. The most skilful architect in the entire empire.'

'Damn right.'

'Who's also an annoying burr under my saddle.'

'Damn right again.'

Severina laughed as the two men pretended to glare at one another.

But Apollodorus's sun-weathered face crinkled into a smile when he turned to Severina. 'A *friend*, Lucan? And such a *beautiful* friend…how delightful.' He took her extended hand and lifted it to his lips in a surprisingly elegant gesture. Even more surprising, the courtliness didn't seem out of place despite the man's coarse appearance. 'It's a pleasure to make your acquaintance, beautiful lady.'

The man was a master. Severina somehow knew it within minutes. His gaze was sharp and intelligent, but he made her feel welcome in spite of such deep scrutiny. There was an innate gentility to the man that defied her initial impression. As Lucan had predicted, she soon found herself drawn to Apollodorus and liking him.

'Lucan, you old bear-chaser,' Apollodorus said, returning his full attention to the younger man. 'How goes it with you? I've been meaning to get back to you about my inspection of those properties you wanted me to look at, but I haven't had a free moment these last few days.'

'You've done the inspection already?'

'Yes, and I quite agree with you. They're in fine shape and have excellent potential. With a few improvements, there could be a handsome profit at resale. I can't do the work right now, of course, but I'll send Omnesimus. Trajan's baths are nearly done, so I can pull him off that job. All that's lacking there now is the ornamentation, some finishing work, tiling…nothing he needs to oversee personally. He can be working on your place within a couple of days.'

'Yes, well…I appreciate that, Apollodorus, but I wonder if Omnesimus might take a look at another smaller project first.'

Apollodorus raised an eyebrow. 'Something else first? I thought you were so eager to reinvest your profit from the sale of that office building, that you wanted to move quickly and—'

'Those properties can wait a little longer. Severina needs the help more right now.'

A smile twitched at the corner of the older man's mouth. 'A project more important than making money for yourself, Lucan? Since when?'

He winked at Severina and suddenly she understood. This wiry little goat-man was definitely on her side. Though she wasn't sure of his full purpose, Apollodorus was giving her information about Lucan she could never have discovered otherwise. It was a game the old man seemed to be enjoying tremendously, while Lucan merely endured it with long-suffering patience.

'Ah, I understand,' Apollodorus said. 'Had I a woman this comely who likewise needed me to give place to her need, I'd surely move heaven and earth to accommodate her, too.' He grinned at Severina. 'Nice to know you matter more to him than gold, isn't it?'

'Apollodorus—'

'Not that Lucan *needs* more gold. He's really done very well for himself.'

'Apollodorus!'

'Added much wealth to his family's coffers, he has. And oh, his parents are so proud. No wonder they want him to come home and marry that sweet little girl they've chosen for him. They'll soon be needing an heir to inherit the family fortune.'

'Apollodorus! That's enough!'

'Is it, now?'

'Past enough, damn it. What do you think you're doing, anyway?'

Apollodorus grinned. 'I'm furthering your suit.'

'That may be true, but I don't need your help.'

Apollodorus shrugged. 'Fine, then. Inspect your own buildings in the future.'

'I don't need your help with *women*.'

Apollodorus laughed softly and scratched his head, leaving his hair in further disarray. 'True, true. You've never needed anyone's help there. Unless you count that time… Remember that whore who went to the commander and named you the father of her babe? You needed help then. The lying baggage.'

Lucan cleared his throat much too loudly.

Apollodorus turned to Severina. 'Lucan's always had a way with women.'

Severina smiled sweetly at the older man. 'Has he?'

'He has. The young fool, he used to boast that he'd bed a thousand women before his thirtieth birthday.'

Apollodorus looked to Lucan, his eyes gleaming mischief. 'And just how did that turn out, old boy? I never thought to ask. Did you meet your goal?'

'Perhaps if you hadn't thought to ask before, you certainly shouldn't think to ask it now.'

'But I've always wanted to know. Donatus swears you gave up trying before you'd quite made it. Says you've given up youthful follies.'

Lucan nodded.

'Lately I've heard Donatus has given up his reckless ways, too. Trajan told me the lad's married a fine-looking woman and sired two healthy sons. Ah, it's good to see you two settling down. There was a time I thought you both quite mad. Thought Donatus might kill himself in those suicidal cavalry charges against the Dacians. Now look at him. A proud papa and serving in the Senate. Imagine that.'

Apollodorus's eyes met Lucan's, gleaming with amusement. 'So when are you going to make a few golden-haired babies of your own? Legitimate ones, I mean.' Apollodorus chuckled.

Lucan crossed his arms over his chest. 'So many questions, Apollodorus. I begin to wonder why I enjoy our friendship.'

Apollodorus's laughter was anything but repentant. 'Because, like any good friend, I know when to dig into tender flesh to draw out the arrow's deadly point. A little pain can be a good thing in the long run, young Lucan.'

'Fine. You can be an army surgeon when you grow tired of the building trades. Now maybe you should stop playing matchmaker and tell me instead what is planned for this magnificent hill. It seems an enormous project.'

The request was like putting flame to a wick.

'Enormous? Of course it is,' Apollodorus said, turning to jerk hard at the flap of the tent behind him. 'Come inside and see.'

Lucan and Severina followed him inside. Though the interior was more dim than the intense glare outside, the tent's canvas panels were lit by enough sunlight that they could easily see that a table filled almost the entire space. Upon it sat a detailed model of the work in progress outside, all in diminutive but perfect scale.

'Good heavens,' Lucan said reverently as he stared at the complex of buildings laid out before him. 'No wonder you've no time for other things, Apollodorus. There are no words for this.' His eyes lifted to those of the architect. 'It's the most beautiful thing I've ever seen.'

Apollodorus acknowledged the praise with a humility Severina hadn't expected. Outside, he'd seemed rather odd—sometimes belligerent, sometimes playful, sometimes demanding.

But here in this room he seemed a quiet genius, an artist whose work would transcend his humanity for all the ages to come, a lowly man whose creative soul had been touched with divinity by the gods themselves.

'Emperor Trajan and I were young together.' Apollodorus spoke quietly, his gaze distant. 'We met in Syria when his father was governor there. Trajan later served that province himself as military tribune. We spent a lot of time together in that place, riding through the territory to inspect bridges and aqueducts and military installations. Our respect and admiration grew alongside our friendship. I stood up with him when he married Plotina. He drank himself into a stupor with me on the long night my wife gave birth to Omnesimus.'

His eyes lifted to Lucan's. 'But in all that time, did we ever feel ourselves destined for greatness? Could we have foreseen where all our service to Rome would lead us? In all truth, we could not and we did not. But, Lucan, it's often said that water will find its level, and so it has. Trajan has become Emperor. And I will use my talents to build for him a legacy that will long outlast our poor, feeble dust.'

He looked down at the model before him, his eyes suddenly glistening with tears. 'It's not a charge I take lightly.'

Lucan's voice had a surprisingly gruff quality. 'With this, your name will always be remembered. Men will come from far lands to survey these buildings. Apollodorus of Damascas, they'll name you in the books to be written of you. They'll call you the most gifted architectural mind in all of Rome.'

The architect smiled and laid a hand on Lucan's shoulder. 'Perhaps they will, my hopeful friend. But even if they don't, I'm proud of my service. I've lived my dream and enjoyed the journey. No man can ask for more than that.'

He tapped the open area in the centre of the model. 'Look here. In this plan, Rome shall have its largest forum yet.'

'Good,' Lucan said. 'The space is badly needed. Our city grows more crowded with each passing year.'

'The design seems complex at first, but look closer. You'll easily recognise the basic configuration.'

Lucan studied it for only a moment before he looked up and smiled. 'An army encampment. It's laid out like an army encampment. A more elaborate one, of course, but with the same basic structure.'

Apollodorus smiled. 'It is. Trajan's idea, not my own. You know, Lucan…one of the things a good architect must do is listen, really *listen*, to the needs of the one whose building he designs. He must hear not only what is said, but what is *meant*, so that his design might fulfil deep emotional needs. Am I making sense?'

'I think so.'

'Well, you were in Dacia, Lucan. You know how Trajan felt about the men who served there. The men who fell and died there.'

'He was and is a great commander of men. It was an honour to serve under such a man.'

'One of the things he keeps saying is that we're building this forum with the spoils of that war so it must be a source of pride for those men who served there and safely returned, and a memorial to those who did not. That it will be the only memorial most of those men will ever have.'

'A noble sentiment.'

'Yes. And soon far more than mere sentiment. Visitors will enter here…' Apollodorus tapped the spot '…coming from Augustus's Forum through this triumphal gate. It will be surmounted with a magnificently sculpted, six-horse chariot. This central open piazza here is quite large and will be flanked, here and here, by two large hemicycles. On three sides it will be surrounded by Corinthian porticoes, whose columns will be of green-and-white cipillino marble from Carystos. The entire open area will be paved in marble as well. An enormous statue of the Emperor on horseback will be here, in the very centre. You'll have to see its size to believe it. Nothing of the like has ever been done for any Emperor before.'

'Trajan deserves the honour. It's absolutely fitting that it will ornament this piazza, the most spacious and lovely place for any large gathering of Rome's citizens.'

'That's the intention. Now here, opposite the entrance and closing off the north-western side of the piazza, there will be the largest basilica ever constructed. Five aisles with huge apses at each end, highly decorated. The main nave will have a wonderful marble frieze of winged victories. The columns of the centre aisle will be large and of grey Egyptian granite. Side aisles will have smaller columns—again, of cipillino marble. The interior will be bright because the upper galleries will have clerestory windows and, of course, there'll be plenty of room for legal offices and shops.'

'Of course.'

'Beyond the basilica will be a column to celebrate the conquest. But, oh, what a column! At the base, a pedestal, elaborately sculpted to represent a pile of captured barbarian clothing and military equipment. Then a shaft, one hundred feet high, made of nineteen huge, hollow drums of Carrara marble. Each will weigh about thirty-two tons, so we'll be using the big cranes to erect it. Once it's in place, the sculptors will come in, the best in all the empire. Starting at the bottom, they're going to sculpt a long spiral frieze that will tell, in stone for all future generations to see, the story of what you men of Rome did in the Dacian campaigns. And at the top, a statue of the Emperor.'

Lucan's gaze met the older man's. 'Incredible.'

'It will be. Trajan's already got artists drawing the artwork for it, and he's making sure it's as authentic as it can possibly be. Everyone will be represented there, Lucan. The Emperor, of course, but also the archers, slingers, boatmen, cavalry…even the barbarians who fought alongside us. Many of the faces you'll recognise. Trajan's called on veterans to pose for the artists so the renditions can have a real, life-like quality. I could still have you and Donatus put into it if you want.'

'No, I can't spare the time. But I do long to see it when it's done.'

'As do I. I will tell you this…' The architect lowered his voice. 'Trajan gets emotional every time he speaks of it with me. He's embarrassed by such feeling, of course, but he's always powerfully overcome. You know…the memories. The friends we lost.'

Lucan nodded, saying nothing.

After a moment the architect pointed out two areas flanking the column. 'Here will be two libraries, one for Latin texts and another for Greek. And past the column, as time and money allow, we've plans for a temple some time in the future.'

Apollodorus directed Lucan and Severina's attention to a new area with a slight wave of his hand. 'Now over here, something to please the lady.' He smiled at Severina. 'A huge market area with a large, vaulted hall. Offices and shops. Lots and lots of shops.'

Severina lifted a hopeful eyebrow. '*Lots* of shops?'

Apollodorus laughed outright. 'About one hundred and fifty of them. You'll have shopping on four different levels, my dear, though we're having to cut away half the damn hillside to manage it.'

Lucan made a small sound of satisfaction. 'So that's what I was seeing out there. Terraces?' He shook his head in amazement. 'Apollodorus. I don't even know what to say. The planning. The engineering. The artistry… It sounds too beautiful to be true.'

'And yet, it *will* be true. Barring unforeseen problems, it will be a reality.'

As Severina watched the two men facing one another over the model on the table, she was suddenly overcome with sadness. She'd never stand with Lucan before the magnificent column with its marble frieze of the Dacian Wars, hearing from Lucan's lips his true memories inspired by its images. She'd never touch the cool, green marble of the Basilica's many columns, or enter the quiet, reverent atmosphere of the libraries. She'd never shop on four levels in one hundred and fifty shops.

She'd probably be gone in weeks, and that suddenly seemed a pain too great to bear.

'Where are you going?' Lucan asked as she gathered her *palla* around her shoulders and lifted the flap of the tent.

'I need a little fresh air. Don't worry or rush your visit on my account. I'll just stroll around the edges of the site and return in a little while.'

Lucan had already begun to move towards her. 'I'll go with you.'

'No,' she protested. 'It's not necessary.'

'It is,' Apollodorus said. 'Lucan's right. A construction site is no place for an unattended female. There are dangers of many kinds. You're certainly welcome to take a look around, but don't do it alone. Let Lucan accompany you.' He smiled broadly. 'That's what *friends* are for.'

Severina sighed as she linked her arm into the one Lucan offered, thinking how depressing it was that a girl couldn't even find a private place to have a good cry when she really needed one.

Chapter Eight

Something was wrong with Severina, but Lucan didn't know what. Was she ill? She seemed pale, but only when underneath the strange, filtered light inside the tent. Back outside in daylight, he was relieved to see that her colour looked normal.

She didn't seem weak, either. She paced the perimeter of the construction site with all the athleticism of a former gladiatrix until she'd worked up a fine sweat in the day's growing heat. It probably didn't help that she wore her *palla* wrapped around herself to protect her shoulders from sunburn and hinder the stares of the sweating men whose labour they watched. It only added another layer to capture heat.

When she was quite red-faced and uncomfortable, he finally convinced her to stop in the shade of one of the water wagons, arguing that it was a good vantage point to see all the work in progress.

'Sit here,' he said, pointing to a smooth, flat stone conveniently situated within the wagon's shadow. 'I'll get the water.'

She nodded and sat, adjusting the long skirts of her tunic modestly around her long legs.

'Lucan?' she said as he moved around the wagon towards the skins of water. 'Have your parents really chosen a wife for you?'

Now he knew what was wrong.

He debated how much to say. 'They have their intentions,' he said finally. 'I have mine. I will choose my own wife.'

'So Apollodorus was telling the truth?'

'Apollodorus talks too much. Ignore it.'

He brought a gourd dipper to her and waited while she drank from it. She handed it back, looking up at him.

She was beautiful. The sunlight had turned her grey eyes to cool, metallic silver. Her skin was flushed and her lips moist with the water she'd drunk. Small wisps of hair had escaped their braid and now, damp with sweat, curled sensuously against her skin.

It always surprised him, the desire for her that came in odd moments, that in the midst of talking or working at some small task together, he'd suddenly want her. His body would twitch to life and swell, and he'd be tempted to lay her down and make her his woman in the most physical and primitive way of all.

'If your father wants you to marry, Lucan, you may have no choice. He's the *pater familias*. You must do as he decides.'

'My father's ageing. He wants grandchildren. But he understands that I'm a man full grown, so he's allowing me some time to find a woman on my own.'

'How much time?'

'Enough. Don't worry about it.'

Severina looked down at her sandalled feet and wiped an imaginary blade of grass from her toe. 'Yet he has a bride chosen for you if you don't produce your own?'

Lucan's jaw tightened. 'Yes.'

'You've seen her?'

'Yes.'

'She is…pretty?'

Lucan's breath hissed out. 'She's a child, Severina, more youthful even than the young sister of Donatus. Imagine Druscilla with freckles and no breasts and you'll have a pretty good idea of how young this girl is.'

He rubbed tension from the back of his neck. 'I could see my younger cousins marrying her, maybe. But me? I hardly think so.'

'Druscilla's changed a lot in the last two years. If it's been a while since you've seen this girl, it's possible she's—'

'She's not the one for me,' Lucan said. 'And let's leave it at that, shall we?'

Severina's eyes were clear and solemn. 'I want you to be happy.'

'I plan to be. That's why I asked you to marry me.'

'We'll have a business arrangement.'

'Perhaps we will not.' He met her gaze. 'Perhaps you'll be so content with me that it will become a true marriage. Perhaps you'll be so happy you'll never ask for a divorce.'

She drew in a breath. 'I've no right to expect such happiness.'

'Why? Because you were the one who walked away before?'

She shrugged.

'The past no longer matters. The place at my side remains vacant and waiting.'

For the time being. He didn't have to add the words. They were simply there, understood, tainting the air between them because of his father's hopes and a freckle-faced child bride.

Lucan knelt beside Severina and slid one large, warm hand to her shoulder, caressing lightly with his fingertips. He leaned closer, his eyes growing dark, longing evident within them.

Severina's gaze focused on his lips, perfectly shaped and beautiful. He was going to kiss her, and she wanted him to kiss her, but…hadn't she decided there'd be nothing between them to cause pain later? Was she so very weak?

She pulled away and jumped to her feet, hearing frustration in Lucan's sharp exhalation. She stood in uncertainty, dancing lightly on the balls of her feet, and gave him the first excuse that came to her. 'I have to go to the bathroom.'

Lucan still rested on his haunches, both forearms across his lean thighs. He bowed his head to look down at the muddy ground and gestured loosely with one hand. 'It's over there. To the right, not far.'

She nodded and moved away. She paused and looked back when she'd gone a short distance. Lucan still watched her, a thoughtful expression on his face.

A loud crack rent the air from somewhere up the hill above them, followed by a deep rumble and the anxious shouts of a host of voices. They both started violently and looked towards the sound.

Lucan's heart skipped when he glanced up the hill, then began to pound. Without thinking, without speaking, he jumped to his feet and raced towards Severina, snatching her hand as he reached her and jerking her along at a run. But she slowed him, her skirts tangling around her legs. With a curse, he bent and lifted her, running in a straight line across the hill, wordlessly praying he made it to safety before the huge boulders tumbling down the incline crushed them.

Time moved with the sluggish unreality of a dream. Details were too sharp: his frantic heartbeat pounding in his ears, the roar and clatter of stone boulders rolling down the rocky Quirinal above him, the taste of dust in his mouth, the heat of Severina's body in his arms. Only in battle had he felt so strangely disconnected, with his body fluidly performing while his mind distanced itself to simply watch.

He reached safety just as the rocks smashed into the water wagon behind him, splintering the wood, breaking its wheels into pieces, slinging skins of water into the air and spewing liquid in all directions.

He lowered Severina to the ground and collapsed beside her.

'Oh, gods. Oh, dear gods.' Severina kept repeating the words, shaken, hardly believing.

Lucan could only concentrate on the physical, the shaking of his hands and legs that he could scarcely control. He'd learned in the aftermath of many battles to breathe hard and deep, clenching and unclenching his muscles to dissipate the excess energy.

'Lucan, are you all right?' Severina asked, a little breathlessly. 'Oh, gods. You could've been killed back there. Those boulders were headed straight for you. If you hadn't acted when you did…if you'd gone down the hill instead of across it… Oh, Lucan!'

Lucan couldn't answer. He could only lie beside her, breath rasping, his back against the pebble-strewn ground while his knees jerked and muscles burned like fire.

'Lucan, are you all right? You're not hurt, are you?'

Severina sensed something amiss and leaned over him, her eyes dark with worry. Her breath blew across his face and he tasted her in it. Her hands moved down his arms, feeling for injury. 'You're shaking,' she said in surprise.

'It'll pass.'

She didn't seem to hear him. Her hands moved over his body. She made a sound of dismay at the spasms in his legs. 'Lucan?'

'It will pass,' he said again.

Her face came back to his. 'How can I help?'

He didn't think. He couldn't think, didn't want to think. He responded instinctively to the nervous tension flooding through his every nerve—and to her lovely lips, mere inches from his own.

He captured her fiercely with one hand, pulling her down to his hungry body, fingers tangled in her hair.

Something hot and needy exploded inside him—relief at survival, and so much more that felt nothing like relief.

Severina's gasp told him she felt the same raw emotion.

He rose slightly in response to the sound and pushed her down to the ground beneath him as he took her lips again. It was an indecent posture—heaving chests, loins together, bodies greedy and grasping and straining for more, oblivious to dust and heat and the stares of onlookers. It went on and on, the touching, the wanting. There was little thought, a scarcity of breathing, only their two bodies shoving and demanding in the thrust towards union. The drive was strong, unrefined and even crude. It was born of need, made of heat. He wanted to take her, possess her, ravage her so fiercely they'd know nothing but this primal fire for ever.

'Lucan.' The voice that intruded into the haze of his emotion was not unkind, but it was firm. 'Lucan, get up. Now.'

Lucan lifted his head, breathing hard. He didn't move.

'This is unseemly. Get up, or I'll have others do it for you.'

Sanity began to flow back in. Lucan shook his head, desperate to clear the confusion. 'Apollodorus.'

The older man knelt beside him. 'It's natural, this madness you're feeling,' Apollodorus said gently. 'A purely physical response to danger, commonly seen in war. But you must rise and get off the lady now.'

Lucan drew in a harsh breath and pushed himself up, ignoring the discomfort of the sharp pebbles that cut into his palms. Oddly, the pain helped clear the haze from his mind.

He became aware of Severina on the ground beneath him, her clothing now wrinkled and dusty and clinging to legs spread wide to accommodate his body between them.

The sight startled him. Had he lost his mind?

He backed away, reeling, shot through with remorse, only vaguely aware that Apollodorus lifted Severina to her feet and soothed her.

'I'm sorry,' Lucan said. 'Severina, I'm sorry.'

Severina withdrew her hand from that of Apollodorus and came to him, her eyebrows drawing into an anxious frown. She lifted her hand to stroke his tense jaw.

He swallowed with difficulty, his throat dry and hurting.

'Return to the tent with me.' Apollodorus's voice held the tone of command.

They followed the architect down the hill. Nobody spoke until Apollodorus lifted the tent flap and motioned them inside. He stood looking from one to the other, ran a callused hand through his disorderly hair and grunted, '*Friends*, you say.'

'Accidents happen sometimes,' Apollodorus said a short while later. 'Fortunately, they're not frequent, but…' he traced his finger along the rim of the goblet of wine he held '…when they do come, there's always the possibility of injury.'

He glanced towards Severina. 'That's why I thought it best that Lucan accompany you. As it turns out, I was right.'

Severina glanced across to where Lucan sat, calmly listening. Probably the wine had helped him. He now seemed as steady as ever.

'I don't know what happened, exactly,' he said to Apollodorus. 'I heard a noise and looked up to see rocks tumbling down the hill towards us.'

'The posts that held the wooden side panels on the wagon must have cracked and given way beneath the weight of their load. It split wide open, spilling its contents down upon you.'

Severina shuddered and made a small sound of dismay. The architect glanced with worry at her. 'It could've been a terrible mishap,' he said. 'As it was, you were relatively unscathed. I'm thankful.'

Severina felt Lucan's attention on her, but he'd avoided making eye contact ever since he'd kissed her so forcefully.

It was impossible to know what he was thinking, but she guessed he was regretting what he'd done. She didn't. It had been pure emotion, an understandable reaction after so narrow an escape.

She'd felt overwhelmed, too. Passionately thankful to live. Ready to yield herself with an abandon close to madness.

A voice from outside the tent called for Apollodorus. The architect excused himself, but returned shortly, looking worried. 'I've got bad news,' he said. 'My site foreman tells me that the accident of which we've been speaking was not an accident at all.'

Lucan's face darkened. 'How do you know?'

'The cart's been tampered with. The ropes tied to the stakes holding the wooden panels in place were purposely weakened, cut through but for the last few strands so they'd give way with only slight pressure. And it now appears the cart was positioned intentionally to cause harm to you. The lad who pulled it there with two young asses says a black-haired man ordered him to place it so, then told him to unhitch his team and move on. That same man was later seen slipping away only moments after the load tumbled down towards you.'

Lucan frowned. 'A black-haired man. With a beard?'

Apollodorus nodded.

Severina's attention snagged on that information. She looked to Lucan, but he hadn't yet figured out what seemed glaringly obvious to her.

Those boulders hadn't been loosed until she'd left Lucan's side. Perhaps *she* hadn't been the intended victim. Whoever had broken the stakes on the cart had given her room to flee, but meant to kill Lucan.

She began to tremble, seeing in that knowledge the answer to her most troubling question. She had no choice left now. There could be no marriage to Lucan. She couldn't stay in Rome any longer. Anok Khai had found her.

'I want to go home,' Severina said suddenly. 'Lucan, please. I must go home now.'

Both Lucan and Apollodorus looked concerned at the urgency in her voice. Lucan rose and came to her, taking her hand, drawing her *palla* more securely around her shoulders.

'I'll look into this incident further,' Apollodorus told him. 'If I discover anything, I'll send word.'

Lucan shook his hand. 'Thank you, Apollodorus. You know how greatly I value your friendship.'

'And I yours.'

Lucan paused when he got to the door. 'Shall I be looking for Omnesimus later in the week?' he asked.

'Aye, I'll send him around.'

Severina hardly cared about her inn at the moment, but she knew that the odd, cold fear that now gripped her would pass shortly. Like a person in a nightmare, she felt an almost eerie calm as she thanked Apollodorus for his kindness and help. He smiled at her, but the worry in his eyes made her feel strange. The entire day had made her feel strange.

And it wasn't even noon yet.

The late afternoon sun slanted low across Rome's red-tiled roofs and pushed long shadows into the city's narrow streets by the time Donatus and Lelia joined Lucan at a table in their favourite *popina*.

Lelia was slightly breathless as she slid into her seat. 'I'm sorry we're late,' she said. 'When Druscilla found out we were coming to join you, she insisted on coming, too. We had a terrible time trying to convince her otherwise.'

'Whatever else you can say about my younger sister,' Donatus said with a smile, 'she's loyal to the ones who capture her heart.'

'He means *you*,' Lelia added, her eyes sparkling with amusement.

Lucan laughed for the first time that afternoon. 'Druscilla's a favourite of mine, too. She's growing into quite a beautiful young woman.'

Donatus nodded, pride shining in his eyes. 'Yes. I'm already practising my stern *pater familias* face so I can sufficiently intimidate her future suitors.'

'Oh, Donatus.' Lelia smoothed a hand down her husband's arm. 'You want Druscilla to marry, don't you? You mustn't intimidate the young men *too* much.'

She smiled at his frown, confident in Donatus's affection for his younger sister.

And what was there not to like about Druscilla? The girl was intelligent and spirited. With her in their home, life was never boring.

Lucan's lips twitched. 'Knowing Druscilla, I'd say she can handle intimidation well enough on her own. She's not exactly the docile sort most Roman lads hope to wed.'

'You've noticed that, have you?' Donatus winced. 'Marriage to my impertinent and loquacious little sister will be an adventure only for the stout-hearted. But I know you didn't ask us here to talk about Druscilla. Your message sounded urgent. What's going on?'

'You remember how I helped you out when your relationship with Lelia was going through deep water? Well, I need a return of that favour.'

Lelia started to stand. 'I'll go order our food and leave you two to talk alone.'

Lucan grabbed her arm and pulled her back into her seat. 'No. I need you, too.'

'Oh, my. This must be bad.'

'No. Well, maybe. It's confusing.'

'Lucan, you're not making sense,' Donatus said.

'Oh, yes, he is.' Lelia smiled at Lucan and eased her chair closer. 'You still love Severina, don't you?'

Lucan looked away, the muscle in his jaw twitching. 'I don't know. Maybe that's gone for ever.'

Lelia's excitement didn't diminish. 'Donatus and I thought that, too, but we were wrong. Tell me this—do you want her? I mean, in a physical way?'

'Lelia. You're forgetting this is *Lucan* you're talking to,' Donatus said.

Lelia frowned in his direction. 'Stay out of this, Donatus. Let Lucan answer the question.'

She turned back to Lucan. 'I've heard you've been seeing other women, but they weren't *her*, were they?'

Donatus growled a low note from across the table. 'Lelia.'

'I thought maybe if I spent time with other beautiful women, I'd forget Severina,' Lucan said to Lelia. 'I thought that if I slept with someone else...but you're right. They weren't her. I couldn't do it.'

Lelia thumped the table with the heel of her hand. 'Proof positive. You're still in love with her.'

Donatus glanced apologetically in Lucan's direction. 'Steady, Lelia. All that proves is that Lucan needs more time to get over her. So stop trying to play matchmaker and let the man tell his story. We haven't all night. Our sons will want their mother back before bedtime.'

The thought made Lelia sigh. She imagined her two sons, their chubby baby arms wrapped around her as she carried them to bed, and their soft baby scent as she drew up the bedclothes.

'I know you want Lucan to have the same happiness we have,' Donatus said, taking her hand. 'But please do back off a little.'

'The kind of happiness you two have seems an impossibility now,' Lucan said. 'But I must take a wife, and soon.'

Donatus's gaze searched Lucan's face. 'Your father has declared it?'

'He has. And there's a young bride waiting if I do not first choose my own.'

'A deadline, too?'

'Of course.'

Lelia frowned. 'How long do we have?'

'*We?*' Donatus's lips twitched.

'Three months.'

Lelia smiled again. 'Plenty of time. Severina will be your wife long before then.'

Lucan shook his head. 'Well, there's the problem. It's why I called you here. I asked her to wed me. *Again.* And she doesn't appear eager to do so.'

'You've asked her before?' Lelia's voice held disbelief. 'She never told me that!'

'Yes. But then, as now, she seems determined to keep her independence.'

'But Severina wants a husband. She wants children. She told me so.'

Donatus's voice was gentle. 'Maybe she just doesn't want them with Lucan.'

'I refuse to believe that,' Lelia said, crossing her arms in frustration. 'She cares for Lucan, I know she does. I won't give up hope.'

'Neither will I,' Lucan said. 'But there's something keeping her from trusting me, something that makes her fearful of commitment. Until I find out what that something is, I may not be able to win her or wed her.'

'Leave this to me,' Lelia said. 'I'll find out or die trying.'

'It may not be as easy as you think,' Donatus said quietly.

Two pair of eyes turned to face him.

'Severina seems the private sort. What do you really know about her past?'

Lucan shook his head. 'Almost nothing. She never talked about it.'

Donatus lifted an eyebrow. 'And you didn't wonder about that?'

There was a moment of quiet.

'You know,' Lelia ventured, looking thoughtful, 'I think she may have once been a slave. She still bears the mark on her left shoulder. Perhaps she was abused by her master. She's an attractive woman, and many attractive female slaves endure that. She was bought by Brocchus at the market in Ostia for his gladiator school about two years before I also sold myself into his service. She's a fearless competitor and taught me much of what I knew about combat. But beyond that I know little else. Strange, to realise that. We've been close. But then, maybe we mostly talked about *me*.'

Donatus chuckled. 'Imagine that.'

'We talked about you, too. You, too!'

Lucan leaned back in his chair. 'So we don't, any of us, know the details of her past.'

'No,' Donatus said. 'Maybe that wouldn't be strange if we were talking about a casual acquaintance. But Lelia has been her best friend for more than two years now. And you were her lover.'

Lucan stroked his chin for a moment. 'There are other things that don't quite fit.'

Donatus grunted. 'The censor. We both know he's out for blood.'

'Maybe more literally than you know. There was an accident today that turned out not to be an accident.'

Donatus and Lelia looked at him in surprise. Lucan began to relate the details of his morning with Severina.

'Early on we were followed by a dark-haired man,' he said. 'I wasn't particularly distressed at the time. Severina's extraordinarily attractive, and a man would have to be blind not to notice. I thought him an admirer.'

Lelia sent a meaningful glance in her husband's direction.

'At first it seemed so. He stopped following after I kissed her.'

'You kissed her? And she allowed it?' Lelia's voice was hopeful. 'Oh, Lucan, that's good. Very good.'

'Stop distracting him, Lelia. This is too important.'

Lucan went on, telling about their visit with Apollodorus and about the rocks that tumbled down the hill, narrowly missing them.

'We were almost smashed along with the wagon of water that stood in the way. If I hadn't snatched Severina up and run straight across the hill, we might have been killed.'

'You're sure it wasn't merely an accident?'

'Apollodorus's foreman found that the ropes to the stakes on the cart had been cut nearly through so they'd give under slight pressure. Besides that, the cart had been intentionally placed in exactly the right place to release its load of rubble down upon us.'

'Did anyone see who placed the cart there?'

'The lad who drove the cart says he was ordered to do it by a black-haired man. That same man was later seen leaving the scene after the rubble went down the hill.'

'The same man who'd been following you?'

'Apparently. I assume he was watching for an opportunity to do us harm all along.'

Donatus made a harsh sound.

'At any rate, Apollodorus is investigating.'

Donatus nodded as he raked a hand through his dark hair. 'Good. Apollodorus is clever and careful, and he has connections throughout the city. If anyone can find the man, he will.'

'I don't like this,' Lelia said. 'It reminds me too much of the danger *we* faced, Donatus. Perhaps they should go to a place of safety until we work out what's going on.'

'But we don't really know that anything *is* going on. Lucan's working on instinct alone. And yet…' Donatus's eyes met those of his friend '…I trust his instincts. They saved my life in Dacia more than once.'

'Severina won't leave right now,' Lucan said. 'Guests are due at the inn tomorrow, a large group from Capua to attend a wedding. Besides that, Severina and I are having work done to the inn. Apollodorus's son Omnesimus will oversee the project. We're to start later this week, and Severina will want to direct the builders herself. She won't trust that to anyone else, not even me.'

'Work on the inn?' Donatus looked at his friend strangely. 'Was this planned before the censor's visit?'

'No. It's…' Lucan looked sheepish. 'It's a recent idea of mine.'

'A recent idea? Why? To prove you're the owner? To gain the testimony of witnesses?'

Lelia laughed. 'To spend time with Severina.'

The flush that immediately appeared under Lucan's golden skin told her she'd hit the mark, especially when his lashes lowered to hide his thoughts.

'It's not a bad idea to stay near her,' Donatus said, pushing away from the table. 'Especially now. Severina's skilled at combat, I know, but having you there to protect her is better.'

'Except you mustn't tell her that's what you're there for,' Lelia added. 'Because it would make her angry.'

Lucan nodded.

'And besides that, it would be a lie. Because you're really there to win her heart.'

'Lelia.' Donatus sighed. 'Give Lucan a rest, will you?'

Lucan flashed his friend a grateful look.

Lelia sighed as she stood and looped her arm through her husband's. 'Oh, well. My babies are waiting, anyway. But don't worry, Lucan. I've got a plan.'

'Oh, no,' Donatus said. 'One of Lelia's plans. This could get bad, Lucan. *Really* bad.'

Chapter Nine

Lelia *did* have a plan. It wasn't much, but it might yield information about Severina's past. It was also something Lucan couldn't do for himself.

She set aside momentary twinges of guilt that she shouldn't be prying into secrets Severina had obviously not wanted to share. Privacy was one thing, but having someone threaten Severina's life…that was another thing entirely.

Lelia loved Severina and she'd be damned before she'd let anything keep her from getting to the bottom of this matter. If someone wanted Severina and Lucan dead, then Lelia and Donatus must do whatever they could to protect them—even if that meant prying out the harsh, painful secrets of Severina's past.

She waited until the following morning when Donatus left for the baths and his work in the Senate. Then leaving her sons in the gentle care of Donatus's stepmother, Faustina, Lelia set off to find Brocchus.

The huge, fiercely ugly owner of the gladiatorial *ludus* had once been Lelia and Severina's formidable *lanista*. He'd pushed his gladiatorial slaves to their limits, imposing strict discipline.

But he was also, Lelia knew from experience, a surprisingly kind man who truly cared and wanted them to survive combat. His training, demanding as it was, ensured that they'd be the best. He knew that only those gladiators who survived through combat after combat would achieve the *rudus* of freedom and be retired from their gruesome work.

Lelia and Severina had been lucky. Donatus had returned from the war and rescued them from the arena. But for most gladiatorial slaves, the only way out was to endure, fight after fight, defeating one formidable opponent at a time. Few would manage that. Of those who did, almost all had been trained by Brocchus.

'Leda!' The slave who met Lelia at the door recognised her immediately. And though it was odd to hear herself called by that combat name again, all the sights and sounds and smells of the place were oddly familiar as she was escorted in to Brocchus's office.

The adolescent slave who accompanied Lelia was almost beside himself with excitement as he studied his surroundings. Lelia had known he would be. Draco was a huge fan of the gladiatorial games. He followed them week after week and could rattle off the names of recent winners and losers complete with statistics. 'Pugnax,' he'd say, 'a Thracian of the Neronian *ludus*, with three fights to his credit, victorious,' or 'Murrans, a *myrmillo* of the Julian *ludus*, with four fights, killed.'

Lelia had chosen him to accompany her this morning because she could use his interest in her favour. 'You may go with me,' she'd told him, 'but only on one condition. You must never breathe a word of this to anybody, especially not to Mistress Severina.'

The young man looked momentarily distressed. She was asking a lot of an ardent fan. But the prize she held out was worth the sacrifice.

Now Draco's dark eyes were lit with excitement as he accompanied Lelia to Brocchus's office. 'Look,' he whispered, pointing towards the open area where a training combat was in progress. 'That's Atticus. A Thracian with *fourteen* fights. Reprieved in his last.' His voice contained awe. 'He's the *best*, mistress.'

She smiled. 'I know Atticus. Fortunately, I never fought him myself, but he was most amiable over the dinner table. He tells fine jokes and has a thousand comical stories. Perhaps Brocchus will allow you to shake his hand later. Would you like that?'

Draco's nod was enthusiastic.

The lad's excitement didn't affect Lelia. In fact, the atmosphere of the place depressed her. The further down the portico she walked, the more the memories seized her. Only her love for Severina kept her from leaving. She shuddered, remembering the heaviness of metal greaves on her legs and the hilt of a *gladius* against her palm. She imagined the salty tang of her own perspiration and overriding all, the sense of palpable despair. She'd felt trapped here.

It was true she'd sold herself into slavery. Her life was dark in those days, so filled with painful losses that she welcomed death.

The only bright spot in the darkness had been Severina. Within days of meeting the tall, athletic woman with the intelligent grey eyes and long chestnut braid, Lelia had felt that someone understood.

Soon she'd shared with Severina all the deep secrets of her life. Somehow, just sharing the pain had brought healing. But as Lelia reflected on those days, she realised that Severina had never been forthcoming about her own hurts. She'd never divulged details.

Lelia's thoughts were interrupted by a familiar voice.

'Leda, my girl!' Brocchus's greeting as he came forwards boomed out so loudly that several sparring athletes turned in their direction. 'What a pleasure! By the gods, it's true!'

He came forwards, his dark eyes shining—at least the one not covered by the eyepatch he wore. Lelia knew it hid a disfiguring scar received from the curved *sica* of an opponent years before.

'Brocchus. It's wonderful to see you again.'

'Is it? Then I must be growing more handsome.' He chuckled and winked at her with his good eye. 'D'you think?'

She laughed as he intended. 'More like…absence makes the heart grow fonder.'

'Ah, well. That's good enough.' He studied her for a moment. 'You're more beautiful than ever. Married life still agrees with you?'

'It does.'

The big man smiled. 'I could tell he was the one for you, that senator. Even though you looked eager to carve him into pieces, there was something…' he snapped his fingers '…something *there*. I'm glad to see I wasn't wrong.'

'You weren't wrong, Brocchus. And for listening to your heart and going with your fine instincts, I owe you so much. My life, and Donatus's…' Lelia's eyes unexpectedly filled with tears. 'Thank you.'

Brocchus put a fatherly arm around her shoulders and drew her towards his office. 'Ah, well. I have a tough job here, and I see too many sad stories. It's good to know that sometimes a story does end happily.' He sighed. 'But enough about that. Tell me why you've come. Do you wish to engage some gladiators for entertainment? I have several who'd suit well.'

Lelia shuddered. 'No. I think not.'

'Too many unpleasant memories? I once felt the same way after I'd won my own freedom. But then I realised I could help others like me, slaves forced into combat, slaves who'd either fight well or die. Their survival became my purpose.'

'I'm thankful it wasn't mine…or Severina's.'

'Severina,' he said. 'And how fares my lovely Persephone?'

Lelia had almost forgotten Severina's combat name. She was impressed that Brocchus still remembered it.

'She's in trouble. That's why I've come.'

Brocchus frowned. 'What trouble?'

Lelia told him everything, stressing Severina's romance with Lucan because it would appeal to Brocchus's soft heart. She told him about the censor's threat, the stranger who'd followed Severina, and the suspicious accident.

'But how am I to help you?' Brocchus asked when she'd finished.

'Maybe something in Severina's past holds the key, but I know little about her background. I'm hoping you can tell me more.'

Brocchus shook his head. 'She was always the private sort.'

'Can you at least tell me how she came to the *ludus*? Didn't you find her at a slave auction in Portus?'

'In Ostia. But she wasn't a slave.'

Lelia's eyebrows shot upwards. 'No? But she said—'

'I'd gone to purchase slaves, yes. But I was introduced to her by a friend of mine, a Nubian trader of Egyptian wheat. Severina was an old friend of his who'd somehow become destitute. He was unwilling for her to sell herself to me, but she was determined to do so.'

'Tell me every detail you remember.'

'The conversation was difficult. For one thing, I hadn't actually put any females into the arena before. Other *lanistas* had already begun doing it and the practice looked to be wildly profitable, but I was still holding out against it, so I kept telling her no. But she simply wouldn't take no for an answer.'

Lelia smiled. 'That sounds like Severina.'

'Except that she was having to talk through our mutual friend. Her Latin wasn't good.'

'But Severina speaks Latin as well as I do!'

'*Now* she does. But not in those days. She knew it, but her use of it was halting. It was faster to use the Nubian as our interpreter.'

Lelia was fascinated. She'd never imagined such a thing. 'What language did she speak?'

'I assumed it was Egyptian at the time.'

'So Severina wasn't a slave, but was destitute enough to become one?'

'I guess so. Though she didn't *appear* destitute. Her clothing was of good quality, and she looked to be well bred. If I'd met her on the street, I would've thought she was of the upper classes. I thought that odd at the time.'

'Brocchus, did Severina ever talk to you about her family?'

'No. There wasn't that kind of relationship between us.' Brocchus thought for a minute. 'All I know is that she hated her father, and I only know that because I trained her myself. Once, while encouraging her to be aggressive, I told her to think of the person she most hated. She told me she hated her father. Afterwards, I used that whenever I wanted her to get tough and fight hard.'

'She never told me that. She knew about my problems with my own father, but she never mentioned hers.'

'That's all I know,' Brocchus said as he stood. 'I wish I could give you more.'

'One more thing,' Lelia said, rising from her chair. 'Could Draco meet a few gladiators before we go?'

Brocchus looked at the young man, recognised the hopeful awe in the boy's face and smiled. 'Of course! Come with me and I'll introduce you to my bravest warriors.'

'Brocchus?'

Brocchus turned back from the doorway.

'May I have the name of that Nubian trader?'

Brocchus nodded. 'I'll have the clerk write it down for you, along with directions to his warehouse.'

'Thank you. I owe you.'

His smile was gentle. 'Just see to it that my girl Persephone has her happy ending, too, all right?'

'If I have my way, she'll be happily married by the end of the year.'

'Uh-oh. I've seen that look in your eyes before. It usually meant somebody was about go down in serious defeat.'

'Severina trained me for combat. And soon she's going to know exactly how well I learned those lessons.'

Brocchus grinned at the lad at his side. 'One bit of advice, young fellow,' he said. 'Whenever you're looking for a fight, stay away from my gladiatrices. They're the best, the very best. In the ring or out of it.'

Brocchus's laughter rang in Lelia's ears long after he'd stepped outside.

'No, no, you're doing it all wrong.' Severina's voice wasn't as severe as it needed to be. She was trying not to laugh.

Lucan eyed her sternly, also trying for severity but not quite succeeding. And he was so handsome it hurt, with his eyes alight with laughter, the rugged cleft in his chin and charming dimple that teased her with its frequent appearance in his left cheek.

'Give me a little credit,' he reproved her. 'You can't deny that I've done well masquerading as the inn's owner during the four days I've been with you.'

'Well…'

'I charmed your guests.'

'You did,' she admitted. 'But Gaius Maximus was in a good mood already, since his daughter was marrying into a senatorial family.'

'Uhm-hmm.'

'His wife, Alva, too.' *The hussy*, Severina was tempted to add, thinking how blatantly the woman had flirted with Lucan.

'She made you jealous.'

'Me? Of course not.'

'Steam was rising out of your ears at dinner when she rubbed her bosom all over me.'

'Don't be ridiculous. I thought it unseemly, but I wasn't jealous.'

'No? Too bad. You're worried about my reputation, then.'

She snorted. 'Hardly.'

'You should be. A man's reputation affects his wife, too.'

Severina fought not to grind her teeth. She should be used to Lucan's sneaky little advertisements for marriage by now. He'd made them constantly during the last four days.

She understood the strategy. He was wearing her down, keeping the issue before her until it stopped causing discomfort. He'd mentioned it so often that she'd stopped reproving him for it. It would mean nothing when she left in a few days, anyway.

She tolerated this marriage campaign only because her slaves would need Lucan when she left. The censor's case was against her, the woman, but he'd be forced to leave Lucan alone after she was gone. She had to be practical now. For Orthrus and Ariadne and Juvenal's sake, Lucan simply had to learn to operate the inn. There wasn't much time.

She put her hands on her hips and glared at him now. It proved a weak defence against his attractiveness when he only grinned roguishly at her.

'Stop trying to annoy me, Lucan, and pay attention to buying good fruit. Or else give me the basket and let *me* do it. I don't think you really know what you're doing.'

'Leave me be, woman,' he growled. 'I know how to buy fruit. I buy it all the time.'

'Not for my inn, you don't. I want it to be perfect. At the very *peak* of perfection. And look, you're not even squeezing it! I always squeeze it. If it's soft, it's too ripe. If it's hard, not ripe enough.'

She jerked at the basket and frowned when he didn't give it up. 'Only a dolt would buy fruit without squeezing it.'

Lucan rolled his eyes and looked towards the heavens. 'Gods, be merciful. If she only knew…'

'If she only knew what?' Severina lifted an impertinent eyebrow.

Lucan grinned so wickedly that Severina's insides flipped. 'If she only knew how this conversation tempts my lascivious male appetites. All this talk of fruit and squeezing and peaks of perfection. And we won't even go into what the words *soft* and *hard* are doing to me. Good Lord, Severina. You're killing me.'

Severina burst into laughter.

Lucan propped against the tall side of a vendor's wooden cart and rested his head on his hand, watching her through the heavy fringe of his gold-tipped eyelashes. A lazy smile played around the edges of his sensual lips. 'I love your laughter,' he said quietly. 'You should do it more often.'

Severina drew in a breath, caught off guard by the husky note in his words.

'You used to smile more. You used to laugh more, when we were together.'

Severina swallowed hard. There was something dangerous about the way he was looking at her.

'Do you ever think of those times, Severina? Do you ever remember the way it was between us?'

She looked away. 'Sometimes. Do you?'

'Too often. You know, I really did try to forget you. I wanted to forget you. But I can't find joy like I had with you no matter how hard I try.'

'I'm sorry.'

'These four days with you have been hell.' Lucan pushed off his prop and came to her, capturing her chin in strong, lean fingers. Her gaze lifted, and the fire in his eyes made Severina hurt.

'Such sweet hell,' he murmured, his gaze fastening on her lips. 'And heaven, too. Working beside you, hearing your voice, watching the graceful way you move…and wanting you.'

He closed his eyes as if overcome by pain. 'I thought I no longer loved you. I thought I was still angry. But now I'm not sure. Now I'm just lonely for that sweet thing we left behind.'

His eyes opened, full of sadness. 'I miss it, Severina. I miss *you*.'

Severina's eyes filled with tears. She tried to lower her head so he wouldn't see, but the light touch of his fingers held her.

A teardrop slid down her cheek. He made a small sound and leaned forwards to capture it with his lips, warmth against warmth, his breath sighing across the wet trail on her face.

The moment was too beautiful, and *he* was too beautiful. She closed her eyes against the pain.

Two more tears slid out. His lips caught them, too, tracing the line of wetness they'd made down her cheek.

Like a woman in a dream, Severina turned her face to his. It was a small movement but Lucan groaned, understanding it for all it was.

Severina waited for him to move. She was confused, full of uncertainty, not wanting to hurt him any more and not wanting to hurt herself. But she longed for him.

Her hand lifted of its own accord and closed around the fabric of his tunic. Whether she steadied herself in the chaos swirling around them, or whether she pulled him with her into the fire, she didn't know for certain. She opened her eyes just in time to see the turbulent emotion in Lucan's eyes as his lips took hers.

Only with Lucan could a kiss be so much. Only with him. It whispered love and sang desire. It coaxed and comforted, pleaded and promised. It tasted of agony and bliss, and ravaged even as it gave.

Her knees weakened and trembled, but he was there, pulling her against the firm strength of his body, aligning her frame with his to support her with tantalising sureness.

In that moment, oddly enough, everything suddenly felt right. The world might crumble around them, reality lost in an inferno of feeling, but there was *this* between them. Even now in a crowded marketplace, with one of Lucan's hands still gripping a basket of fruit, there was this.

It was oddly reassuring. She'd been afraid of losing him though she had no right to this moment of passion and pleasure. She'd been the one to walk away.

Yet here, now, he was still *hers*. It seemed miraculous, as if the Fates had, for once, chosen to be kind.

Except that now, even in this, they were still cruel.

Only a few days more and she'd leave him for ever. There'd be no more of Lucan where she was going, no opportunities to see him, nothing of him in the faraway place to which she'd flee.

'Where are your thoughts?' Lucan whispered, stroking the smooth skin of her cheek with his thumb. 'When your eyes get soft and that distant look comes into your face?'

'In the past.'

'I prefer the future,' he said slowly, his eyes dark. 'You say we don't have one together. You're afraid to marry me, but when I hold you, your body and your kisses tell me something different. You're not afraid of me, Severina, and you're not afraid of my touch. Focus on that, and we might still find happiness together.'

Severina closed her eyes. For one moment, only for a moment, she wanted to pretend the world was a beautiful place and that even she, the rebel daughter of the great Anok Khai, could still find joy within it.

'Let's try that,' Lucan whispered, his breath sighing across her lips. 'Let's push past fear and find some beauty together, one moment, one hour, one day at a time. Will you allow that much, Severina?'

What could she say?

He wasn't speaking of marriage. He didn't ask for for ever. He held out only the promise of pleasure. This might be had without guilt.

Or could it? Her conscience pricked her. Did she use Lucan selfishly? Did she show too little regard for his feelings? Perhaps she shouldn't allow him to put new rules to the game and then play it out only to suit her own desire.

But she'd hurt so much. She'd known so little happiness. And Lucan stood there now and held it out to her. Was it wrong to want it? To want him?

She would hurt Lucan now or she would hurt him later. She regretted that, but she couldn't avoid it.

Coward that she was, and selfish, the choice was clear.

'Yes,' she said, not quite daring to meet his gaze. 'Let's find beauty together. Then no matter what happens in the future, we'll always have sweet memories.'

Something flickered within his eyes. 'We begin tonight.'

Her eyes widened at his boldness, and he smiled. 'But perhaps not with whatever you're imagining.' He lifted her hand to his lips. Her skin suddenly seemed extraordinarily sensitive, and she shivered at the gentle caress. 'Tonight we'll host your guests on this last night before they leave. And tomorrow night we have another dinner party to attend, if you'll allow me the honour of being your escort. Donatus and Lelia sent over an invitation this morning. It isn't to be a grand affair, but there will be other guests. In her typical fashion, Lelia said we were both expected to attend and that she'd not take "no" for an answer.'

Severina smiled. 'Then of course we must go. As sweetly annoying as Lelia can be as an ally, she's even more formidable as an enemy.'

'I tremble at the thought.'

Lucan's gaze focused on Severina's lips. Amusement fled away. She was suddenly unable to swallow, unable to breathe.

'When those obligations are done, we will be together,' he said quietly. 'Though I wonder if either of us knows what we've begun.'

Severina lifted an eyebrow.

'In every life, some decisions are momentous. They change one's destiny, or mark a new era. Those moments usually feel different somehow, carrying such a stunning amount of weight they're easily recognised. Do you know what I'm talking about?'

'Yes.'

'I've had maybe a dozen of those in my entire life. The night I lost my innocence at fifteen. The day I left my parents for a life of my own. The morning I signed my name to enlist in the army, and then again when I was baptised as a Christian…I knew those moments, that they'd change me for ever.'

His gaze found hers. 'I feel that right now. I'm afraid of what it might mean.'

Severina looked away from the intensity on his face. Was he a mystic? Did he sense the future? For a moment she feared for him and grieved for the hurt she'd cause.

'If you're unsure, you can always change your mind,' she said.

'I will live dangerously,' he murmured, pulling her into his embrace. 'As long as you will live it with me.'

Severina felt strangely unsettled as Lucan took her lips. She'd known danger, but she and Lucan were agreeing to become lovers, and that seemed more dangerous than anything she'd known before.

Like Lucan, she sensed a moment of destiny and trembled.

Chapter Ten

Lucan hoped the departure of guests from the inn would bring a slower pace and time alone with Severina, but he soon found his desire thwarted.

Onesimus arrived early the following morning, along with five donkey carts straining under their various loads of wood and sand and brick. The young architect had received the plans Lucan had sent several days before and now was eager to get started. A small army of workers arrived with him; even more arrived within the next hour, cursing and perspiring as they tried to guide the strong work mules pulling a wheeled Tryphystos crane through narrow, cobbled streets.

When Lucan sent a quizzical glance in Onesimus's direction, the builder simply shrugged. 'Don't know if I'll need it,' he said, 'But better to have it and not need it, than to slow everything down with a lengthy wait when I'm ready to lift stones up to that second-storey addition.'

Lucan had to laugh. He knew Onesimus well. They weren't far apart in age and had both served Emperor Trajan together in Dacia—Lucan as a cavalry officer, the *vexillarius* of his *ala*, and Onesimus as one of the huge team of builder-engineers who built the massive bridges and siege structures designed by Apollodorus.

Lucan knew the son to be much like the father—goal-oriented and driven, ruthless in pursuit of excellence, keen-eyed in attention to detail, a true lover of architectural beauty.

Also like Apollodorus, Onesimus in the midst of any project was part-friend and part-tyrant, switching back and forth between the roles so seamlessly you could scarcely tell one from the other, but admired him in either. It was a task few men could pull off with such capability.

By afternoon Severina's once-beautiful courtyard was a mess of debris. The roof had been taken off the kitchen and two large wall portions demolished by well-muscled men who pounded them with weighty iron hammers. Onesimus himself stood in the sun, watching every aspect of the work as it progressed, sometimes helping with it, sweating alongside his crew of slaves and breathing in the acrid dust as he barked orders that were followed immediately and to precision. *Wood beams, place them there. Use chisels to attack the old mortar on those bricks. Tiles? Separate them, broken ones in that cart to be hauled away and the rest, saved for re-use.*

Lucan was paying for the work and for all the material and labourers, but he found himself being ordered about by Onesimus as curtly as were the slaves. Even Ariadne and Severina worked, bringing water out at regular intervals and setting up their noon meal on outdoor tables made of wooden planks and oak barrels.

Yet even though the work progressed with almost stunning rapidity under Onesimus's demanding scrutiny, the atmosphere all around seemed pleasantly jovial. There was good-natured teasing among the men and much deep-voiced male laughter. Brickmasons laid new foundation walls and teased their fellows about who among them used the proper amount of mortar. Carpenters sang out of tune as they measured and cut floor joists, wall studs and rafter beams.

Lucan didn't mind spending his day as a labourer under such circumstances. He relished physical outdoor work. To feel his muscles tight and straining as he lowered beams and carried stone made him feel alive.

Several times he sensed someone's attention and looked up to find Severina staring at him from across the courtyard, admiration and desire shining in her eyes. That, too, made him feel good, comfortable in his own skin and eager to experience more of the subtle nuances of the flesh.

'Four days,' Orthrus said in a low voice beside Lucan, drawing his attention back to the wide-mouthed wooden barrel in front of him and the mortar they mixed together inside it. 'Onesimus says it'll take only four days to get the new structures up. Finishing might take a day or two more, but we'll be painting and decorating in another week.'

Lucan nodded without speaking, putting most of his effort into shoving a large wooden paddle through the heavy slop of concrete.

Orthrus drew a tired, grimy hand across his forehead and straightened, stopping his churning paddle for a moment. 'I know it's what the mistress wants, but this bothers me, all the chaos, having workers in and out constantly with carts and equipment. There's too much opportunity for something to happen. For something to go wrong.'

'Work sites are dangerous. You can't do anything about that.'

'It's not the work site that worries me. It's those who might try to pass themselves off as workers and not really *be*.'

'What are you saying?'

'I've seen men watching this building.' Orthrus glanced quickly towards the shaded portico where Severina and Ariadne poured cool drinks. 'I think they're watching the mistress.'

Lucan nodded. 'You're right. There *are* men, Orthrus, four of them. Usually one at each corner, hidden from view on nearby rooftops, looking down into the courtyard and watching who passes by on the streets.'

'They don't just watch, either. There's one in particular. He doesn't just watch.'

'I know. The tall one. With black hair and beard.'

'Yes. He follows Mistress Severina when she and Ariadne go off on errands. He followed her to the Forum Holitorium yesterday afternoon.'

'I know. His presence accounted for my sudden desire to help Severina buy fruit.'

Worry still clouded Orthrus's expression. 'So what do you think? Is there danger for her? For Ariadne? Will these men try to hurt the women?'

Lucan frowned and tamped his paddle against the rim of the barrel, knocking off chunks of wet concrete. He called for two slaves nearby to take it away.

'I don't know,' he said. 'Perhaps Marcus Terentius is only gathering information to use against us in the hearing. In that case, I welcome his spies. Let them go back to that greedy bastard with plenty of news to make him squirm, that Livius Lucan is living at his inn and spending his gold to make improvements to it.'

Lucan looked up, scanning the rooftops that overlooked Severina's inn. Was he being watched even now?

'For safety's sake, I might take Severina to another location. But she'll fight me like a tiger; she'll not go willingly.'

Orthrus smiled crookedly. 'Perhaps you can make her an offer she can't refuse.'

'I'll give it some thought. Until that day comes, let's give that censor all we can. Let him hear about everything from the passionate kiss I gave Severina yesterday in the Forum to a detailed description of the work progressing today. Let's light a fire under him, shall we?'

Orthrus lifted an eyebrow. 'You kissed Mistress Severina? In the Forum? In front of everyone?' He laughed softly. 'Ariadne will be glad to hear that. She…you know how women are. She's hoping something will develop between you.'

Lucan rolled another barrel into place and stood it upright to expose its open end. He dumped a few spadefuls of sand and limestone into it. 'Ariadne mustn't be too hopeful just yet. It might work out with Severina, or it might not. I do, however, intend to give it my best effort.'

'Women can be hard to understand sometimes.'

'Agreed. At any rate, I'm to escort Mistress Severina to a dinner party tonight. Donatus is sending an armed escort to lead us through the streets to his home. He's aware of our situation here and is rather concerned about it.'

'I'll go with you. I can wield a sword.'

Lucan shook his head. 'No. Stay here and watch over the inn. With me, Severina will have full protection. But her property will not, and I wouldn't put it past Marcus Terentius to take advantage of our absence. He's a crook, Orthrus, a ruthless criminal. I'd feel better knowing you were watching over things here. It would ease my mind and help me enjoy my evening with Severina.'

A look passed between them, male to male. 'Certainly you should enjoy your evening, Master Lucan,' Orthrus said. 'May there be much pleasure in it for both of you.'

'Like I said, I'll give it my best effort.'

Late afternoon had come, along with the long, slanted red-tinged rays of a lowering sun and the slight dissipation of the day's heat. Severina usually liked this time of day. Her guests were ordinarily quiet during these slow hours between noon and dusk. They napped in their rooms or wrote letters or played at one of the many games she provided for their entertainment.

For Severina, it was the most peaceful time of day. Ariadne and Cook liked to work together in the kitchen in advance of the evening meal, giving Severina time for relaxation beside the fountain or a stroll among her well-tended beds of irises and lilies.

She avoided looking at the courtyard this afternoon. She'd spent most of the day there already, and though she was excited by the almost unbelievable pace at which Onesimus and his crew were completing their work, she was tired and didn't want to think about it any more today.

Besides that, she had more intriguing things to consider. Lucan had sent a message that he wanted to see her. There'd been something odd in Orthrus's expression when he'd knocked at her bedroom door to tell her that Master Lucan would be joining her later in her bedroom. She could have sworn the handsome slave knew more about her newfound agreement with Lucan than she'd like to admit.

Orthrus hadn't said the matter was urgent or that Lucan would be coming to her swiftly, so she took time to wash and change.

Since they'd soon leave for the dinner party, Severina went ahead and donned her best tunic. It was of deep indigo blue, its fabric soft and fine. Tiny beads of jet sparkled at the neck and hem, a subtle accent that made her feel rich and tasteful. The garment clung well to her body. She'd retained most of the sleek muscle of her days as a gladiatrix. Her waist and hips were still trim, her abdomen flat. The garment's fit made the most of her curves, so she hadn't worn the *stophium* that ordinarily bound her breasts. That tight leather strap only made her feel confined, and she was in the mood for freedom tonight.

She drew her hands down the sides of the tunic and sighed at the feel of silky fabric against her fingertips. She imagined Lucan's hands sliding down it, too, and smiled with anticipation.

Lucan's hands.

His hands fascinated her. They were warm and knowledgeable, the fingers elegant and graceful. He had the hands of a musician or an artist. An artist, she decided, because there was infinite skill in the way he touched her, such marvellous creativity in his hands.

But maybe he was more the musician. She always made music when those gentle fingertips strummed with purpose across her body, wonderful little female sounds of pleasure that excited them both.

This was madness, to want him so.

Perhaps it was only that the tunic made her feel extravagantly feminine. It fit beautifully, sweeping gracefully down to the floor, a fluid, sensual eroticism against her bare legs whenever she moved. Even the garment's deep ocean colour suited her to perfection. It made her eyes darken nearly to charcoal, and her skin glow like warm alabaster.

Ordinarily she never considered herself beautiful, but the woman who stared at her in the looking glass now did almost appear so, with her pale lips slightly parted, her eyes dark and glittering, her hair in deep, russet-touched waves against her bare shoulders. Too bad she'd have to braid her hair and fasten it up in keeping with current fashion. She preferred to wear it loose to caress her neck, back and shoulders. Odd, how she'd never noticed the sensitivity before. Odd, how—

A knock at the door startled her.

Lucan stood on the other side. His eyes widened when he saw her. He seemed unable to do anything but stare as she faced him.

For a long moment, raw emotion passed between them. It expanded, filled the space, snatched away the air she tried to breathe. 'Come in,' she said.

He entered, still looking at her as if he wanted to devour her.

She waited for him to speak.

He gave a soft, self-deprecating laugh after the silence had lengthed. 'There was something I needed,' he said, looking slightly embarrassed. 'But I'm having trouble remembering what it was.'

But Severina knew what he needed. She saw it in his eyes.

He swallowed, hard and convulsively. His hand clenched and un-clenched at his side, not quite under his control. She doubted he was even aware of it.

'Dear God in heaven,' he breathed. 'Severina…'

'I've been waiting for you. I received your message,' she said quietly, tilting her head. Her long hair stroked her backside when she did that, a pleasantly arousing sensation.

Lucan seemed to suddenly discover the small box of tooled leather he held in one hand. 'I brought you this.'

Her laughter was low. Its throaty, seductive quality surprised Severina.

It also surprised Lucan. There was a swift, hard intake of his breath. He seemed relieved to move away from her, to turn his back and set the box on a nearby table. 'It's a gift. For you.'

She moved towards him. One step, two. Even that slight motion felt wonderful as silken fabric slid against silken limbs. Her long hair swayed against her hips and buttocks. Bare feet sank into the plush wool rug, heel first and then toes, one at a time.

It was amazing, how alive she felt. She wanted to laugh at this and share the joy with Lucan. All because she'd seen it in his eyes, that she was beautiful. That he wanted her.

He opened the box and took a small steel dagger from it. 'I want you to have this,' he said, holding it by the blade so she could grasp the hilt. 'I want you to wear it from now on, every time you venture into the streets.'

She took the weapon. Long familiar with instruments of combat, she sensed the fine quality of this one. The steel was clean and sharp, the balance superb, better even than the ones used by the *retiarii* in the Flavian Amphitheatre.

She frowned. 'Why?'

He shrugged. The indifference on his face made her wary. 'Just being cautious, that's all.'

'You know something.' She moved closer, as if touching him would make him truthful.

His body tensed. Something fierce flared in his eyes. He subdued it. 'You don't have to worry, but the streets of Rome grow more dangerous every day, and I'd feel better knowing—'

'Then give me your *spatha*.'

'My *spatha*?'

'Yes. A dagger is fine. A *gladius* is better. But a *spatha*…now there's a weapon for a gladiatrix. I fight best with a *spatha* and yours is—'

'Mine.' There was steel in his voice.

Severina smiled and laid one palm to his chest. The muscles tightened as he drew in air.

'I really like your *spatha*, Lucan. Of all your possessions, it's the one thing I covet.'

His eyes closed. 'It's the one thing I could never give you, Severina. You don't understand what it means. You weren't in Dacia. You didn't fight there. You couldn't know—'

'I fought in the Amphitheatre. I do know.'

He opened his eyes. The muscle tightened in his jaw until Severina wondered if his teeth would crack.

She didn't know why she asked this of him. If street fighting was the issue, she could easily protect herself with a dagger. All gladiators trained with a variety of weapons, from the curved *sica* to the mace. The dagger was an easy weapon to use and she was skilful with it. Furthermore, in a street fight, she'd have the advantage of surprise. Nobody would expect combat skill or courage from a woman.

'Take the dagger, Severina. Forget my *spatha*. I'll never give it up. Not to you, not to anybody.'

She searched Lucan's face. He meant every word. She'd never seen him look so determined.

'I never considered that it might mean so much to you,' she said. 'It has sentimental value, then?'

'It's more that I'd feel vulnerable without it, out of control, like I couldn't influence my own destiny. To surrender it…that's something I'll never do.'

There was a long moment of silence.

'Fine, then. I'll take the dagger.' She was quiet for a minute, then turned to smile at him. 'You give odd gifts, Lucan. A dagger's not a man's usual gift to a lover.'

'You're not the usual sort of lover.' He took the weapon from her hands and placed it on the table so he could take both her hands into his own. 'What we have will be extraordinary. What we do…will be unforgettable.'

The coolness left his eyes. She drew in a deep breath to steady the sudden tumult of emotion. His eyes dropped to her breasts.

'Thank you for the dagger,' she whispered. 'I'll wear it, if you wish, but not tonight.'

'No?'

She swallowed hard at the hunger in his eyes. She knew where his imagination had gone. She was envisioning the same thing he did—their two bodies, naked and entwined, with no leather thong holding a dagger to her sleek thigh.

'It would ruin the line of my tunic,' she said. 'There'd be an unsightly bulge beneath my fine clothing.'

His smile was wicked. 'Then there'd be two of us.'

'Your *spatha*?'

'Hardly.' His laughter was soft. He kissed her hands, one at a time, and let her go. 'One more thing… Pack some extra clothing. Tell Ariadne we won't be returning for at least two days. We're leaving Onesimus to handle the construction here and going away for some peace and quiet. It's been clearly established now that I'm the inn's official owner. I see no further need to endure the mess and chaos of the building process, do you?'

Severina stopped breathing. 'Go away? Together? Alone?'

Amusement lit his eyes. 'Yes. That's the way it usually works best.'

Her knees suddenly felt unsteady. She reached for the back of a chair and held it so tightly her knuckles turned white. 'You mean…you and I?'

The corner of his lips turned upwards. He had such beautiful lips.

'Yes, you and I. Unless you had other plans. You didn't have other plans, did you?'

'No. Oh, no.'

'I didn't think so.' His voice was low, disturbingly masculine, with a seductive quality that caused desire to shudder through her.

Her tingling breasts firmed against her garment. Lucan noticed it and reached out to touch her nipple with a fingertip. He squeezed it—gently, firmly—and she sucked in her breath as pleasure shafted through her.

His eyes were burning now, fiery molten gold.

And her flesh was molten, too, a hot river between her legs, flowing with need for him.

'Perhaps we'll leave Lelia's dinner party early,' he said.

'She'll understand,' Severina whispered.

'Maybe we'll also be late.'

Severina groaned softly as Lucan pulled her into his arms. She watched in helpless fascination as his face drew near to hers, eyes glittering, jaw determined, a powerful eagle intent on prey.

She lowered her lashes at such magnificent beauty, bowing to the inevitable, acknowledging his right to possess, frightened at how eagerly she wished to be devoured. *'Dominus,'* she whispered, and the word rolled through her core until she trembled.

Lucan's gold-tipped lashes lifted. He searched her face and saw her willingness and her vulnerability.

'Trust me,' he commanded.

'Yes.'

His mouth came down on hers, fierce and hot, and their bodies collided with sweet and gentle force.

'Dear gods,' Lucan said when the long kiss ended. His voice was tinged with awe. 'Do you give to me or take from me?'

The rasp of his breath in her ear caused her to whimper and press closer. She was as startled with the passion as he, and hurt when he took his lips away.

He relieved the ache with gentleness, sliding warmth and pressure into the sensitive hollows of her neck, drawing heat down to her collarbone. She held herself still, scarcely breathing. The jet beads on her bodice clicked together daintily when he fulfilled her wish and closed his hand around her breast.

She looked down, perplexed, intrigued by her own surrender, aroused by the sight of Lucan's hand, callused, strong, the rugged hand of a man who laboured. Of the rough fingers that cradled her, caressing her fullness, his thumb sliding across the taut fabric that stretched over the peak.

She could hardly bear so exquisite a torture. She couldn't breathe. The lack of air made her dizzy. Lucan bent as if he sensed her weakness, catching her up into his powerful arms and carrying her with two long strides to the bed. She was laid like a pagan offering on an altar, her hair tumbling into disarray, her skirts riding up her calves.

'Please…' she heard herself say, trying to slow the spinning of the room, the thudding of her heart, the pounding of blood in her ears. Her voice sounded strange—plaintive, tormented.

'Ah, love,' Lucan murmured, his body coming alongside hers. 'Let me answer your hungers.'

He didn't do what she expected. He didn't cover her with his heat or weight even though she longed for him.

He moved towards the foot of the bed. She jerked with surprise when his huge, rough hands closed around the smooth skin just above her ankles. 'Easy,' he said, his palms sliding upwards with slow deliberation, taking the hem of her tunic higher, carried upwards on his wrists.

She gasped, startled that his touch could wield such pleasure. It intensified when his fingertips skimmed lightly over her knees. It became painfully acute when his fingertips slipped over the sensitive skin of her inner thighs.

'Lucan…oh!'

He pressed firmly, sweetly, against the soft fold between her legs. Sensation sheared through her body so that she twisted hard against the bedclothes, convulsing, moaning.

He slipped one finger into her slick, moist cleft and then parted her, opening her to his gaze, and to his lips when he lowered his head and tasted her.

To be touched that way shamed her. 'No, Lucan,' she murmured, plucking at his tunic, trying to pull him away from a vulnerability she could hardly endure.

He resisted her meagre efforts and centred his mouth over the bud at the top of her labia. She could no longer protest; sensation overwhelmed her. His tongue, his lips—oh, they were so wicked and so sure.

She was daunted by the knowledge that he'd known about this all along, that he'd always understood such naughty pleasures existed and that he could make her willingly cry for them.

And there were still other things he knew that she did not. She sensed this in him and it maddened her; she couldn't bear that he might restrain himself or withhold such treasure as she felt now, soaring higher, flying nearer to an elusive blazing glory.

Her muscles clenched hard, tightening to the point of pain. Her hands clawed at Lucan's shoulders and fisted in his hair. She was mewling, moaning, writhing beneath his hot mouth.

She thought she could endure no more. Yet this was Lucan and so there *was* more. Even now he intently watched her face and felt her muscles throb beneath his lips, and he called on all he'd ever learned during his long intimacy with sin.

He knew the moment, chose it well. In the instant she felt she'd break into pieces or die, Lucan gave her more, pushing his finger hard and deep into her body, possessing her so fully that she screamed his name and hurtled over the edge into pleasure rich and fine, sanctified by pagan fire.

She had cried his name.

Lucan pulled away from her, and let the wonder of the moment sink in.

He'd been right to seduce Severina towards intimacy. His name on her lips in that moment of wildest abandon proved it. Already the bond was forming. Already she was closer to becoming totally, irrevocably his.

She lay wearily on the crumpled bedclothes, eyes closed, chest softly heaving. Spent.

Her thighs remained parted and Lucan feasted on the vision of her body open to him, glistening wet and still swollen with passion. It made his engorged flesh throb still, but denial was no stranger to him these days, and he preferred to wait for other worlds to conquer. Severina would become his woman later that evening and that would be soon enough.

He performed loving service to her now and pushed her thighs together, pulling down the hem of her gown to restore order to her world. She opened her eyes and looked at him.

'Lucan?'

'Hmmm?'

'I don't know what to say. I feel so…'

'Relieved? Pleasured? Satisfied?' Lucan smiled down at her. 'A simple "thank you" will do.'

She blushed furiously and looked away as if she couldn't bear this moment of emotional nakedness.

He was tempted to be hurt at her withdrawal; he'd hoped for better. He sensed now the return of her fears. Already she distanced herself from him and fought for her sovereignty.

Trust was a fragile thing.

He'd been foolish to believe she'd give it easily. Her willing vulnerability in these past moments changed almost nothing between them. There had been only a momentary triumph, he understood that now. The next time he touched her, he'd be back at the beginning and would labour again just as diligently to carve his niche into her deep soul. The campaign for Severina would not be won in one decisive moment; it would be won in skirmish after skirmish over long months of effort.

But she'd be worth it.

He looked down at her again, and couldn't resist the urge to caress her cheek. 'This was only a sample of the delights to come for you tonight,' he said. It was a promise he meant to keep.

She nodded, her eyes still not quite meeting his.

His hand slipped down and around to curve against her nape, his fingertips smoothing over her skin, smoothing over…a gold chain? He hooked it with one finger and lifted it, pulling it towards him and the heavier weight that hung from it out from its hiding place within her bodice.

She gasped and reached up to stop him when he would have taken the prize into his hand.

'No.' He scowled at her. 'Let me see it.'

Her breasts heaved in and out with her long, deep sigh.

He studied the object in his hand for a moment. It was beautiful, crafted of burnished gold and elaborately carved with Egyptian motifs, adorned with one large ruby surrounded by pearls and diamonds. It was worth no paltry sum.

'Explain this,' he said quietly. 'Why do you wear another man's ring on a chain around your neck?'

She wouldn't meet his gaze and that worried him.

'It's nothing,' she said, taking the ring from his hand. She unclasped the chain and took it from around her neck, placing it on the nearby table. 'Just a memento, a reminder, a sentimental thing.'

His heart began to hurt. 'A memento? A reminder of whom, Severina? A past lover?' He forced out the words. 'A husband, perhaps? Is that why you won't marry me? Are you already married to someone else?'

Her startled gaze flashed upwards to his face. 'Sweet mercy, Lucan. Of course not! Do you think I'd let you touch me like you just did if there were someone else...?' Her laughter was low and nervous, filled with incredulity. 'Is that what you think of me?'

'I don't know what to think.'

There was a long moment of silence. Severina's eyes looked everywhere but into his. He waited in the quiet, silently willing her to give up her secrets, to tell him something to lessen the ache in his chest.

She did not.

When the silence had stretched long between them, Lucan spoke. 'If you possessed a token of such value, why did you not sell it to purchase your freedom from gladiatorial slavery? Or use it to buy the inn for yourself?'

'I would never sell it. I treasure it more than gold.'

Another long silence.

'I see,' he said finally. But he did not see. And she didn't offer any further information. She wouldn't tell him about the man who'd worn that ring. She wouldn't explain how she'd come to own it or why it mattered to her more than gold.

This moment shouldn't hurt so much. He'd known she had secrets. He'd known something kept her from marrying him. This new discovery had given him nothing he didn't already know, but his soul felt the knife's keen edge all the same.

He suddenly needed to be alone and turned to leave her.

'Lucan?'

He halted.

'Have you ever given a dagger to any other woman?'

'No.'

Her voice was subdued. 'Not every woman would understand such a gift.'

He turned his head until his eyes met hers. 'You're not every woman, Severina. You're *my* woman.'

She didn't say anything to that.

He accepted her silence. Further acknowledgement was unnecessary. They both knew a line had been crossed.

But Lucan did not smile as he closed the door.

* * *

Time was a confusing thing. Learned men might say that every day was composed of equal units, but Severina knew better. Time was a perverse and slippery thing with a stubborn will of its own.

Earlier it had moved with the pace of a tortoise, lumbering and slow. During the morning she'd watched Lucan work on the inn, eyeing him from across the courtyard, her attention never far from him even when she poured drinks or talked quietly with Ariadne.

He'd moved through his tasks with the sensual grace of a feline. She'd been fascinated by the flex of muscles in his back and legs as he hefted beams and carried brick. Sunlight gilded his hair, darkened his skin, fired the warmth in his leaf-green eyes. His smile came often, a flash of white against bronzed skin. His laughter was deep and satisfying. She wished she could have a lifetime of hearing it.

Lucan had watched her, too. She was aware of his attention, tingling with it, aching because of it. When the men came to get drinks, she could hardly pour his goblet for the trembling of her hands.

He'd noticed. His fingertips brushed over hers in a reassuring caress as he took the vessel from her hand. 'To tonight,' he had said quietly, lifting the glass in a subtle salute. She hadn't realised that she held her breath until he turned to go.

To tonight. To tonight.

All afternoon the words had beat hard against her heart, hammering the man's virile presence into every crevice of her soul. And time had passed slowly, simply because she'd begun wanting him so much.

Neither of them had been prepared for the passion that had overtaken them in her bedroom. A sample of delights to come, he'd called it, somehow knowing it would only whet her appetite for more.

He'd been right, and now the night had come. He rested beside her in an ornate litter as they travelled to their friends' home. Lucan's warm hand settled on her thigh, not moving, not encroaching, simply resting there. But it was, she knew, both a statement and a question. She covered it with her own hand, a caress. She knew she'd given the right answer when he turned to her and smiled.

Oh, Lucan. When she breathed, she breathed in his scent. When she moved, her thigh rubbed against the firm length of his. The touch held such agony, such sweetness. She would memorise every moment.

And the minutes that crept with agonising slowness earlier in the day now spun away so quickly she wanted to cry. If only time would move slowly. She desperately wanted to savour every moment. But they always fled before she could capture every delicate sensation.

Lucan glanced out through the curtains. 'We're almost there.'

Of course they would be. Soon they'd have to chatter and laugh and make conversation over a good meal when all Severina really wanted was to have Lucan to herself. She craved his touch, his warmth wrapped around her, his body filling hers.

They would make love tonight.

Lucan had carefully withheld himself from her before. She'd been content to have it so, understanding that he, the reckless lover of so many, had wanted this relationship to be different.

But their kiss in the Forum had marked a change in their relationship. They both understood that a new set of rules had come into play. Tonight they dealt only in hours and minutes; they weren't discussing for ever.

She was comforted in this. She'd not have to promise him a future in order to lie with him tonight. She'd not have to surrender freedom to enjoy this fleeting happiness.

If guilt intruded, she pushed it away. If reason reminded her that loving Lucan might endanger him, she hushed it.

Time was running out. Her future would be uncertain and lonely. But she could have this one night and Lucan as her lover for the duration of it. To have that, to have *him*, was worth any pain or risk. It would be a warm memory for colder days to come.

If only she could make time move more slowly.

It seemed only seconds later that they stopped before Donatus and Lelia's palatial home. The litter was lowered to the ground and Lucan helped her out of it.

Lelia met her at the door with an enthusiastic embrace. 'Severina, you're stunning,' she said. 'Absolutely stunning. That colour looks beautiful with your complexion…and, oh, those adorable jet beads!'

Severina scarcely heard. Her gaze was centred on Lucan, on how manly he looked as he shook hands with Donatus, on how sensuously he moved, on the warmth of his large hand against the small of her back as they were led forwards through the foyer and into the atrium.

The room was large and spacious and fragrant with the waxy scent of a multitude of candles. But…

She turned to Lelia with a puzzled expression. 'Where are the other guests?'

Lelia laughed. 'They'll be arriving shortly. Donatus and I wanted to talk privately with you and Lucan before they got here.'

Donatus drew Lelia against his side. 'Let's offer them something to drink first, shall we? We shouldn't be impolite. Besides, they might need it, once they hear our news.'

'What news?' Lucan looked from one to the other, his face lit with interest. 'Don't tell me you two are already expecting another child.'

Donatus and Lelia both laughed his comment away, but Severina thought Lelia blushed slightly, and that she turned away too quickly to request four goblets of chilled wine from a nearby slave.

It made Severina wonder if…well, why not? Lelia was deeply in love with her husband, and he was a bold man. If being in love made a woman fruitful, then Lelia would one day have a house full of children.

'No, no. Not that,' Donatus said. He caught Lelia's eye. 'Though I won't deny that I'll welcome the news each and every time it comes.'

Lelia's blush deepened.

Severina's heart twisted hard, watching the two of them. They were happy together, so much in love. If only…

'This news is something else entirely,' Donatus said, turning back to Lucan. 'We wanted you two to be the first to know it. Lelia and I, we're soon to be baptised as Christians.'

For a moment, nobody spoke.

'That's wonderful,' Severina said as the quiet lengthened. She moved forwards to embrace Lelia. 'I wish you the best. I want you and Donatus to have whatever you want, and if this is what makes you happy—'

'Oh, it is!' Lelia's voice was excited. 'We've been moving in this direction for a long time now. In fact, Lucan was the one who first caused us to consider it. We saw the peace his faith gave him, and the good changes in his life…and then he brought his Christian brothers and sisters here, and they used our large banquet hall for their feasts. Donatus and I listened to their ideas and found them odd at first, but gradually we came to understand. Now we've committed our lives to Christ and we—'

'No.' Lucan's voice was sharp. 'You're being misled, and I regret that I had any part in that.'

Donatus's face hardened slightly. 'Lucan, I know you—'

'No—' Lucan held up a hand '—you don't know, Donatus. You've just begun with this faith, but I lived it. I was faithful. I prayed and fasted and sought God. *Nobody* tried harder than I did. But what good did it do?' He looked down, rubbing the rim of the goblet he held with an agitated motion. 'When I needed God most, he wasn't there. When I truly needed peace, I didn't have it.'

Donatus's voice was gentle. 'It would've come, Lucan. You shouldn't have given up. God's ways aren't always clear to us at first. But if you had kept on believing, if you'd waited—'

Lucan's growl was low and deep. 'Don't blame me,' he said, his eyes sparking fire. 'You think I wanted confusion and pain?' He shook his head. 'I wanted to know God was there for me, that he really cared, that he heard my prayers and answered them. Unfortunately—' his voice held a bitter edge '—I never became convinced of that.'

Severina winced. *She* had been the cause of Lucan's crisis of faith.

Lelia was quick to soothe Lucan. She moved to him and stroked her palm gently down his arm. 'We understand, Lucan. We don't blame you.' She glanced at Severina. 'We don't blame either of you.'

'She's right.' Donatus came to Lucan and held out his hand. When Lucan grasped it, Donatus pulled his friend into a strong embrace. 'You've been my good friend for years. Many times we've disagreed. Sometimes I questioned your choices. Sometimes you questioned mine. But that's never kept us from our friendship, and it won't now.'

Their gazes locked.

'I wish you well with your decision,' Lucan said quietly. 'But please understand if I don't attend your baptism.'

'Rufinus will baptise us, he wants you to come. He asked me if—'

'No.' Lucan's jaw tightened. 'I won't be there, Donatus. You and Lelia have my best wishes. You could do worse than to live the moral life to which Christians hold themselves. But don't make the mistake I did and hope that faith in their God will give you any help when you need it.'

The men studied one another for a long moment. Finally Lucan looked away. Severina wondered at the unnatural brightness of his gold-flecked eyes.

'Tell Rufinus that I've left the faith,' Lucan said quietly. 'I'll look elsewhere for my answers in the future.'

Donatus's reply was gentle. 'You might leave God, Lucan. But God doesn't ever leave *you*.'

The pain in Lucan's face told Severina everything about the hurt she'd caused him. She'd never seen such longing or grief. For the first time she understood how much she'd stripped from him. And she despaired, because she'd never be able to give any of it back.

Lelia came forwards and linked her arm into Severina's, her voice full of forced cheer. 'Oh, well. At least we've cleared the air and we all know where we stand. Time to change the subject now.' She gestured towards the *triclinium*, which was large and spacious, with an abundance of silk-cushioned couches and tall lamp-stands that sent flickering light over the mosaic tile and coloured marble friezes decorating the walls. 'Our other guests will be arriving any moment and I'm still not sure if I've chosen the best seating arrangement. You'll help me decide, won't you, Severina?'

Severina glanced back at Lucan. Though he followed her and Lelia towards the warmly lit room, his face was as cold as the marble on its walls.

Chapter Eleven

Donatus and Lelia were excellent hosts. As their guests arrived, each one was treated to the lavish attention of a bevy of servants—mostly freedmen, Lucan noted. Donatus, like his father before him, believed that slaves released from servitude and paid for their work were happier and more trustworthy than those forced to serve.

Lucan tried to enjoy the benefits of their service. Normally, he liked having his feet washed and his limbs massaged with warm, fragrant oils. Normally he enjoyed the conversation and laughter of other guests as it flowed around him. Normally he applauded the gentle tones of the lyre, harp and flute played while everyone socialised. He might even hum along; he was a fair musician himself.

But tonight he felt out of sorts. He'd been startled by Donatus and Lelia's announcement of their conversion to Christianity. They'd been right to tell him about it in private; he hadn't reacted well. He shouldn't have responded with such bitterness. He knew Donatus and Lelia understood and that they would graciously accept any apology he tendered, but it galled him that an apology was needed. He'd been reared to show better manners than those he'd displayed tonight.

And that wasn't the only thing bothering him. He'd worried all day about his earlier conversation with Orthrus. The younger man's anxiety matched Lucan's own and had led to his decision to take Severina away to safety.

Lucan hadn't been completely honest with her about it. He didn't want to frighten her when all he had was a vague unrest. It was easier to let her believe he was leading her to a romantic tryst.

But that wasn't actually a lie, either. During the last two days, ever since their agreement in the Forum, there'd been a heightened sexual awareness between them. Even a less experienced male hunter than he would have sensed the change and responded accordingly. Severina's gaze now followed him, intent and hungry. Her manner was subtly alluring, leading his imagination to all kinds of wayward places.

There had been that passion between them in her bedroom earlier. He hadn't expected it, but he'd made good use of the opportunity.

Her response had aroused and excited him, but it angered him, too, that she'd give herself so willingly when he promised her no future, nothing but the pleasure of a moment. Yet she fled whenever he spoke of love and commitment, of marriage and a lifetime together.

The irony chafed him raw. He'd used countless women for pleasure and nothing more. Now he rebelled at being used by Severina in exactly the same way.

He was caught on the horns of a dilemma. He could hold out for something lasting, but that hadn't worked before and was unlikely to work now. On the issue of commitment, he'd seen no change in her.

On the other hand, he could simply give in to the strident urging of his body and take her on the terms she offered. He knew he could give her pleasure. He was an accomplished lover; he knew his level of skill. It was no idle boast that he could easily have her begging, pleading, crying for release. He'd make her shake with need, then take her to a climax so fierce that all memory of anything less would be forever banished.

He could give her this, and he wanted to.

But there was the slight problem of his own heart.

It pained him to realise that he wanted Severina to care something for him before she gave herself fully to him.

It was even worse to admit that he wanted their sexual union to bring her to the place where she'd willingly wed him.

He knew what lay ahead if she never came to that place.

He'd hurt like hell, worse than he ever had before, worse than the time she'd left him and worse than every lonely night since.

Because once he took Severina, flesh to flesh, soul to soul, he'd be unable to sever the bond.

Was he willing to hurt that much? Perhaps not.

Until he thought of Severina as she'd looked earlier, her sleek thighs open to him, her body swollen and ready for his possession—and he knew with unsettling inevitability that he would take the risk.

Donatus's voice at his shoulder pulled him away from his thoughts. 'You're being too quiet, Lucan. You're still upset about my decision to adopt your discarded faith?'

Lucan shook his head, suddenly grateful that he reclined next to Donatus in the place of honour. They could talk without being overheard. 'No. I did behave badly about it, though. I'm sorry for that.'

'Forget it.' Donatus smiled. 'But think of this. When we rode as cavalrymen, it was always the chafing under the saddle that made the horse buck and rear.'

'Meaning what?'

'Meaning that, oddly enough, your reaction did much to reassure me. You're not too far away from the faith you think you've lost.'

'You speak in riddles.'

Donatus laughed softly. 'Do I?' He reached for a dish of appetisers. 'Here,' he said, passing it beneath Lucan's nose. 'Forget deep thoughts for now and enjoy these. Sea urchins in clove sauce.'

Lucan spooned a couple on to his plate, lifted one with his fingers and tasted it. He made a sound of pleasure. 'Wonderful,' he said. 'Better even than the snails and spiced eggs last time we dined with you.'

'I thought you'd like those.' They ate in silence for a moment. 'If you're not sullen tonight because of what Lelia and I told you,' Donatus ventured, 'then there's something else bothering you.'

Lucan made a low sound in his throat.

'Sounds like sexual frustration to me,' Donatus said with a smile. 'Am I right?'

Lucan's lips tightened. Sometimes Donatus knew him too well.

'Ah, don't worry. The women will soon return to the table. Lelia took them out to show them her new additions to the flower garden.' He shrugged. 'Not that they'll be able to tell much about it in the dark, with only torches to light the paths. But I'm just a man. What do I know?' He leaned closer and grinned. 'When they return, you'll be pleased to note that Lelia put two people per couch. Severina will dine with you.'

Lucan immediately imagined he and Severina lying close together. Her breasts would be close to him, perhaps touching his arm every time she reached for another bite of food.

He changed the subject. 'One couch is still empty. Someone's arriving late?'

Donatus nodded. 'A Nubian trader from Ostia. An interesting fellow. Lelia and I met him earlier this week. He should prove most entertaining.'

Something in Donatus's manner made Lucan look at his face. 'I look forward to meeting him.'

'Perhaps he'll arrive soon. But look, here come the ladies. Lelia's directing Severina this way.' Donatus quirked a mischievous eyebrow. 'Anything I can do to relieve the pain?'

'Just don't say anything to the crowd when I slip away to the nearest bath. I'll probably need cold water in the worst kind of way.'

Donatus's laughter caused Lelia to turn and smile in their direction. Severina started their way.

The seating arrangement was, Lucan decided, a jest his hosts played on him, maybe testing whether he'd go insane because of unfulfilled desire. Either that or they thought it funny to see him embarrassingly prominent in all the wrong places.

Either way, he wasn't laughing.

'Lucan?' Severina halted at the foot of his couch, looking as hesitant as he felt.

He smiled and held out his hand. 'Come and dine.'

Her face betrayed her confusion. 'This is an odd arrangement, don't you think?'

'No one will make an issue of it. And I promise to behave myself, so none will question your virtue.'

She relaxed and sat down on the couch near his feet. 'Lelia's probably trying to encourage something.'

He laughed softly. 'I'm sure of it.'

She pulled back. 'In that case, maybe I should…'

'And deprive your friend of the most fun she's had in weeks?' Lucan slid far to the side and gestured for her to share the wide couch. 'There's room.'

Severina moved into place. Lucan looked away to avoid the pleasure of seeing her body stretched out next to his.

'Cold water,' Donatus muttered beside him. 'I might need some, too. Now that Lelia's got all her guests into place, she's coming to share this couch with me.'

Lucan grinned at his friend.

'The sea urchins are good,' Lucan said, turning back to Severina. 'Try this.' He placed a morsel to her lips.

Lelia overheard him as she slid into place beside Donatus. 'Oh, yes. I hear they're powerful aphrodisiacs.'

Severina choked on the bite she'd just taken.

Lucan handed Severina his napkin as he glanced at Lelia. 'They're *what*?'

'Aphrodisiacs. They make for good…you know.'

'Sex,' Donatus said in a low voice. 'For good sex.'

Lelia smiled at Donatus. 'That's what I heard.'

Donatus drew his wife closer against his body. 'And you thought…what? That we needed some help?'

'No. I didn't think that. I was thinking about others. Not everybody here is as blessed as we are.'

Severina cleared her throat. 'I think I'll pass on the sea urchins.'

'I think I'll take a double portion,' Lucan said, grinning roguishly at her.

Lelia laughed at the way Severina's eyes widened.

'Oh, go ahead and eat some, Severina,' she said. 'If nothing else, it'll whet your appetite for the huge sausages to come.'

Severina's gasp was so loud Lucan was sure Lelia and Donatus heard it, but they graciously pretended not to.

Lucan suddenly wanted to laugh, though he wasn't sure if Lelia was helping his cause or hurting it. He was fairly certain that she and Donatus were enjoying the show, however.

A slave entered and brought the second course, a roasted wild boar. The guests broke into applause.

Lucan was pleased with the diversion created by the food as it was sliced and served to the guests. In all the chaos, he had the opportunity to observe the woman lying beside him without others noticing.

'You're hungry?' he asked her, noticing her parted lips as she watched big slabs of roasted pig being forked on to plates.

'Starved.'

He smiled, unable to look away from her. 'I'll call for a servant to fill your plate.'

'That's not what I'm hungry for.'

He met her gaze. Her eyes were dark, the pupils wide.

'I want to kiss you,' he murmured.

'I'll die if you don't.'

Lucan heard Lelia's soft gasp behind him when he lowered his head to Severina's and took her lips. That slight sound was enough to keep him clinging to sanity. His lust didn't spiral far out of control; he pulled back after only a moment, leaving Severina's eyes glazed with need and her breath passing hard through moist, parted lips.

'This isn't the place,' he said in a low voice. 'We can't dishonour our hosts this way.'

Severina nodded, still looking slightly dazed. 'Later?'

She was killing him. Sweet mercy, she was killing him.

'Is that what you want?'

She swallowed. 'Yes.'

He looked away, tension tightening his jaw.

'We'll see,' he said. 'For now, we'll eat and enjoy the night's entertainment. I hear Lelia's written a play.'

Lelia overheard his last words. She swallowed the bite of food she'd been chewing and nodded enthusiastically. 'Oh, yes! And Druscilla's playing the lead role. She loves playacting, you know, and thinks it's appalling that females aren't allowed to act in Rome's theatres.'

Donatus snorted. 'You shouldn't be encouraging her, Lelia. She should be settling down to learning the skills she'll need as a wife, not learning lines of dialogue to perform for our guests.'

'I think it's wonderful,' Severina said. 'Playacting is one of the most useful skills of all.' Lucan and Donatus turned questioning gazes in her direction and she shrugged. 'Don't you men use it all the time? When you go to sell a mule? When you convince your colleagues in the Senate to pass your legislation? When you buy a piece of property?'

'That's not playacting,' Donatus answered. 'That's just…'

'Just what?' Lelia demanded.

'Just…business.'

'But you're doing it with a fair amount of make believe, you've got to admit. Not so different from playacting.' She glanced at her friend. 'Like Severina said, it's a useful skill.'

'I thought women used playacting all the time,' Donatus said with a grin. 'Like when they tell their husbands how little their *stola* cost, or how they acquired the new gold ring.'

Lelia lifted a haughty eyebrow. 'Or perhaps when they moan with pleasure in the marriage bed.'

'Ouch.' Lucan winced.

'What's the play about?' Severina asked as she daintily tested her meat. 'And did you say you *wrote* it, Lelia? Since when do you write plays? Is this a recent interest?'

'Fairly so. I hope you'll like it. It's a love story.'

Severina scowled hard at her food. 'It ends tragically, I suppose,' she said.

'Oh, no. But I won't spoil the surprise.'

A tall servant stepped to the door of the *triclinium*. 'Another guest has arrived, my lord,' he announced in formal tones. 'Shall I escort him in?'

Lelia clapped her hands. 'What perfect timing. Yes, please do bring him in.' She glanced towards Severina. 'Donatus and I met the gentleman only this week, Severina, but already we feel like we've known him for ever. You'll like him. I know you will.'

'The Nubian?' Lucan asked Donatus.

'A trader from Ostia, very wealthy. Owns a fleet of grain ships, among other things.'

Lucan turned to see the tall black man enter the room. The trader stopped and quickly surveyed the scene before him. Then as if he'd been looking especially for her, his sharp, black-eyed gaze found Severina.

Lucan felt the sudden tensing of Severina's entire body. Time seemed to hang in odd stillness as each studied the other. Something unspoken passed between them. Jealousy bit into Lucan, hot and horrid.

Severina was the first to look away. She turned to Lucan. 'The veal cutlets in garum sauce are delicious. Would you like some?'

'No.' He studied her a moment. Over her head, he saw the newest guest making his way towards their end of the room to greet Donatus and Lelia as proper etiquette dictated. Lucan lowered his voice. 'Severina, do you know that man?'

Her laughter seemed forced and was accompanied by a theatrical wave of her hand. He thought again about her comment that playacting was one of the most important skills a person could have.

'Know him? How would I know a grain merchant from Ostia?'

Lucan turned her face until he could look into her eyes. 'Then maybe I'm a fool, but there almost seemed to be something between the two of you when he entered. Between just the two of you.'

She didn't look away. Her gaze was touched with soft amusement. 'You're imagining things, Lucan. The only man I want to share anything with right now is you.'

Lucan wasn't completely reassured, but he swept aside the odd feeling. Maybe he really was imagining things. He hadn't felt quite himself all evening, not since he'd found another man's ring around her neck.

He watched her closely for the remainder of the evening. Nothing else seemed out of place. Severina watched Lelia's play in utter fascination, applauding Druscilla's performance with sincerity and complimenting Lelia on her skill as a playwright. She ate heartily, especially the sausages served with oysters. Her tongue licking over them made Lucan almost wild with lust, but he refused to give Lelia the satisfaction of knowing that.

Some of the guests had begun to depart when Donatus turned to Lucan. 'Lelia and I have something urgent to discuss with you.' He glanced towards Severina. 'Alone, if you don't mind. It shouldn't take long.'

Lucan turned to Severina. 'I'll be right back. Will you be fine without me for a moment?'

Her eyes darted towards the tall Nubian before she thought. Lucan's fears surfaced again. 'Of course,' she said. 'Take your time.'

Lucan followed Donatus, glancing backwards as he slipped through the doorway.

Severina wasn't looking in his direction at all. She hardly seemed to care that he'd left. She was staring at the Nubian trader.

Lucan wasn't used to the emotion he felt right then.

He didn't like the feeling. Not at all.

Severina pretended to watch the servants as they took out the table with the main course and replaced it with the second table carrying desserts. She focused on a large bowl of figs as the Nubian sat down on the couch beside her.

'A pleasure to see you again, Aloli,' he said in a voice so low and deep it was barely audible. 'You're looking well.'

'Thank you, Semni. You always were kind to me.'

He reached past her and took one of the figs from the dish, bit into it and chewed. 'Have you heard? The drought continues to ravage our two homelands.'

Severina frowned. 'I'm sorry to hear that.'

The dark-skinned man lifted an eyebrow. 'Are you?'

'Of course. I don't wish for any to suffer.'

'And yet, here you are.'

Severina glanced towards the doorway. 'Our hosts will be returning soon. Shouldn't you return to your own seat?'

'Our hosts are already aware that you're not all you seem.'

Severina jerked around to look at him. 'How do you know that?'

'They sought me out earlier this week. They asked questions. Lots of questions.'

Severina's breath hissed out. 'And what did you tell them?'

The man's dark gaze found her. 'Relax. I told them nothing, but neither did they believe me. That we're both here, invited to this same party…no mere coincidence. They watched you when I entered. They looked for your reaction, and mine.' He bit into another fig. 'You played the part of stranger beautifully, but…' he leaned down to whisper the words near her ear '…they *know*.'

Sudden nausea assailed Severina. She fought panic.

They'd never use the knowledge to hurt her, would they? Donatus was Lucan's friend. Lelia was hers. Even if their affectionate friendship caused them to meddle in something they barely understood, surely they'd never—

'The man you're with. What is he to you?'

'A friend.'

'You remain a virgin, I hope.'

Severina scowled. 'That shouldn't matter to any but me.'

The Nubian chuckled. 'No. Perhaps not. One favoured as you are by the goddess might, after all, do whatever she pleases.' He reached across to take a honey cake from a bronze tray. 'But the drought in our region is severe. Your father, all the priests, the nobles of Egypt…they're more desperate than ever to fulfil the prophecy.'

Semni tasted his food, closed his eyes at the sweetness, opened them to focus hard on her. 'Anok Khai's zeal now borders on madness. He's close to finding you.'

'How do you know?'

'He knows you came to Rome aboard one of my grain ships. He questioned me months ago, but I feigned ignorance. So many grain ships, how was I to know the cargo and passengers of every single one?'

He held up a hand. The two smallest fingers were missing. 'He didn't take me at my word in the beginning, as you see.'

Severina shuddered. 'I am unworthy. Thank you, Semni.'

The black man shrugged. 'No matter, now. As mad as he is, and as cruel, he would've killed me had I spoken the truth. My lies that day kept me alive for this one, and I'm still able to do almost anything…except maybe play the harp.'

He leaned forwards, his face serious. 'I will offer you one piece of advice. Leave this place quickly if you want to keep your freedom. It's taken him five years to run you to ground, Aloli, but he's within days of capturing you.'

Severina closed her eyes.

When she opened them again, Semni had returned to his own dining couch, smiling and laughing with the other guests as if he hadn't just brought destruction crashing down on her world.

She glanced around. Donatus, Lelia and Lucan were still in Donatus's office. They could return at any time.

But her father was nearer than she'd thought. The moment she'd dreaded was nearly upon her.

And what about Lucan?

She thought back to the previous days. The censor's visit—her father's doing. The black-haired man who'd followed them—one of Anok Khai's spies. The accident with the cart of boulders—no accident at all. She was certain now.

She wasn't afraid for herself. Her father must take her back to Egypt alive. But Lucan?

He'd kill Lucan.

Severina bit her lip, her thoughts whirling. She had to protect Lucan, but if she stayed with him and especially if they became lovers… She'd put him into danger.

If Lucan loved her tonight, he'd unknowingly be guilty of a heinous sacrilege. If he tore through her virginity, her father would have him killed for it.

Anok Khai burned with zeal for the goddess Isis. He was her High Priest and would allow no man to live who profaned anything sacred to her. And he fervently believed Severina had a destiny to fulfil for the goddess.

Severina had been only fifteen when Isis had appeared to Anok Khai in a dream, promising him immortality when his eldest child was wed to the eldest child of Egypt's ruler. The marriage would bring fertility to the Nile and ensure the blessings of the gods.

Severina was his first-born.

Aided by her old nurse and Semni, she'd fled Egypt before her father could fulfil his plans for her. She'd gone first to Athens and then to Rome. Taking on a new identity, she'd so far outwitted Anok Khai and outrun him. But now he'd found her.

Severina looked again towards the door. Still no sign of Lucan.

She mustered her courage, stood and walked to the couch where the tall trader reclined. He looked up at her, not surprised that she spoke quietly in her native language.

'The next grain ship. When does it leave?'

'Two days' time. Bound for Britannia.'

Britannia. That was further that she'd expected. Even her father would have trouble finding her there. It was a mysterious land filled with the Celtae, a wild and savage people. It was unknown and frightening.

But it would suit her purpose well. Two days would also give her time to prepare documents of manumission releasing her slaves. She'd miss Ariadne's wedding, but that couldn't be helped now.

'You'll escort me to the ship?' she asked Semni.

His eyebrows rose. 'Tonight?'

'Yes, tonight. Immediately. Before our host and hostess return.'

'And the golden-haired man. He will not follow you?'

She thought of Lucan and felt pain. 'No, he won't,' she said. 'You'll see to it. You'll tell a male guest here that I…that I offered myself to you and you couldn't refuse.'

The Nubian's dark eyes studied her for a moment. 'You love him,' he said. 'You love the golden-haired man. But you'll hurt him like that?'

'You know I have no choice.'

There was regret in the man's face. 'Very well. Gather your things and meet me near the front door. I'll take you to the ship.'

Chapter Twelve

Lucan stood at the window that faced the private courtyard outside Donatus's office. He shoved his hand through his hair.

'You're sure?' He turned back to Lelia. 'You're sure about this?'

Lelia nodded. 'Brocchus wouldn't lie. He had no reason.'

'We substantiated part of the story,' Donatus said quietly. 'Brocchus was right about the trader's name, his nationality, the street on which he worked. We must assume he was right about the rest even if we can't prove the details.'

Lucan began to pace. 'An Egyptian. But Severina said—'

'She never really *did* say,' Lelia interrupted. 'She never lied about her past or her identity. She simply didn't disagree with the assumptions we made.'

'So we don't, any of us, know the truth.'

Lucan fought hurt, but he could scarcely blame Lelia. Severina had been secretive with him also. 'This trader from Nubia. He brought Severina to Rome?'

'Brocchus said he did, but the man's denied knowing her.'

'We invited him here to see if he remembered her when he saw her face, to see their reaction to one another.' Donatus scratched his head. 'It was disappointing. They didn't seem to know one another.'

Lucan thought again of the fascination Severina had shown for the Nubian. Had he been the only one to see that, or was his desire for Severina making him crazy?

He thought again of the ring she'd worn. It had been carved with Egyptian symbols. Nubia was very near to Egypt…

'Maybe we were wrong. But you must ask her, Lucan. Confront her and demand that she explain all this to you.'

'Confront her? Demand it?' Lucan shook his head. 'I don't think so. She must tell me her secrets willingly, or not at all.'

'Desperate times call for desperate measures,' Donatus said.

Lelia touched Lucan's sleeve. 'We're frightened for her, Lucan. Something's not right. Severina loves you, but she'll not wed you. Why is that? And why is her inn threatened, and maybe her life as well?'

'I don't know. But I doubt she'll tell me anything. She—'

'Shh!' Lelia suddenly motioned for quiet.

'What?' Donatus mouthed silently.

'Out there.' Lelia jerked her head towards the open window and the courtyard beyond.

Both men heard the slight noise, iron scraping against stone. A shadow moved in bushes near the far wall. Lucan caught Donatus's gaze. Wordlessly, they agreed on a plan of action.

Donatus eased forwards, opened a chest on his desktop and retrieved a dagger. He handed it to Lucan. He drew a *gladius* for himself from a drawer. Then they were through the door and gone, leaving Lelia alone.

There was silence as Lucan and Donatus crept closer to the bushes. Gingerly, Donatus pulled back the large branch to reveal their adversary and there was…nothing.

Nothing except a heavy, rectangular iron grill on the ground in front of a dark hole in the stone wall. It had been laid into place neatly, intentionally.

'What's that?' Lucan whispered, gesturing towards the hole which would easily have accommodated a small man.

'An old sewage drain, no longer in use. There was a kitchen here before my father made changes to the house.'

'Where does it lead?'

'I don't know, but maybe it's time I found out.'

'You can't fit in there.'

Donatus studied the hole. 'No. Can you?'

'I can,' Lelia said from behind them.

Donatus made a sound of disapproval. 'No. We don't know what we're facing here. It could be the men who've been following Severina or—'

'All the more reason to go in. Besides…' she put one hand on her hip and faced Donatus down '…I'm better than average in a fight.'

He frowned.

Lelia moved to the hole and peered into it. 'I see light. Someone's in there.' She raised one foot and started inside.

'Lelia, no.'

'Hush, Donatus, and give me your *gladius*.'

Her tone was so commanding that Lucan wasn't surprised when Donatus sighed and put the weapon into her hand. As agile as a cat, Lelia slipped her other leg into the hole, slithered her hips through the narrow opening and disappeared.

Long moments of silence ticked by. Neither man moved.

'I hope I did the right thing,' Donatus whispered. 'Maybe we should go and get someone—'

Lelia's head popped back through the opening. She was laughing. 'It's Druscilla,' she said, climbing out. 'That little minx, she's always up to something!'

Donatus helped Lelia stand. 'Druscilla?'

Lelia peered into the opening. 'Come on, Druscilla. Come out right now or there really *will* be problems for you.'

She stepped aside and let Druscilla wriggle out. Lucan caught her, only noticing after she'd righted herself that she was dressed as a boy in a short tunic that exposed bony legs and feet shod in hobnailed boots. Her black hair, usually long and lustrous, was hidden beneath a dark cap. A nondescript brown cape completed her attire.

'What the hell—!' Donatus looked her up and down. 'What foolishness is this?'

The girl lifted her head. 'My business shall remain my own.'

'I'm the head of this family. You will tell me.'

Druscilla snorted. 'Enjoying the role of *pater familias*, my brother? Oh, please.'

Lelia stepped forwards, eager to soothe her husband's growing anger. 'Donatus, maybe you should let me talk to her.'

'I won't tell you, either,' Druscilla said. 'It doesn't concern you.'

Donatus's eyes narrowed. 'You're slipping out to meet somebody? A lover?'

The denial was vehement. 'No! Nothing like that!'

'Then what? Tell me or I swear—!'

Lucan decided it was time to step in. He took Druscilla's hand, careful to meet her gaze. She was intelligent and headstrong, but she'd always been susceptible to his charm.

'Druscilla,' he said gently. 'Severina's being followed by strange men and is perhaps in danger. Last week an accident that nearly killed us turned out not to be an accident at all.'

Druscilla's eyes widened. 'Somebody's trying to kill you?'

'Possibly. We thought at first you might be one of those who threaten us.'

'I'd never do that. Never. I was only…' She paused, looking anxious.

'You can tell us. It will be all right. Won't it, Donatus?'

Donatus scowled. 'I suppose.'

Lucan smiled encouragingly into Druscilla's beautiful dark eyes. She really was an entrancing young woman. Much too young for him and not his type, but still curiously attractive.

'I use the drainage tunnels sometimes to get from place to place. They're spacious, with vaulted arches. I have a boat and a lantern. It's like travelling by river. I can go many places within the city, unhindered, unnoticed.'

'That's why you're dressed as a boy?'

She frowned. 'Partly.'

'Partly?'

'Well…' Druscilla drew in a deep breath. 'I'm an actor.'

Donatus swore under his breath.

Lelia laughed. 'A real, honest-to-goodness actor? Like those at the Theatre Marcellus?'

'Just like them,' Druscilla said proudly. 'In fact, I *am* one of them.'

Donatus swore louder.

Lucan exhaled his relief. 'All right. At least now we know. Donatus, she's not a threat.'

'So I can go now?' Druscilla asked in a hopeful voice.

'No,' Donatus said. 'Go take off those clothes. Playacting is for the low-bred, not for a lady from one of Rome's finest families. You'll give up this nonsense immediately.'

'No!' Druscilla was frantic. 'Donatus, no! I can't! I'm to do a play tonight! I'm late already!'

Lelia touched Donatus's sleeve. 'Let her go for the moment,' Lelia said gently. 'We'll deal with this later. Right now, we must return to our guests. We've been away too long for good manners.'

'But she's— What will her mother say?'

'Faustina's already abed. You and she can talk in the morning. For now, just leave it alone.'

Donatus scowled, but he didn't stop Druscilla as she crawled back through the hole and disappeared.

'No wonder I've been reluctant to wed,' Lucan said to Donatus. 'You were a commander of men in Dacia, but here enemy forces outwit you on every hand.'

Donatus rubbed tension from his neck. 'Just wait until you're wed to Severina. You'll not be so cocky then.'

'If I ever *do* wed her. And with what you two have told me tonight…'

'Maybe when you two talk, all will become plain,' Lelia ventured.

His voice betrayed his scepticism. 'I can only try.'

Donatus led the way back towards the *triclinium*. The raucous laughter of their guests let them know they'd already enjoyed a generous amount of Donatus's best wine.

Lucan thought of Severina. Wine always relaxed her and lowered her inhibitions. Maybe later tonight, in the sweet afterglow of pleasures enjoyed, she'd be persuaded to share her secrets.

Lucan's gaze searched for her when he entered the room. She wasn't there.

Lelia realised the same thing. 'Severina's not here,' she said. 'Oh, no, Lucan. Could somebody have—?'

Donatus strode forwards. 'The woman who sat there beside me—' he asked a guest, gesturing '—where is she?'

The man glanced around. 'I'm not sure.'

Another man answered from across the table. 'The pretty lady with the reddish hair?' He began to laugh. 'Ah, yes. She got a craving for dark meat tonight, if you know what I mean. She left with the Nubian. He said she'd made him an indecent offer no man could refuse, the lucky fellow.'

Lucan felt the floor drop out from beneath him.

'That's not like her.' Lelia's voice came near his shoulder. 'Don't believe it, Lucan. Don't.'

'I'm not really sure what I *do* believe any more,' he said. 'It seems none of us knows the real Severina, not even you.'

The beauty of the morning mocked Severina and did nothing to lift her spirits as she travelled towards Ostia in Semni's horse-drawn *raeda*. She was leaving Rome behind, the life she'd built, the friends she'd made. She was leaving Lucan.

He hadn't followed her.

And the night that would have been a dream of pleasure in his arms had become a nightmare. Whenever she thought of her in the future, there'd be anger and bitterness, not the sweet memory she'd hoped to leave behind.

But maybe her decision hadn't come too late to save his life.

Semni had been kind, sensing her distress.

He'd always been kind to her, even in the early days of their friendship when she'd been only a girl and he, a youth just beginning to make his way in the world.

They'd met by accident. She and her nursemaid had ventured too far from the palace and had been set upon by robbers in the street. Semni had come running from the shop in which he worked and had driven the criminals away. He had lifted her from the dust and carried her inside. He had bathed the dirt from her face and spoken kind words to calm her.

She'd loved Semni from that moment and made her old nurse take her frequently to visit him.

By the time her personal crisis came, Senmi had increased in wealth and status. He was also her trusted friend, the only one willing to help her escape, the only one not afraid of Anok Khai.

But now her father had discovered Semni. Like Lucan, he could suffer for his involvement with her. So this journey would be the last favour she'd ask of him. She'd disappear into Britannia and never contact Semni again.

She was truly leaving behind every friend.

Because she and Semni were being careful, she'd adopted yet another identity. Semni introduced her to his captain using a false name and a story they'd invented together. She was now a young widow bound for Britannia where a soldier in the Twentieth Legion awaited her companionship.

The captain looked at her strangely, but that didn't seem unusual. Many seamen disliked having females aboard their vessels. Or perhaps he resented giving up his quarters for her sake.

But Severina understood that strange look better once Semni left and the captain led her to her quarters. She'd only barely shut the door behind her when a movement in the room made her gasp.

Lucan unfolded his lanky form from a stool beside the narrow bed.

Severina's heart began to pound. For a moment she was so light-headed she thought she'd faint. 'Lucan,' she whispered. 'How did you find me? How did you know?'

His hard gaze never left her face. 'I'm not a stupid man, Severina. Even if I do keep returning for more of the hurt you so carelessly inflict.'

She didn't know what to say. Her heart ached, knowing that he'd cared enough to come, and seeing the anger and regret in his eyes. But if Lucan had found her, then her father couldn't be far behind.

'I don't inflict hurt carelessly,' she said. 'I know it seems that way, but there's much you don't understand.'

'Then you will tell me.'

'I can't.'

His eyes glittered anger. 'This time you *will* tell me, Severina. No more secrets. No more lies.'

She hesitated. If she refused, he'd leave and it would all be over. That would be best. But did she have the strength to do it?

She looked away, afraid he might read pain in her eyes. 'Let me go, Lucan.'

'I would, if I thought that was what you really wanted.'

'You don't understand.'

'No, I don't. You've told one lie after another. Your whole life now appears to be a lie. But, Severina…' he pulled her into his arms '…*this* does not lie.'

His lips came down on hers, fierce with the anger and frustration within him, yet she revelled even in the harshness. It might be all she'd have, the last touch, the last kiss, the last memory.

He hadn't shaved. His beard scraped her sensitive skin. She found pleasure in it.

His hands held her hard, roughly, without forgiveness for her deception. She wanted that rough touch everywhere.

His lips were not gentle. She enjoyed the brutal taste and gave her mouth willingly to his questing tongue.

'Oh, God,' he moaned, pulling her body more firmly against his own. 'This does not lie.'

He kissed her again and then with a growled oath he released her and stepped away. His eyes glittered, his jaw worked with tension.

'Last night you let me believe…' He let out a hard breath. 'You didn't want me to follow you. Why not?'

'It's dangerous.'

'I've faced danger before.'

'This isn't the same.'

'Explain.'

'Lucan, please…I cannot. You must simply trust me.'

He snorted. 'Trust you? Liar that you are?'

That stung. Her eyes filled with tears.

He made a strangled sound deep in his throat and pulled her back into his arms. 'I'm sorry. I didn't mean to hurt you.'

She thought of how often she'd hurt him, and how deeply, and she began to cry.

For a long while he held her, soothing her with deep-voiced murmurings.

'This can't go on,' he said at last. 'We're tearing each other apart. You won't explain; I can't bear not knowing. Either we find a compromise or…' he drew a heavy breath '…we end it for ever.'

Severina swallowed convulsively.

'What's your true name?' he asked.

Severina gasped. Lucan had asked the question in her native tongue.

'Tell me,' he repeated in Egyptian.

'How…how do you know?'

'Know what? Know that you have another name? Or know how to speak your language?'

'Both.'

'I speak Egyptian, though poorly. I was once assigned army duties in Alexandria and found that I acquired the language easily. As for the rest, Lelia discovered from Brocchus that you were Egyptian. Based on that, I simply guessed that Severina was not your birth name.'

Severina stared, scarcely able to comprehend everything at once.

He lifted an eyebrow. 'Well? Your birth name. What is it?'

Severina bit her lip. Dare she tell him? Would it matter now, when she'd soon be gone from Rome for ever? It was a small thing, but if her father later caught Lucan and tortured him, even so small a thing might bring him death.

His green-gold gaze watched her intently. 'Trust me.'

She looked away.

'If you can't give me even that much, then I'll go. There's no hope, nothing for us in the future.'

Tension exploded. 'There's no hope for us *now*!' she cried. 'If only you'd believe me! You *must* leave me, Lucan, or die.'

'What are you afraid of? *Who* are you afraid of?'

She shook her head.

'If I'm in danger because of you, then you owe me that much. Tell me exactly what to expect. Don't let me be found butchered in my bed some day, ripped open from groin to throat because I never knew what—or who—I faced. Allow me to die like a man, on my feet with *spatha* in hand. For God's sake, tell me the name of my enemy.'

Should she? Severina thought of Semni, of the missing fingers on his right hand.

Lucan's fate would be worse. Her father was good at long, agonising deaths. He especially liked to emasculate the men, bit by painful bit, making them suffer the utmost humiliation before they died. Lucan had no idea... She shuddered.

'Anok Khai,' she said. 'His name is Anok Khai.'

'Who is he?'

'Chief priest of the goddess Isis. Supreme Counsellor to Trajan's appointed Prefect in Egypt and the self-appointed leader of the nobility there. A powerful man with many resources at his command and spies everywhere throughout the empire.'

Lucan sucked in his breath. 'Sweet hell. Who *are* you?'

Severina lifted her head. 'I am his daughter.'

Silence.

'Lelia believed you were once a slave,' Lucan said at last. 'Was that another lie?'

'I was reared in the palace of the Temple of Isis. Yet I was as bound to my father's will as any slave could be.'

'The mark on your shoulder?'

'Put there by Semni, to give authenticity to my claim.'

Lucan snorted. 'You thought of everything, didn't you?'

'Not everything. I didn't expect to meet *you*, Lucan, in front of the granary that day on Donatus's farm. You were handsome, so bold. I wasn't prepared for what happened between us, for the way it felt, for how it would...change everything. I knew my father might someday find me. I feared what would happen if he did. I should never have brought you into my nightmare, but I…I wanted to be happy for just a little while.'

Lucan's expression softened. 'And were you happy?'

'Yes.' Her eyes squeezed shut. A tear slipped down her cheek.

'You're sure we could never be that happy again?'

She didn't answer.

'Let me protect you. I'll take you anywhere. To Britannia or Bithynia. To Syracuse or Seleucia. I don't care, just anywhere you'll never know fear. Let me marry you, put babes in your womb and happiness in your heart.'

Severina was torn. Her father had spies in many places, but surely not in every obscure hamlet. Could she and Lucan find a secure hiding place? Could Lucan take on another identity? Leave behind his friends? His family?

His family.

Severina thought of his ageing parents. They looked to Lucan for heirs. They needed grandchildren. If Lucan fled with her now, they'd never know they had any.

'I can't let you do that,' she said. 'You'd eventually regret the choice. You'd despise living in lies and secrecy as I've done all these years.'

He studied her intently. 'Why do *you*? Does your father seek to kill you?'

'No. He won't kill me. I dare not explain, but he needs me to return to Egypt alive. Besides that—'

She absentmindedly reached for the ring that usually hung around her neck. It wasn't there.

She moved her hand as if to conjure it. 'Oh, no!' she cried. 'The ring. It's not here!'

Lucan frowned.

'I took it off, remember? I thought I'd return home, but then… Oh, Lucan! The ring's back at the inn!'

'Why does that matter? What does that ring mean to you?'

'It's one of three rings sacred to Isis. It's a powerful talisman of protection and gives its wearer power over death. I can't leave Rome without it!'

Lucan scowled. 'That's why you wouldn't sell it to pay your way out of slavery.'

Severina made an exasperated sound. 'No, it was because I *chose* gladiatorial slavery. It was the one place my father would never look for me, don't you see? And while I wore that ring, I had the protection of the goddess.'

Lucan looked momentarily stunned. 'You *wanted* to be a gladiatorial slave?'

'Yes. The training was hard and I didn't enjoy the combat. But I was safe in that world. The life was structured, all my needs supplied. I rarely left the *ludus* and so I rarely risked being discovered by my father's spies. I used a combat name and wore a helmet that hid my face when I fought. The situation was ideal, as long as I wore the ring. Only when Donatus redeemed me from slavery did problems begin.'

She sighed. 'He meant well. I love him for it. But you see, I really do need that ring. I have to go back.'

'It's not safe. The inn's being watched.'

Severina's head jerked upwards. 'You knew this and you didn't tell me?'

'I thought it the censor's doing. I didn't want to frighten you.'

'But the ring…I must have it.'

'You'd risk being captured?'

Severina's gaze met Lucan's. 'The power that ring wields is strong. I'll need it where I'm going.'

Lucan's eyes darkened with worry. 'Then I'll go to the inn with you,' he said.

She started to protest, but he put his fingers against her lips. 'I know you're determined to leave Rome, and now I understand *why*. But please…let me give you this one last thing. Let me protect you.'

He kissed her fingertips, one by one in slow, unhurried adoration. Severina held back a sob. 'Oh, Lucan,' she breathed, 'I could have loved you for a lifetime. It would have been good between us.'

He pulled her into his arms. 'It would have been unforgettable,' he said as his lips descended. 'You would have been the only woman with whom I'd ever truly *made love*.'

His kiss broke Severina's heart.

His gaze burned hot when at last he lifted his head.

'Lucan?' she whispered.

'Hmmm?'

'My name is Aloli.'

Lucan tried the word. On his tongue, it sounded sensual. Severina imagined him whispering it as she lay beneath him.

She suddenly wanted to give him everything.

'My father was visited by the goddess Isis in a dream,' she said in a rush. 'He was promised immortality when I was wed to the son of Egypt's ruler. He believes the union will bring the abundance of the gods to the land.'

Lucan was slow to answer, but she saw understanding come into his eyes. 'No wonder you've been fearful. No wonder you refused to wed me.' His gaze connected with hers. 'Your father worships his god; I was likewise faithful to mine. To surrender your will to me would be like surrendering to him…'

'Shh,' she whispered. 'In my mind, I've always known the difference. Only my heart had to come to understand.'

With one finger Severina slowly traced his high cheekbones, his well-shaped brow, his beautiful lips. 'I pray I've done you no harm by telling you this,' she whispered. 'You're the only man with whom I've ever willingly shared this secret.'

'Your trust is all I ever wanted.' He leaned down until his breath washed softly over her sensitive lips. 'And I refuse to believe that I've finally won it, only to lose you again. We will have a future together, Severina. Somehow, I will make it so.'

He took her sob into his own throat, and for the first time Severina understood that a man's faith could be both a blessing and a gift.

Chapter Thirteen

Severina had to be tired, Lucan thought as they made their way through Rome's dark streets. She'd travelled to Ostia and back in less than a day. He'd also ridden the same distance, but he was a seasoned veteran of war and accustomed to such demands.

He sometimes struggled to remember that she'd been a gladiatrix. He was glad he'd never seen her fight. He couldn't imagine her drenched in sweat and blood. He preferred the graceful creature who blushed easily, whose laughter made music, whose eyes changed from the grey of dusk to the rage of storm and sea.

But soon, if she had her way, that fascinating creature would be lost to him for ever.

Lucan did not intend to let her have her way.

He didn't yet know how to prevent it. He understood instinctively that Severina valued independence above all else. He wasn't sure how to change her mind, but neither was he convinced it was a hopeless cause. She had finally shared herself and parted with her secrets. He'd finally won her trust.

Now he wanted everything else, but he knew of only one way to win that. If they made love, and especially if they made a child…

Lucan thought this through.

He knew he could seduce her. He'd won women far less willing. Once Severina conceived, he had only to play on her natural feminine tenderness. She was sensitive, easily aroused to pity. He only needed to paint the right picture in her imagination.

A man alone, never to know the child he'd sired.

A child alone, growing up fatherless in a harsh world.

Guilt could be an effective tool. It would get him what he wanted and bind Severina to him for ever. He'd make her happy, protect her, give her security and a pleasant life.

But his conscience screamed at him.

Lucan frowned, already knowing the truth. He couldn't make love to Severina, not like that. He couldn't manipulate or coerce her. If she accepted him as her mate, the choice must be her own.

If she didn't, he'd lose her for ever.

Severina was anxious. As she and Lucan neared her neighbourhood, the sense of foreboding increased.

It was always dangerous to travel through the city at night. The streets were dark and the buildings tall, blocking out the light of stars and moon. Criminals lurked in alleyways and behind arches to make victims of the unwary.

She sensed Lucan's tension. He was alert, stopping often to scan the shadows, his right hand never far from the *spatha* belted over his tunic.

They moved like wraiths through the darkness—cloaked, hooded, speaking in whispers.

But as they neared her neighbourhood, the silence changed to confusion. People moved about with torches, all heading in the same direction. They talked in anxious voices. Something was wrong.

'What's going on?' she asked Lucan.

'Fire, I think. Take a deep breath.'

She did. The air smelled of smoke. There was a fire, a distance away.

Fire was not unusual. It was a constant threat in this congested city where residents used open flames for cooking and oil lamps to light their nights. Night after night, the *vigiles* patrolled the streets, ever alert to the danger. Even small fires had to be quickly contained or whole neighbourhoods could become cinders within minutes.

The closer Lucan and Severina came to her home, the thicker the air became. Fire carts passed, their drivers screaming to the crowds to move aside and let mules and equipment through. Voices grew louder, more frightened and strident. The press of bodies in the narrow streets became harder to squeeze through.

'We can't pass this way,' Lucan said, raising his voice to be heard over the clamour. 'Your street's blocked.'

He led her around, his larger body parting the crowd so she could follow. She couldn't see over all the people, couldn't discern particular sounds in the indiscriminate noise of the chaos, couldn't breathe in the heavy, smoke-laden air.

They must be very near her inn now. Lucan pulled her around a corner.

He stopped so suddenly that she pushed into his broad back. 'Oh, no. Oh, dear God, no!' she heard him say.

She tried to peer around him, but he was turning to her, blocking her view.

'Severina…' His face was taut, his eyes dark, his tone distressed. And she knew.

'No!' She pushed herself around him, and saw her inn fully engulfed in flame.

She would never remember exactly what happened next. There were people, so many people, and they were in her way. She was frantic to get past them, frantic to close the distance, frantic to reach the edge of the crowd. She clawed and shoved, pushing through with strength she didn't know she possessed—and all the while, eerie orange light jumped and danced over her, and her lungs burned in the acrid air.

She'd nearly reached the edge of the crowd when she saw Orthrus. He writhed on the ground and screamed. Men held him down, several strong men, and he fought them. It took Severina a moment to realise what that meant. Ariadne hadn't made it out of the building, and Orthrus was frantic to go in after her.

Severina looked towards the flames and knew it was hopeless.

Lucan grabbed her as she started forwards. 'No!' he shouted above the confusion. He jerked her backwards, at the same time covering her bright hair with the hood of her cloak. 'No, Severina, no!'

'But Orthrus! He needs me! Ariadne, she's—!'

'It's a trap!' Lucan yelled. 'Think, Severina! Your father!'

She gasped as reality flooded in.

'His men are drawing you out,' Lucan said, pulling her backwards with him through the crowd. 'They don't know where you are. They lost you after Lelia's dinner party. You didn't return home. But they knew you couldn't stay away from *this*! And when you returned…they'd be waiting.' He gestured to the rooftops surrounding the flames. 'There. There. And there.'

'But Orthrus…!'

'Orthrus will survive. But you won't, not unless you listen to me. Your father's men, they aren't playing any more. They mean to capture you, Severina, don't you see? They mean to take you now. This fire was no accident. They wouldn't have gone to these lengths unless… Oh hell, I've got to get you out of here!'

He pulled her back through the press of people, his face hard with determination.

Numbness filled Severina. She was too tired to go on, too tired to fight. Lucan commanded and she obeyed. He halted and so did she. He looked up to rooftops and she shuddered, pulling her cloak more tightly around her face.

He stopped three streets away, looking up and down the street before squatting on his haunches beside a wall. As Severina watched, he carefully removed a thick metal grate from its place.

He looked at her when he'd laid it aside. 'I'll go first. Give me a minute to get my bearings, then you follow. Wait until the street's empty so nobody sees you.'

'I don't understand.'

'I'll explain later. Just trust me and do what I say.'

Lucan lifted himself into the hole, the muscles in his arms bulging as he pushed his rangy body through the tight space and disappeared. Severina waited through a slow count of ten, looked down the empty street, then followed him into the darkness.

She gasped when she fell into water, cold and deep. The darkness disoriented her and she panicked, bobbing to the surface, sputtering, flailing.

Lucan caught her against his warm body. 'I'm here,' he said. 'It's all right. I'm here.'

'Where are we?' she gasped.

'A drainage tunnel. Can you swim?'

'Not well.'

His grip around her tightened. 'Never mind. I'll help you to the wall.'

He pulled her with him through the water. 'There's a ledge. You can rest there.'

He gave a grunt of satisfaction when he found it, loosening his hold until her feet found the bottom. Severina realised she stood on a narrow concrete ledge that seemed to run the entire length of the wall.

'I've got to go now,' Lucan said.

'Go?' The darkness made Severina anxious. 'Don't leave me, Lucan. There could be snakes. Rats.'

His laughter was soft in the darkness, punctuated by gentle splashes of water. 'Ah, Severina. Where's my fearless gladiatrix now?'

Severina didn't know. Somewhere away from here, with this water and this damp wall and this stifling darkness.

His body was suddenly against hers, warm, comforting. 'I'll be back soon. This tunnel connects with the one underneath Donatus's home. Druscilla has a boat and some torches. I'll find them and come back for you.'

'Druscilla?'

'Long story, best suited for another time when you're safely away from all snakes and rats.' He kissed her clumsily in the darkness. 'Be brave, love. I'll hurry.'

His warmth pulled away. Severina listened until his splashes became too distant to hear any more, and experienced the most aching loneliness of her entire life.

She was beginning to need Lucan, to depend on him. That terrified her more than anything—even more than dark water, snakes and rats.

* * *

Lucan was exhausted. By the time he'd found Druscilla's boat and returned to Severina, it had been late into the night. By the time he'd rowed them through the maze of drainage tunnels, eventually reaching the River Tiber, dawn's opalescent shades of rose and gold had painted the sky.

Now another full hour later, he'd finally reached his destination, a deserted farm on the outskirts of the city. The farm was pleasantly situated on the river and Lucan was glad of it. His muscles ached with rowing. He craved the closest bed.

Severina had dozed off and lay curled like a child in the bottom of the boat. She groaned in protest when he shook her awake.

'Come, love. We'll sleep more comfortably in the house.'

She sat up, her hair tousled, her eyes red-rimmed from the previous night's smoke and lack of rest. Her tunic was still damp, stained with the muddy water of the drainage tunnel. But she was beautiful.

Fierce protectiveness bolted through him. For the moment, she was safe. He'd done that for her. She'd trusted him and he'd managed to outwit their enemies. It was a tenuous security, but at least he'd bought them both a little more time.

Now they needed rest. And food. His stomach was gnawing at his backbone.

He helped Severina from the boat. She looked at her surroundings in confusion. 'Where are we?'

'Down the River Tiber, about a mile outside the city. There's a farm here, no longer occupied, but the house is in good repair. I visit the place now and then. It's peaceful and private. And the fishing's good.'

Severina yawned. 'The owner doesn't mind?'

Even weary as he was, he found humour in that and smiled. 'Not at all.'

'What's funny about that?'

'I *am* the owner.'

'Oh.' She shook her head, still groggy. 'Then I guess it's all right.'

He pulled the rowboat higher on to the bank and tied it to a tree. 'This way.' He started up the grassy bank. 'The house is just beyond these trees.'

'Lucan, it's lovely,' Severina said when they stopped before the quaint stone structure.

'It's small, I know, but clean. A woman from the neighbouring farm comes weekly to attend it.' He rubbed the tired muscles at the back of his neck. 'It's a good thing I'm so tired—I could sleep anywhere. There's only one bed.'

He opened the door and gestured for Severina to enter. Every movement, every line of her body proclaimed her utter exhaustion. Her face was oddly without emotion; grief had passed there and stripped away feeling. It hurt him, to see her so weary and passive. He touched her arm as she moved past him. 'The situation's grim,' he said. 'But it's not hopeless. We'll sleep now and make decisions later.'

She nodded.

She stood beside the bed so long that Lucan began to wonder if she'd fallen asleep on her feet.

She turned finally. 'There's room enough here for you, too.'

'Severina, that's not really—'

'I know it's not necessary.'

Lucan smiled. 'I was going to say it's not appropriate.'

Her voice was weary. 'Does that matter? It's just you and me. We've been through a terrible night. We're tired. We're filthy. We're running from an enemy we can't see. I think we could forget about propriety for now and share this mattress, don't you?'

Sweet hell. He was tired, but was he tired enough?

Severina sat down on the edge of the bed. He knew from experience that it was soft and comfortable, the bedding crisp and fresh-smelling. She sighed and stretched out, kicking off her sandals. Within minutes she breathed deeply, already asleep.

Only then did Lucan relax. He was dirty and smelled of smoke and sweat, so he removed his tunic, drew a basin of water from the well outside and washed. Then, still clad in his undergarments for modesty's sake, he lay down to sleep beside Severina. His last thought, just before he drifted off, was that she smelled sweet even when she was dirty. And he wondered if she smelled that good everywhere.

Chapter Fourteen

Severina awoke to hewn rafters overhead, and to an unfamiliar quiet. She looked around at her surroundings.

Too quickly the pain returned. She remembered now why her skin smelled of smoke and why she'd whimpered as she floated in dreams.

The pain was sharper than she expected. The inn was gone.

But worse, there was the other memory, that of Orthrus writhing on the ground, fighting against all restraint, screaming out the agony of his loss.

Ariadne…could it be true?

Pain wanted to rush in. She loved Ariadne.

But Severina had learned much as a gladiatrix. Friendships then had ended in a moment, on the curved blade of a *sica* or under the heavy weight of a mace. Life wasn't always beautiful, nor was it always fair.

You swallowed down the hurt, sucked up the pain, treasured the friendship in whatever odd moments it returned to you in memory. And you moved on.

You had to, if you wanted to survive.

She couldn't allow herself the luxury of grief just now. She'd cry later, when she was safely away. Ariadne would understand. She'd want it that way.

Severina wiped her eyes with her hand, sat up and looked around. She vaguely remembered that Lucan had slept beside her.

She remembered his body, the sound of his breathing. She wondered where he'd gone.

She went to the door and looked out. It was nearly dusk; she'd slept through most of the day. Light waned, the glow from the west was angled and diffused.

She saw Lucan in the river, bobbing among the currents as he scrubbed ash and grit from his hair.

She acted on impulse, slipping across the grass to stand beneath the trees. He faced away and didn't know she was there, so she watched him surreptitiously, enjoying the flex of muscle in his arms and back. His skin was golden everywhere, in shades that varied from pale sunlight to deepest amber. Rivulets of water trickled down his sun-bronzed neck, down his back to his waist. She suddenly wanted to lick the water from his skin, to see if he tasted warm like the sunlight he seemed made of.

Fascinated, she edged closer and sat on the roots of one of the large trees. Darkness was fast approaching; sunset turned the water that pooled around Lucan's waist to ripples of magenta and plum.

He turned in her direction and shook the water from his hair, carelessly brushing the wet strands from his eyes. He waded nearer. She started to stand, meant to stand, but stopped instead to stare.

She hadn't realised he was completely nude.

As he waded closer to the river's edge, enough of him was becoming visible for her to clearly see that.

She should call out now, before it was too late. He could still step backwards and hide himself if he wanted. Propriety demanded that she make her presence known.

But Severina was fascinated by the display of broad shoulders that tapered to a trim waist. And below that—angular hips and his male sex, intriguing because his anatomy was so different from her own.

She didn't say anything. She wanted to look at him. There was much she didn't know. She watched Lucan leave the water, enthralled by the sight.

He stepped out on to grass and reached for the linen cloth nearby, towelling himself. Severina tilted her head as if that gave her a better viewing angle.

His legs were long, muscular and lean. Every part of his form fit perfectly together with every other part. There was an aesthetic sense of unity and balance.

His flanks, his buttocks, they weren't curvaceous like those of a woman. Perhaps a man's frame couldn't truly be called beautiful, but there was something of beauty in the austerity, in the corded muscle, the sharp definition, the economy of movement.

Not exactly beautiful, but certainly majestic.

She understood now why Roman sculptors carved nude men into their marble friezes. The male form was pleasing. It spoke of strength and of something divine.

But only if every man were formed as Lucan.

Severina didn't really know. She was only somewhat familiar with the male body. What little she knew had come from her days at the *ludus*. Overall, she considered herself appallingly ignorant.

She was twenty years old and yet remained a virgin. Other girls younger than she were married already, with children. It chafed her that she knew little of men and of the mating act.

Her father's fault. She'd been kept like a prize in the palace of Isis, guarded by eunuchs. Afterwards she'd been too busy running, too busy fighting, too busy trying to survive.

She'd never cared about what she didn't know until Lucan. He'd taught her of desire and how a man's caress could sharpen it.

She knew there was more even beyond that. Studying Lucan's body now, she imagined what she did not yet know.

She wasn't sure at exactly what moment he became aware of her. She'd been too caught up in her study of him. But gradually she became aware of something different in the air all around her—a hum, a tension, the energy of lightning striking the ground.

The atmosphere wasn't the only thing growing tense. Lucan's body was changing, too, his male parts growing longer and thicker, standing erect. She knew she ought to look up to his face, but she couldn't. The sight was fascinating, and she wanted—

'Severina?'

She looked up. Lucan's eyes were lit with strange fire, even as darkness closed in around them.

Her throat tightened. She licked at lips gone dry. Feeling clumsy and awkward, she scrambled to her feet.

'How long have you been sitting there?'

'A while.'

'You've been watching me?'

She was suddenly embarrassed about her ignorance. It frustrated and angered her, and she didn't want to confess to Lucan how little she knew. 'I wanted to know.'

He seemed amused. 'A curious little cat.' He looked down at his body and then back up to her face. 'And was your curiosity completely satisfied?'

'Maybe.' She bit her lip. 'You are beautiful.'

His lips curved. 'Beautiful?'

'Not beautiful like a woman. Just…beautiful. I like looking at you.'

His eyes flickered. 'Then I'm sorry to disappoint you, Severina. But we'll both be in trouble if I don't get some clothes on. Now.'

He seemed agitated as he wrapped the linen around his loins. His erection stood like a tentpole beneath the thin cloth. 'You might want a quick dip in the river now that it's dark. It'll refresh you and…' his grin was wicked '…I promise not to watch.'

He tweaked her nose with one finger as he walked past, disappearing into the stone building.

Severina walked towards the river, wondering what was wrong with her. She wanted a bath, but she wanted…more. She felt nervous, edgy, uncomfortable, as though she didn't quite fit into her own skin.

She took her clothes off and was surprised by how good it felt to be naked. She did this every day, but she couldn't remember that it usually felt so good. She was aware of every breeze blowing across her skin and the dampness of the dark air.

She stepped gingerly into the water. It was cool. She waded out deeper, luxuriating in the sensation, letting the liquid wash over her. It soothed her, cooling her heat. She washed her hair, her face. Her arms, one at a time, marvelling in the softness of her skin. Her breasts were also soft, and full, with nipples hard and pebbled.

Would Lucan think her body beautiful?

She imagined him sitting beneath the trees, watching *her*. It was a titillating thought. She imagined the display she'd give him, the slow stroke of delicate hands against smooth female skin, cupping one breast and then the other, rubbing her palms against her nipples.

His organ would grow hard at the sights she'd give him. When his desire became unbearable, he'd stand and come to her. Their eyes would meet as he came to the river's edge. She'd smile when his clothing dropped to the grass. In another moment, their bodies would make contact, warm skin to cool. Hard man to feminine softness.

The thought made her shiver.

She imagined Lucan's large, warm hands encircling her breasts, his thumbs stroking the hard peak of her nipples. He'd bend, cover her with his hot, wet mouth, tease her with his teeth, suckle her.

She groaned softly as the heat within began to burn unbearably hot.

Was it wicked, to want Lucan? Was it wrong for her body to crave his touch?

The unrest increased. Her body was alive, tingling all over. She was drowning in feeling—the slide of her palms along the curve of hip, the lap of river current and wave against her softest parts…she could scarcely bear so many sensations, all of them abnormally intense, all of them abnormally pleasurable.

Suddenly she wanted to go to Lucan and ask him to soothe her. He'd know how to settle the tension. He'd know how to calm the anxiety.

She wanted him to love her. She'd wanted it for a long time. Lately it had been all she could think about.

She had feared her father, but who was her father, to keep her from living her life as she wanted? If she'd been born a lowly peasant, she would have had freedom to choose. She'd have loved by now, mated, given birth. She would have *lived*.

As it was, she sat on the edge of life, watching others find happiness while she merely existed. Always holding back, afraid, expecting danger.

No more.

She suddenly wanted to snatch back everything her father had taken. She wanted knowledge. She wanted pleasure. She wanted, more than anything, for her choices to be her own.

She would choose to love—only once, and only here in secret, to protect Lucan from her choice. But for tonight, she'd take this thing she wanted.

She came reborn from the water—joyful, powerful, eager for experience. She didn't dry the water from her skin. It was cool and wonderful. She didn't pick up her garments as she ran across the grass to the house.

Chapter Fifteen

Lucan lit a lamp to banish the darkness and decided the room looked cozy.

While Severina had slept through the afternoon, he'd slept only briefly. He'd awakened and gone about providing for their needs.

His neighbours had been surprised to see him at their door, but they didn't question the story he gave to explain his bedraggled appearance and need for food and clothing. Boats overturned all the time, and any neighbour who suffered such mishap certainly needed help. Arturus and Julia were kind people; they'd been generous.

When Severina returned from her bath, she'd be surprised to find a well-laid table and plenty of food. He'd also placed clean clothing on the bed for her—men's garments, unfortunately, since asking for female apparel would have raised eyebrows. But she could wear them until her own clothing had been washed and dried.

His stomach rumbled with hunger. He'd been given a large slab of salted pork, two entire loaves of bread and a generous portion of cheese. He was pouring two goblets of wine from a clay amphora when the door burst open behind him.

'I've got our *cena* ready,' he said, without turning around. 'No doubt you're as hungry as I am.'

He turned. And lost his breath.

He'd spent the last several minutes denying himself the fantasy of Severina's body as she bathed.

Now that fantasy stood before him in commanding glory.

He'd never seen Severina fully naked before, but in his fantasies he'd held her, touched and tasted her. He'd imagined the feel of her skin, the weight of her breasts in his palms, the scent of her secret places.

Now she watched him with a heated expression, breasts heaving as if she'd run. He forced himself to breathe. The desire in her face was plain to see, so intense it hurt.

Lucan knew what he needed to do. He needed to think clearly and with something besides his male organ. But his body betrayed him.

If he stepped away from the table, Severina would see that his calm was merely feigned. He remained where he was.

'There's clean, dry clothing for you, over there.'

She stepped into the room and turned to close—and latch—the door. He noticed that she latched the door.

Ordinarily he'd find humour in that. He might tease about whether she meant to keep intruders out or her lover imprisoned within, just before he willingly surrendered to whatever bondage that tight latch implied.

But there was no humour here. Conflict raged within him. As much as he wanted her, as often as he'd dreamed of this moment, he wasn't sure he should succumb to Severina's beautiful temptations now, when soon she'd be leaving him.

But he saw the plea in her eyes, burning hot. Already the heat of that flame was spreading, licking at his body, tearing through his resolve.

'Lucan, please...' she whispered. 'Please.'

He could no longer pretend he didn't know what she asked. The tension between them was too strong. He cleared his throat and spoke with difficulty. 'It's not wise, Severina, not if you plan to leave. It will make our parting all the harder. There'll be a deeper bond to sever.'

She made a soft sound of distress. 'I know how much it will hurt. But, Lucan...I *need* to do this.'

His eyes narrowed as he considered her meaning. 'Why?'

'All my life, my father's been a menacing shadow over me. I did what *he* chose. My wishes were never considered. My dreams didn't matter. I had no choice. But now, tonight, I do.'

He heard the hurt and it touched him, so he went to her. It was dangerous, he knew, to be near her. Her fragrance twined around him, delicate and alluring.

He lifted one hand to stroke her cheek, marvelling in the softness of her skin and in the length of her dark eyelashes as she closed her eyes. Her damp hair tickled the back of his hand.

'If we make love tonight, you'll only cede that power of choice to me,' he said gently. 'One man's power determined your past. Another man's passion—mine—should not decide your future. If we become lovers and you take my seed, there could be consequences, hard ones, for you. There could be a child.'

She turned her face into Lucan's palm and nuzzled his hand. 'But I want that. I choose that. Even if there should be a child.'

Merciful God in heaven.

Feeling burned through him, and if it was lust, it didn't seem so. He felt wanted. Needed. A man called to join his woman in the mating bond of a lifetime.

But it wasn't for a lifetime.

Severina still meant to leave him. He remembered that, and fought hard to keep his wits together.

Her next words flung a sharp javelin straight into his heart. 'I'm a virgin,' she said quietly. 'Let me give my innocence to you. I want it to be you.'

A virgin.

The wonder of that assailed him. He hadn't expected it, he didn't know why. Maybe because he'd been with so many women of a different sort. Maybe because he'd lost his own innocence at a young age.

'Come here,' he said, and pulled her into his embrace. It was a loving action born only of his admiration for a woman rare and fine. There was no lust to mar the simple beauty. He took her chin and raised her gaze to meet his.

'I'm honoured to be the man of your choosing. And humbled beyond belief.'

She nodded.

'I understand the fires that burn in you tonight.'

'Lucan, please don't say—'

He put his four fingertips against her lips. She fell silent. 'I know the fire. I understand the need. I honour the choice.'

'Then you'll make love to me?'

He was slow to answer.

'Yes,' he whispered finally. 'I'll make love to you.'

It wasn't quite a lie. All he did for her, all he gave to her, would be an offering of love. With all the reverence he'd never shown any other lover, he'd place her trembling, hungry body on the altar of human love and kneel before her. He'd pour out his soul, a worshipful libation to his own beautiful, beloved goddess. He'd pour out his soul, but not his seed.

God help him, he would *not*.

Severina looked suddenly unsure. 'Should I go to the bed and lie down?'

Lucan smiled at the sweet naïvety of the question. 'No, Severina.' He chuckled. 'You should dress in clean clothing and eat the *cena* with your lover.'

She looked startled.'

'He must have sustenance to find strength for the exertions ahead. You wouldn't want him to prove inadequate due to hunger, would you?'

Her blush was entrancing. It reminded him, ever so delicately, of the enormity of the moment. Severina would leave innocence behind for ever, an irrevocable crossing into carnal experience.

He'd never before taken a virgin. And he'd never once, in all his hundreds of sexual encounters, unselfishly cared for the woman with whom he shared intimacy.

For each of them, this joining would be a first.

She dressed and came to the table. Lucan had already put food on their plates. He was hungry. He hadn't teased about needing strength. It had been more than a day since he'd eaten.

Severina looked strangely at him when he said a quick, silent blessing over his food. 'You still do that?'

He felt foolish. 'Some habits are hard to break.'

She nodded and bit into her meat, chewing it hungrily. 'You still do believe in the god of the Christians, don't you?'

He swallowed a piece of pork and tore off a bite-sized hunk of bread. 'Maybe,' he said. 'But this wouldn't be the best time to remind me of it.'

'Why not?'

'Because their God takes this thing we're about to do rather seriously.'

'In what way?'

Lucan hesitated, wondering what she'd think if he told her. He decided not to hide the truth or soften it. She had asked.

'It is the act of marriage. An irrevocable covenant of blood.'

Severina choked on her food.

He handed her a goblet of wine.

She took a drink. 'So you're telling me that after tonight, I'd be your wife. And you'd be my husband.'

'In God's eyes, yes. And in the eyes of all Christian believers who serve and obey him.'

She thought about that for a while, eating in silence. 'I like their way of looking at it,' she said.

Lucan lifted an eyebrow.

'It's limiting, I know, but the view has merit. No man who believes the act to be so important could use a woman for careless entertainment.'

Lucan nodded.

'And no woman who believes the same would allow herself to be merely a man's plaything. I like that they each, man and woman, place such value on their joining. It seems better, somehow.'

'You'd make a very fine Christian,' Lucan teased. 'So…shall I sleep on the floor tonight?'

'No. I know what I want, but, Lucan…I also place great value on our joining. It's not something I do lightly.'

'I understand.'

'It's not merely about the pleasure. It's not even about having the freedom to choose my own way.'

'Of course not.'

Silence descended again. Lucan ate quietly and waited, letting her have time to work everything out in her mind. It seemed important that she have the chance to think the decision through, or even to change her mind.

'Could we believe as Christians in this?' she asked him suddenly.

The question surprised him.

'Severina, if you'd later regret this, we don't have to do it.'

'No. No regrets. But I'd like…could this be…?'

He met her gaze. 'Our marriage union?'

She looked away, blushing to the roots of her hair. 'Yes.'

Lucan was silent for a moment. 'You do know what that would mean?'

Her eyes darted back to his face.

He took her hand and raised it to his lips. 'It would mean that I'd never take another woman as long as you, my wife, yet lived. The same would go for you. Any further sexual relationships would be adultery, a very grave sin.'

She looked nervously down at their joined hands. 'I could never ask that of you.'

'You think me incapable of such fidelity?'

'Men have needs.'

'Women do, too. Would you willingly forgo all future fulfilment just to have this one night with me?'

'Yes,' she said. 'I would.'

His heart lurched in his chest.

Feeling shone from Severina's dove-grey eyes, washing through him with a sweet, purifying stream. It was altogether the most humbling, and the most exalting, experience of his life.

Her words and the love in her face made Lucan suddenly desperate to have her, though he tasted his future hurt even as he rose and pulled her into his arms.

'I thought you were hungry,' she said as his lips descended.

'Ravenous.'

Severina moaned in soft accord as his lips took hers and gave herself up to sensation. She wrapped her arms around his neck and pulled him against her body. Her breasts, so sensitive, scrubbed against his chest.

The kiss he gave her was full and demanding. His tongue entered her and stroked, dancing with hers in a breathless preview of the mating ritual to come. He did not hurry, and Severina was glad. She wanted to savour the warm, rich tastes of man and wine. She wanted the pleasure of her taut nipples against the rough texture of their garments and his two large hands as they rested against the small of her back, holding her in place against his big, rangy body.

He withdrew from the kiss and Severina had only just enough time to breathe again as he buried his face against her neck. He nipped at her skin, one kiss, two, three, before he returned to her mouth and drank deeply again.

He slid his hands into her hair, tangling his fingers in the length of silky, still-damp curls. His kiss was firmly possessive—not quite brutal, but certainly anguished and demanding. Lucan wanted her, needed her. He would soon possess her. That knowledge excited her.

The kisses went on and on—slow, drugging kisses that lasted so long she felt disoriented. He explored her mouth, tasting her deep and hot, then withdrawing to lick across her lips. He found other, equally sensitive places and pressed heat there. To her cheek, her ear, her neck. He moved lower, to her collarbone. His mouth was hot upon her skin and his heat must have somehow transferred itself to her. She was growing hot, too, feeling flushed and faint and weak and greedy.

The warmth in her expanded, centering itself in her secret places. Her breasts ached. Her most intimate parts, too, plagued by a strong throbbing that softly hurt.

Dimly she became aware that as Lucan kissed her, he was slowly, slowly pushing her backwards towards the bed. When her legs finally touched the frame, she opened her eyes. Lucan's face above hers was harsh with emotion that almost looked like pain. His gold-flecked eyes glittered with an unnatural brightness.

'You're sure this is what you want?' he asked. The question seemed forced from him, as if to hear her deny him would hurt.

'Yes.'

He released a long, pent-up breath. 'We'll take it slowly. I want it to be beautiful, Severina. The most beautiful thing we've ever known.'

Beautiful enough to last a lifetime. He didn't say it, but the thought hung there in the air between them.

His fingers shook as he grasped the hem of her tunic and pulled it over her head. She wore nothing beneath it. His gaze heated as it passed slowly over her, and her body fired hotter beneath his intense scrutiny. Admiration shone in his eyes. She felt womanly and pretty.

He lowered her to the bed. Even there she found sensual pleasures. The bedclothes were cool and crisp against her bare backside, and his tunic was rough along her front as he lay down against her.

'Lucan?'

'Hmmm?' He was already busy nuzzling her neck.

'I'm not experienced with this, but shouldn't we both be naked?'

He lifted his head to look down into her face. 'I didn't want to frighten you.'

'I'm not. I saw you at the river.'

He hesitated.

'I like looking at you. Your body is magnificent.'

He stood. With an impatient jerk he loosened his undergarment; it fell to the floor. Severina drew in a hard breath. He *was* magnificent. He was also large, even larger than he'd seemed before. Despite what she'd just told him, she had a momentary twinge of panic. That all of him would fit into all of her—*could* he?

She reached for him. He groaned when her hand closed around his shaft. She glanced up. His eyes had closed. There was a pained grimace on his face.

'I'm hurting you?'

'No. Touch me, Severina. Oh God, yes, touch me.'

She explored him freely, feeling, stroking, learning of him. She knew she was pleasing him and that excited her, too. His body twitched and jerked with each small thing she did. He made low, guttural sounds. Manly sounds. His face, his dear and handsome face, became harsh with need.

After a while his hand closed around hers. 'That's enough,' he said hoarsely. 'I can't take any more.'

He eased into the bed beside her and drew her into his embrace. His body was warm and big. It felt heavenly against hers, even that proud and alien hardness pressing against her thigh. She didn't realise she trembled until he pulled back to look into her face. His hand came up, four lean fingers barely touching the side of her cheek, his thumb feathering across the sensitive skin of her lips.

'You're trembling. And look, my hand isn't steady, either.' His voice held amazement. 'I'm shaking. That's…odd.'

Severina's brow wrinkled. 'Odd?'

His laughter was soft, touched with wonder. 'As many times as I've done this, I can't remember ever trembling with such need or wanting any joining so badly. This means so much, Severina. You mean so much.'

Severina's heart twisted.

His face came close to hers. 'I never answered your question.'

'What question?'

'Whether we might regard this as the marriage rite between us.'

Severina groaned. 'Please forget I said it. It was a foolish request. I shouldn't have asked that of you.'

Lucan placed warm fingers over her lips. 'Shh. It's not a foolish question. It's a perfect question.'

He took her hand. His expression was solemn. 'By taking you tonight, I make you my wife for as long as I live. I promise to forsake all others and to cherish only you for as long as I live. As God himself bears witness, I pledge this to you.'

Severina's eyes filled with tears.

'I needed to tell you this,' Lucan said quietly, 'before I lose myself to you. Already I'm near madness.' His gaze lowered.

Like one in a dream, Severina watched in helpless fascination
as he closed the slight distance between them. His lips parted. His
mouth closed over her nipple.

She gasped at the shocking sweetness. His tongue was warm and
wet, and his teeth gently pulled at her, torturing the exquisitely sensitive peak. He tasted, he suckled. He teased with both mouth and
hands until she moaned. She dug hard into his shoulders with her
fingers, only half-aware that she held him there.

Sensation shot straight to her feminine core; every slight tug of
his mouth pulled hard at her body. She twisted, she melted. She
became molten liquid, hot and fine.

She wanted, and Lucan gave. He held her tightly, murmuring
deep-voiced, incomprehensible words against her skin as he
moulded her in his hands, toyed with her, teased and tasted and
tempted.

It was never enough. Every craving he satisfied led to another.
She was wild with pleasure, but she couldn't get enough.

His hand moved lower and touched her in her most intimate
place. She jerked hard and cried out; the pleasure was too intense.
With his skilful hands, Lucan parted her feminine fold. His finger
traced a path through it, so slowly up and back down again,
bringing pleasure as sharp as pain.

'Yes, love,' he murmured against her hair. 'Relax your thighs
now and let me give you this.'

Oh, he was good. His fingers knew exactly what to do, exactly
where to stroke her. The pressure was perfect, not too light, not too
hard. The rhythm was perfect, lifting her up on a wave of wanting,
letting her ebb downwards, pushing her high again. Her arms
straightened, her fingers clawed into the bedclothes as he brought
her towards fulfilment. She mewled and arched her body hard
towards him, wanting, craving, needing, begging.

Lucan knew from the increasing tenor of her cries and from
the forceful arching of her hips that she was ready for him. He
shifted slightly and replaced his fingers within her moist, scented
fold with the sleek tip of his manhood. She was so hot, so slick;

the press of her soft heat against him was driving him mad. He stroked her with himself, the pressure growing firmer, the pace moving faster.

He watched her; her body tightened with bliss. She panted and she cried, writhing beneath him on the bed.

Lucan watched her; his timing must be perfect, not off by even a few seconds. Their joining was imminent now, and he longed for it. To be the man to lead her through the rending of her virtue was no small thing to him. There'd be pain for her, and he regretted that. But past that, there'd be wondrous experience, as all her muscles spasmed around a man's thick length for the first time. He wanted badly to give her that.

But the timing would be tricky, if he would keep from spilling his seed inside her. He usually knew instinctively when the moment was nearly upon him. One stroke more, perhaps two, and he'd be past the point of withdrawal.

Severina was wild beneath him now. He'd imagined her this way many times before, but the reality exceeded his fantasies. Her eyes were closed, her features drawn, her hair tangled wildly around her shoulders, breasts heaving with her laboured breaths and the frantic, sweet cries of a woman's desire.

He slipped himself in to her soft, slick entrance, taking just a little of her.

She misinterpreted his hesitation. 'No,' she moaned. 'Oh, no. Don't stop!'

'Shh,' he gentled her, putting one warm hand on her lower belly. 'It's all right. I promise it'll be all right.'

She opened her eyes, her body tensing slightly as he eased further in. She was beginning to understand.

'It's time,' he rasped. 'God knows I don't want to hurt you, but I can't hold off any longer.'

He was more clumsy than he meant to be, trembling and too eager because she felt so damned good. Smooth and tight, she enveloped him in heat as he took her inch by careful inch. By the time he came to the barrier of her virginity, he was almost sick with tension, his skin flushed and damp with sweat. He tasted its salty tang on his lips and in every breath, mixed with the heady scent of sex.

He paused, unsure whether to push through slowly or rend her in one quick, hard motion. Which would be less painful? He cursed his inexperience with virgins.

Severina took the choice from him.

In a surprising move, she locked her arms around his neck and drove her hips upwards, shoving him deep inside, impaling herself on his hard rod. She gasped as pain tore through her.

'Sweet hell,' he groaned, unable to contain a shudder of pleasure at finally being in her deep places. 'You shouldn't have done that. I would've spared you—'

'It's over,' she breathed. 'I wanted it done.'

He was silent for a moment, then kissed the soft skin of her shoulder. 'My sweet, brave wife.'

Her eyes locked with his at the declaration. She forced a smile, even though he was sure the hurt still throbbed deeply. 'I'm yours completely now,' she said. 'It's all right. It's what I want.'

He kissed her and began to move, carefully at first. Severina soon caught on to the rhythm, her hips joining him in the dance, meeting each one of his long, smooth thrusts.

'Oh, Lucan,' she moaned, eyes closed. 'Oh, yes. Oh, please!'

The words were a blessing and a curse. He needed to stay focused on doing everything so carefully, but her excitement and the sublime feel of her body writhing beneath his…it threatened to sweep him away. Even the smell of her all around him…. Could he do this?

She was forcing him to a quicker pace now, slamming their bodies hard together. He put his hands on her hips to slow her. He *had* to slow her. *Now.*

'No, no, no!' she protested wildly, jerking against the restraint. 'I'm so…oh, I need…it's so close! Please! Lucan, please!'

They both gasped for air in the thin ether near the peak. She was close, but damn it all, so was he.

'Oh, oh!' Her cry was frantic, anguished. Her body was strong and rigid beneath his, bucking slightly, jerking as she neared climax. Lucan knew a surge of fiercely male satisfaction, that he'd brought her through the pain to this moment, and she was almost, *almost* there.

He wanted to give her a powerful orgasm. He wanted to experience it with her, to feel the tightening of her deep muscles all around his shaft. It would be glorious beyond belief. He'd dreamed of having her that way more than once.

But he was too close. He desperately needed to pull out of her, and soon. His love for her, his need for her made this harder than it should have been. It frightened him, that he might not be able to hold back long enough.

He fought to give her one stroke more, and then another. He distracted himself with thoughts of the weather, of the food on the table, anything but—

Her scream of pleasure sent him over the edge. His ejaculation began almost before he knew. His stomach clenched, his mind screamed the betrayal, but he couldn't prevent himself from the agonising and wondrous pleasure of emptying his hot seed into her womb.

They collapsed on to the mattress together, limbs tangled, breathing hard, smelling of sex and sweat and heat.

'I didn't mean to do that,' Lucan said. 'I'm sorry, Severina. I didn't mean to do that.'

She turned her head to face him, the joy in her eyes dimming slightly at the sharp regret she heard in his voice.

'I didn't mean to loose my seed in you,' he clarified. He didn't want her to think he regretted their lovemaking or the promise he'd made to her. 'I meant to withdraw before that happened, but I couldn't.'

She put her fingers against his lips. 'Shh,' she whispered. 'Don't spoil this for me. I wanted you, Lucan, all of you. The whole experience. Even that. Especially that.'

'There could be a child.'

She was silent, unable to deny the possibility. He rose up on one elbow and looked into her eyes. 'If there should be fruit of this,

Severina, how will I know? If you leave me, I don't want to spend my lifetime wondering if we made a child together.'

Her eyes didn't mirror the anxiety he felt. Lucan had the sudden, strange feeling that maybe Severina had actually wanted him to climax within her. That maybe she'd already examined the possibility of pregnancy and accepted it.

But that same thought *he* couldn't endure, of a woman bearing a child alone. *His* woman. *His* child. Alone, without him.

Severina broke their gaze, looking up to the rough-hewn rafters above them. 'There's little possibility of a child,' she said quietly. 'It was just one time, Lucan.'

'Yet it happens. Even with just one time.' He grasped her chin and forced her to look at him. 'And if it did happen, Severina... what then? Would you come back to me? Would you let me wed you and give my child an honourable name?'

Her frown gave him the truth. She didn't answer.

Lucan closed his eyes against the pain. 'Then for mercy's sake, let me go with you.'

'I can't let you do that. I thought we'd already—'

'That was before we made love. Before we pledged a lifetime of faithfulness to one another. Before I loosed my seed in you. The situation's different now.'

Her lashes lowered, partially hiding her eyes. She sighed. 'You're right. Everything's different now. The changes come too fast. I'm confused and don't know what's best.' She reached up, stroking gently against the stubble of his beard. 'You have a right to be concerned, but I can't make a hasty decision. Give me time to think it through.'

It wasn't what he wanted to hear. He lay back against his pillow with a heavy sound of exasperation. 'All right,' he said at last, drawing her back into his embrace. 'Think it over.'

She turned her face into the cleft of his shoulder and yawned. Her voice was sleepy. 'I will, Lucan. I promise. I'll do what's best for both of us.'

Within a few moments the sound of her breathing changed and

Lucan realised she'd drifted to sleep. Ordinarily, he'd join her, relaxed and satiated from the intimacy they'd shared. But tonight, he was brutally unhappy. The pleasure had only tortured him. He lay a long time in the quiet and thought about the future.

He loved her.

He realised it now. He'd never stopped loving her, never, not even when he'd been most hurt and angry. If he hadn't loved her, he'd have felt nothing.

He wanted Severina, not just because he needed to marry and get an heir. Not just because they'd spent this night in passion, not just because they might have made a child together.

He loved Severina: her wit, her smiles, her graceful femininity. He loved her, secrets and all, danger and all, past help or reason, past all care for pride or pain.

He loved her, but he would soon lose her.

It was nearly dawn when Lucan finally reached a decision. He rose in the dark and dressed. 'I'll be back soon,' he whispered to Severina as he left her. She muttered a soft response, rolling on to her side.

Lucan smiled. If he had his way, he'd awaken with her at his side every morning of every day for the rest of his life. He only had to convince Severina of that.

To that end, Lucan turned sharply on his heel and strode out, latching the door securely behind him as he left.

Chapter Sixteen

Severina was jolted from sleep by the feel of cold metal beneath her palm.

She'd been restless, dreaming that she and Lucan were being pursued by her father, always close to being caught, running out of breath, running out of time, running…

In the dream, her father had caught Lucan. She'd turned to see her lover flailing on the ground, fighting for air as her father choked life from him. She grabbed a sword…

She awakened to find that her palm rested on the hilt of the weapon Lucan had left on the pillow beside her.

His *spatha.*

Lucan had left his *spatha?*

She realised that he'd meant to, and imagined the care with which he'd placed it beside her.

In that moment she knew without a doubt that Lucan loved her, even though he hadn't declared it. He'd been more guarded with his affections this time around.

The *spatha* said it for him. He'd gone back to the city, back into danger, but he'd gone unarmed so she'd wake with his sword beside her. It was the ultimate declaration of his willingness to be vulnerable for her sake.

She rose, flinching at soreness in unaccustomed places. It made her remember her night with Lucan. She'd lost her innocence, a momentous thing, but she didn't regret that. She'd given it to the man she loved. Her father hadn't won.

Even if he captured her now, even if he dragged her back to Egypt to be the unwilling wife to a stranger, she'd have outwitted him in this one small thing. To her, it wasn't a small thing at all.

It hadn't been a small thing to Lucan, either. He'd offered her a lifetime of fidelity. She'd remember that always, and every shimmering moment of the past night because it was all she'd ever have.

Unless she had his child.

She touched a hand to her bare belly. Strangely, she hoped the seed had taken. It would be something of him, a reminder of their love. Maybe the child would be a boy with Lucan's curiously slanted green-gold eyes and tousled curls.

She felt guilty that Lucan would have no opportunity to be a father. He clearly wanted it. She respected him for that; he was a man of honour. But she could say nothing to erase the worry from his eyes.

Child or no child, Lucan couldn't be part of her future. She'd be leaving him this morning. She only prayed that with the slow turn of years, he'd eventually forgive.

She'd do it for him, leading danger away so he'd never suffer for having loved her. It was especially important that she protect him now that they'd been lovers.

Leaving him was the only way.

She couldn't go to Britannia. Lucan might look for her there. She'd not go on one of Semni's grain ships, because Lucan had found her that way before.

Leaving this time would be trickier. She'd have to ensure that Lucan couldn't follow her. But that her father *could*.

She must go like a wily female fox, leading the hounds on a chase to some place far distant from the man she loved. Only after she'd done that would she disappear for good.

She picked up Lucan's *spatha* and drew it slowly from its scabbard. It was heavy, made of fine-quality steel. She imagined Lucan in war. She imagined the fierceness on his face and the ring of steel as blade met blade. The *spatha* in her hand had often been in his.

She looked at the hilt. Much of the decorative engraving had been worn away by the frequent touch of his callused hands.

His hands.

They'd touched her body last night, gentle and warm. A sharp pang hit her heart. He'd never touch her like that again.

She slid the sword back into its scabbard. Even that reminded her of Lucan, of his body sliding into hers. She'd never know that beautiful joining again.

For the first time, Severina let tears come. For years she'd been strong. She would be strong again. But right now, with Lucan's sword in her hand and his scent still clinging to every part of her, she simply wanted—*needed*—to grieve.

Donatus's river barge was large and luxurious, his wedding gift to Lelia. As he approached it now, he decided Lucan was wise to meet him there. These docks along the Tiber were nearly empty. Most of the workers had gone home for their mid-day meal and would nap through the hottest part of the day.

He'd got Lucan's message early. He and Lelia were still in bed when it had come, but they'd immediately arisen and dressed. Either their friend had lost his mind or he was in some kind of trouble.

Donatus knew Lucan well. They'd been through war together and survived—he, as a *decurion* over an entire *ala* of cavalrymen, Lucan as the *vexillarius* who rode beside him, carrying the standard. More times than Donatus could remember, Lucan's cool-headed instincts had saved both their lives.

So, if Lucan were in trouble, Donatus would do whatever was needed, even if the requests in Lucan's message were strange ones.

He found Lucan waiting on the river barge. He hadn't shaved. His hair was unkempt. Deep lines of tension marred the usual beauty of his face. He looked haggard and weary.

'You look terrible,' Donatus said as he stepped aboard. 'Worse than anytime since we pursued Decebalus in Dacia.'

'And a good day to you, too.'

Donatus ducked inside the curtains that enclosed the barge's private area. 'I got your message. Lelia and I did all you asked. But maybe you'd better tell me what in hell's going on.'

Lucan sat down with a weary sigh. 'It's a long story.'

'I have time.'

Lucan related Severina's bizarre tale. 'She's in real trouble,' he said as he finished. 'I must help her.'

Donatus toyed with the strap of the leather bag he'd set on the table and considered this. 'The world's a big place. Surely Severina could find safety within it somewhere, even without your help.'

Lucan glared at him, and Donatus had his answer. Lucan was in love. He'd not be letting Severina go, not without him.

'You'll need to see to the welfare of Severina's slaves,' Lucan said in a thick voice. 'Ariadne didn't make it out of the fire. Orthrus will need extra care.'

'At least in this, I have good news. Ariadne's alive. She wasn't in the inn during the blaze. She'd awakened and heard noises, gone to investigate and seen men dousing walls with oil. She immediately knew what was going on and ran for help. It was only because of her that the *vigiles* got the fire wagons into place as quickly as they did and kept the fire from spreading.'

'Severina will be glad to hear it.'

'The inn's gone, though.'

'Yes. But the property still has value because of its excellent location. Consider it yours now. Severina will no longer need it. She'll understand if I sign it over to you.'

'Which brings us back to business.' Donatus reached for the bag, taking out a thick sheaf of papers. 'I didn't have time to inspect all the details of your holdings, Lucan. There are too many. I didn't realise what an empire you've been building. But if you're still determined to sell everything, then I'll give you the price you're asking. I'll hold the properties for a year until you know how things go. You can take them back if you change your mind.'

'I won't change my mind.'

Donatus sighed. 'Maybe not, but you're no seer, either, and you don't know the future.'

Lucan nodded. 'Agreed. Let me sign the papers and we'll consider this done.'

Donatus placed the documents in front of Lucan, noticing the strain in his friend's face as he signed them all. Donatus had been amazed at the variety of Lucan's investments. It must have taken several years to accumulate so much. Yet Lucan was setting aside all of that now. He meant to leave Rome for good.

It saddened Donatus. He cherished Lucan's friendship. But if Lelia were the woman in trouble, he'd be doing the same thing.

Lucan scrawled his signature across the last sheet of parchment.

'The gold's in there, along with clothing enough for a journey of two weeks,' Donatus said. 'Lelia also packed a generous amount of dried meat and fruit and cheese.'

He pulled out another document. 'This was harder to come by, you know.' He handed the sheet with its official seal to Lucan. 'You'll notice that your signature and Severina's are already on the page. Amazing, how enough gold and the right social connections make possible even false signatures on a marriage licence. We senators really ought to do something about the rampant corruption in our city, don't you think?'

Lucan smiled and bent his head to study the parchment. 'What about the elders of the church? Did you arrange that as I asked?'

'Titus will be here in three hours to perform the rite.' His gaze met Lucan's. 'I must tell you…the Christian brothers were rather concerned. You're marrying an unbeliever. It's not forbidden, but it is discouraged. I convinced them of the necessity, but…please forgive the damage to your reputation, and Severina's. I told them you'd fallen into sin and seduced a virgin, but now wanted to do the honourable thing to make it right.'

Something odd passed over Lucan's features.

'Oh, hell,' Donatus said. 'I didn't lie, did I?'

Lucan didn't answer.

'Never mind. Just know that Titus might ask you to confirm my story. He'll also ask why you want a Christian ceremony at all. And I admit, I'm wondering the same thing.' Donatus's dark gaze met Lucan's. 'Have you, or have you not, left the faith?'

'That's really not any of Titus's business. Or yours.'

'Maybe it's not Titus's. But I do believe it's mine. You're my best friend, and a big part of the reason I'm a believer today. I wanted the same peace you had.'

'Maybe that peace wasn't real.'

'Lucan. I was there, remember? I saw the changes in you and they *were* real. The peace was real. The happiness was real. You weren't the same man you'd been before. Have you forgotten all that? You yourself told me how hollow your life was before, how you'd wake up beside a girl and hate yourself because you couldn't even remember her name. How the wineskin was never enough and never made you feel better. But then after you decided to serve the Christ—'

'My need for the Christian God has passed. He wasn't there for me when I needed him.'

'Ah, so you're a fair-weather soldier, then.'

Lucan's eyes narrowed. 'A *what*?'

'You heard me.'

'I was not a fair-weather soldier for Rome, and I was never a fair-weather believer in Christ. I served the Lord faithfully.'

'Until a cold wind blew.'

'Meaning what?'

'Meaning that maybe *you're* the problem. Maybe you were simply investing in religion like you invest in properties. Put in your gold, get out a bigger return. Put in enough prayer and good deeds, and somehow get a perfect life, right?'

Lucan was silent. The anger on his face told Donatus that he'd rubbed him on the raw.

'I'm going to forget you said that,' Lucan said. 'But only because I'll be gone in another day and I don't want our long friendship to end this way.'

'No. *Don't* forget it. I don't want you to forget it. I want you to

think about it, Lucan, long and hard. Maybe faith's not an immediate fix for every problem like you wanted it to be. Maybe you
found out the hard way that even a devout believer is still vulnerable
to pain and loss. But what did you do? You cut and ran. Dropped
the sword and left the field in full, shameful retreat.'

Lucan's eyes narrowed. 'What was I supposed to do? Stay on
fighting even if I no longer believed?'

Donatus's voice gentled. 'No, you change strategy. You do like
we did at Sarmizegethusa. You dig in and prepare the siegeworks.
You know why Trajan won that one, Lucan? Because he saw the
big picture. He had a plan. It wasn't easy and it wasn't quick, and
there were problems. Some days were bitter cold on that plain.
Bridges and siege ramps didn't get built quickly enough. The *bal-
listae* didn't always work. Sometimes the ropes snapped; other
times the wood splintered. Trajan lost good men to the archers and
slingers on the walls and to illness within the camp. But did that
deter him? No. He kept his focus on the ultimate victory and that's
why he accomplished it.'

'Are we talking about war or faith?'

'Don't miss the point because of the analogy. You had some dis-
appointments. The break with Severina hurt you. But that didn't
mean the Lord wasn't still guiding your life. He's the general,
Lucan. And like Trajan did in Dacia, God focuses on the big
picture of our lives, the overall prize to be accomplished in the
shaping of character. Pain, hurt, tears…yes, we're always vulnerable to those things. But life isn't ours to control; it's God's.
And sometimes bad things come along because he's got a bigger
victory in mind. He allows suffering because our character matters
far more than our comfort.'

'You're saying I left the battle too soon?'

'Yes. And that you're trying to assume the general's role when
you have no right.'

'No right? It's *my* life.'

'Tell me…when we fought, where did the general position
himself? On the highest hill, right? So he could see the entire field,

the action of every unit. He alone knew where the assault prevailed, or where a line was breached. Could any individual soldier fighting down below see the same things as he?'

'No.'

'Neither can you. You want control. But you can't see the whole field. So you might want to talk to the general again. Find out what *his* orders are and trust them. Because Lucan, faith may seem like the ultimate vulnerability, but it's really the ultimate strength.' Donatus eyed his friend solemnly. 'Will you at least think about that?'

Lucan looked away. 'I'll think about it.'

Donatus handed over the leather bag and stood. 'Good enough. You've got to be going now if you mean to have Severina here in time for a wedding. I'll stay and wait for Titus.'

Lucan pulled the strap over his head and started over the side of the barge.

'Donatus?' he called, once he'd settled himself in the small rowboat. 'I really will think about it.'

Donatus grinned down at him. 'I know. That's why I brought it up. Now go on, get your woman. I'm eager to see the marriage noose slip around your neck. I don't want to be the only one tied for eternity to a strong-minded former gladiatrix.'

Lucan laughed and pushed off.

Donatus watched him for a moment and then turned away, hoping his words would help Lucan through the tough decisions still ahead.

Have you, or have you not, left the faith?

Donatus's words were repeated with each pull of the oars.

Because faith is really the ultimate strength.

Lucan's mind was weary, dull with lack of sleep. Still it refused to move away from these painful thoughts.

Was Donatus right?

All the way back to the farm Lucan thought about these things. Occasionally he stopped rowing to rest weary muscles and drifted with the current. The day was glorious, warm with sunshine and the song of birds.

But Lucan paid little attention. He felt sick inside, sick and lonely, filled with an ache he hadn't acknowledged until now.

He was hungry for belief.

He'd felt this way once before, when he'd been sent by his legion commanders to Antioch, a punitive action because of his adulterous affairs with the wives of high-ranking officers.

In a strange place, lonely for friendship and weary of his sinful lifestyle, he'd been miserable until he met Philemon, a friendly bear of a man who introduced Lucan to the Christian brothers who worshipped in the city.

At first he attended their meetings only for the social aspects. But their beliefs began to provide answers for the emptiness he felt.

He'd been so sure of God's love then. What had happened to change his mind?

Maybe Donatus was right. Maybe he had expected immediate reward for living a righteous life, and maybe he'd expected that reward to be Severina. When that hadn't happened, anger had replaced faith.

Nobody likes to be vulnerable, but life isn't ours to control.

Lucan had never been one to lie to himself. He didn't now. He saw his fear and admitted it.

It was the same fear that had made him hesitant about leaving his *spatha* with Severina. He'd overcome vulnerability then by turning to look at her. She'd looked delicate, like an angel. Love prevailed. He'd unbelted the weapon and left it with her.

He realised now that he'd never be totally free of anxiety. Any human who lived would be vulnerable to pain and loss. He could no more control that than he could stop breathing.

But he could love.

He thought again of the night he and Severina had shared, of the gentleness and sweetness between them. He'd willingly handed over his heart, even knowing she planned to leave him again.

Because faith remained.

Somewhere, somehow, faith still lived within him, enough to

believe that his love for Severina would be enough, and that victory would come for him some day.

So why had he given up on God, the creator of such love, the author of such faith?

Had fear simply overcome, for a while, all he'd believed?

He knew a sudden, strong urge to pray. It would be the first time he'd really prayed in months and so he felt obliged to make it something of a formality. He rowed to a grassy bank, tied up to a low-hanging tree and climbed out. When he found a sheltered place beneath the trees, he knelt there.

It didn't take long. God already knew his sins and regrets. But when he stood a few minutes later, he felt like a new man. Good. Clean. And finally ready to listen to the general instead of issuing all the orders on his own.

Neither the strenuous rowing nor his own weariness bothered him when he started back down the river to go to Severina. He finally felt ready for the future, whatever that future would hold.

Semni's face held disbelief when he entered the room where Severina stood, nervously pacing. He glanced towards the slave who'd summoned him, however, and wisely held his surprise.

'I must send Nebibi on an errand,' he murmured to Severina. 'He's a curious lad and prone to talk too much.'

Semni turned to give low-voiced commands to the slave, waiting for the boy to leave and his footsteps to fade before he spoke.

'Why are you here? It's not safe.' His voice was sharp with tension.

'I need your help. I swear it'll be the last thing I ask of you, but I have no one else.'

'If you need transport, you're too late. The grain ship for Britannia has departed. There's not another leaving until—'

'I can't use your ships. By now my father will know you've seen me.'

Semni nodded.

'That's too risky now, but there are other ships, and other captains who are your friends. Can you arrange something?'

'Maybe, but not until morning. Does the destination matter?'

'No, but I'll need another favour. Give me three days' lead time and then somehow let my father know I've gone. And to where.'

Semni's eyebrows rose.

'His men must follow me.'

Semni scowled. 'That's too risky. Suppose your ship is delayed. Suppose the winds don't blow fair. Then your father's men would be upon you.'

'Trust me. I have a good reason for asking this. You must help me.'

The tall Nubian folded his arms and studied her. 'It's the golden-haired man, isn't it? You're protecting him.'

Severina saw no reason to lie. 'Yes.'

Semni's breath released in a long sigh. 'All right. I don't like it, but I'll help you.'

Severina raised on tiptoe to put a quick kiss on his cheek. 'Thank you, Semni. I knew I could count on you. You've always been a dear friend to me.'

A deep voice from the doorway startled them both. 'Don't be too hasty with your praise, Aloli. Even one who seems a friend can be a serpent in disguise.'

The voice was only too familiar, though she hadn't heard it in years. Severina gasped and turned to confirm her worst fears. 'Rashui.'

The huge man she'd once known as captain of the temple guard laughed unpleasantly and made a mocking bow. 'At Egypt's service, of course.' He turned to Semni. 'You've done well, Semni.'

The words hit Severina like a blow. She turned to gape at Semni. 'You *betrayed* me?'

He held out his hands in a gesture of supplication.

'The drought's wasted our homelands,' Rashui said. 'Semni's reliance on Egyptian grain has caused him to be more willing to negotiate than previously.'

Semni's expression held regret. 'I'm sorry, Aloli. I had no choice. My mother, my sisters…they depend on me. Without my grain, they cannot eat. They wouldn't survive.'

Severina didn't respond. Her mind was already leaping ahead. She scanned the room for a way to escape.

Semni saw her intention. 'Don't try it. Your enemies are too many. They've surrounded this house. You'll never escape and I don't want you hurt in the attempt.'

Severina's eyes narrowed. 'Don't pretend concern for me now, Semni. Not when you've just sold me into slavery.'

Rashui laughed. 'Oh, come now! To be wife to the son of a ruler of Egypt…*slavery*? To be dressed in fine silks and collars of gold, to have servants attend your every need…such slavery!'

Severina's eyes narrowed. 'I'd rather die than be a stranger's brood mare.'

'I see. You'd prefer your Roman lover, Titus Livius Lucan?'

Severina's gasp made him smile.

'Oh, yes. We know all about him. And I will tell you this…' His eyes glittered coldly. 'Things will be bad for him if you don't come willingly now.'

'Lucan's done nothing,' Severina said in a tight voice.

'That doesn't matter to your father or the nobles of Egypt. Your rebellion's lasted too long. They grow weary of the dearth in the land and the cries of their people.'

'I can't heal the drought.'

'Your father says you can. You're his first-born daughter and must give yourself to the ruler's son. Then our land will see prosperity.'

He lifted her chin. 'One way or the other, you will return to Egypt. Either proudly, as befits your noble status, or in chains, as befits a rebellious slave.'

'In chains, then, so all may know the truth of what I've become.'

Rashui dropped his hand. 'As you wish. But I will then order that your Roman lover be captured and brought along to face your father. Because he, too, should pay for his part in your rebellion.'

'No! Lucan had no part in my decisions.'

'Then come with me now, and do it without a fight. Only if you willingly submit to your destiny will he be spared.'

Severina had dreaded this moment for five years. She'd never imagined she'd give up her freedom willingly. But that was before Lucan.

Her eyes narrowed as she eyed Rashui. 'You give your word? No harm will come to Lucan if I go now of my own free will?'

Rashui nodded. 'I swear it.'

Severina closed her eyes. This was all she could do for Lucan now, her final gift.

'All right,' she said. 'I'll go without a fight.'

Rashui's laughter was grating. 'I had a feeling you'd see things my way. Come. A sleek Egyptian ship is anchored nearby, awaiting command to sail. We'll be in Egypt within days.'

Severina felt sick. Her life would never be the same, but she could live with the choice she'd made.

She had protected Lucan.

Chapter Seventeen

'No, no. You're not paying attention! My jackal has captured your queen again!'

Sheriti threw down the gamepiece in disgust. 'I don't know what's wrong with you, Aloli. You used to be good at this game. You won every time we played.'

A gentle voice from a nearby chair soothed the tension. 'Let it rest, Sheriti. Your sister's still tired from her voyage.'

'I'm not tired from the voyage,' Aloli snapped, regretting the harshness when her mother and grandmother showed distress. 'I'm just…tired of being imprisoned in this apartment.'

Her mother, Nafrit, set aside her sewing. 'I understand. But truly, your father's dealt gently with you.'

'Yes,' seconded her grandmother, Esho, whose dark eyes missed little. 'We feared it would be much worse than confinement here with us in this luxurious apartment.'

It could have been worse, and Severina knew it. In fact, she'd returned to Egypt expecting her father's fury. She'd expected humiliation, a public beating or torture, or worse.

Instead, expert as he was in manipulation, he'd sought out her one weakness and threatened Lucan.

That threat had been enough to keep her in compliance with his will. She wouldn't see Anok Khai again until her betrothal ceremony. When that day came, he'd be arrayed in the full regalia of the High Priest. She'd also be dressed in finery, with the golden crown of Isis on her head, carried on a litter of gold and jewels. The ceremony would be ostentatious and public, for this marriage was meant to restore blessing to Egypt and hope to her people. Her father believed it would bring him immortality.

Every day a group of bald, clean-shaven, white-robed priests came to speak with Nafrit. They brought news of the wedding preparations and enquired about her daughter's medical condition, a subtle way of asking if Severina had begun her monthly flow.

She hadn't, not yet.

Each night she lay in bed and wondered what would happen if she carried Lucan's child. Anok Khai had rightly guessed that she and Lucan had been lovers. It had angered him, but not deterred him from his plans. Her lack of virginity made no difference to him, but a child…now, *that* would make a difference.

She both wished for pregnancy and feared it. She'd begun to fear the consequences of the choice she'd made.

Would it be bad for Lucan?

Would her child be forcibly taken from her?

Severina hadn't yet had the courage to ask these questions. Instead, she waited and worried.

'Aloli?' Her mother's voice brought her back to the present. 'Are you all right?'

'I'm unnerved by so many changes.'

'It's common for a woman to be nervous before her wedding,' Esho agreed. 'And with this marriage so important to Egypt's prosperity…well, of course you'd feel unsettled.'

Sheriti glanced towards her sister and frowned. 'Especially when your future husband wants nothing to do with you.'

'Sheriti!' There was sharp remonstrance in her mother's tone.

'You shouldn't be unkind,' Esho said reprovingly. 'Besides, it's not as if you know Kahotep's thoughts.'

Sheriti's chin rose. 'But I *do*. Don't forget, Grandmother, Kahotep and I were in the schoolroom together. We've always been close. I spoke to him after word came of Aloli's capture. He does not want her.'

'Perhaps he's simply startled by the suddenness,' her mother countered. 'Don't despair, Aloli. Kahotep's a good man, and he'll treat you kindly. He's half-Egyptian, so he truly does want the best for our land. He'll do what he must to ensure prosperity for us all.'

'He'll do it only because his father demands it of him,' Sheriti persisted. 'But Kahotep doesn't want this marriage. He's in love with…someone else.'

Her mother's eyebrows shot up. 'Sheriti! You must never say such things!'

'But it's true.' Sheriti looked angrily at her sister, her ebony eyes glistening. 'He loves another, Aloli. He will *never* love you.'

The tears that had threatened all morning suddenly blurred Severina's vision. 'That doesn't matter, does it? I don't want Kahotep, either. I haven't even seen him since he was a scrawny boy. And yet, it's already decreed that in a matter of days he'll take me to his bed and rut on me.' She covered her eyes with her hands. 'How will I *bear* it?'

Sheriti jumped to her feet, her fists clenching and unclenching. 'I hate you! You'll make him unhappy, and I hate you for it!' She wheeled around and fled the room.

'Let her go,' Nafrit's voice came softly as Severina wiped at the tears sliding down her cheek. 'She's young, and so is he. They'll get over their feelings, eventually.'

Severina turned to her mother. 'They're in love? With one another?'

Her mother lowered her gaze without reply.

'No wonder Sheriti's upset. I'm so sorry.'

'You can feel tenderness for Sheriti even after she spoke so hatefully to you?' Her mother's voice was touched with awe. 'Oh, Aloli. Sometimes you're so much like your father.'

'I'm *nothing* like him. How could you say such a thing?'

Esho cast them both a sympathetic look. 'Your father was once a very different person from the harsh, arrogant man you know of today.'

Nafrit sent Esho a grateful look.

'Anok Khai, different? I can't imagine.' Severina stood, pushing her chair back from the table.

Her mother gasped, pointing to Severina's skirt. 'You've started your flow.'

Esho clutched her sewing to her breast. 'Bless the gods. They've shown mercy.'

Severina was unable to move, unable to speak. She closed her eyes and opened them again. The blood was still there, a spot of red nearly the size of her palm, staining the garment upon which she'd sat. She stared at the fabric stupidly, blinking back tears.

She'd thought…she'd hoped…

Feeling formed into words slowly. *Oh, Lucan! I wanted your child so much!*

Her mother jerked her head up in surprise at the sob that came from her daughter's lips. It was a ragged sound, unnatural. Severina covered her mouth with the back of her hand in a futile attempt to hold back the pain, but then her shoulders began to shake—hard, silently, a convulsion of sorrow.

'Aloli?' Nafrit moved nearer.

Severina went like a child into her mother's embrace, clinging while Nafrit held her, rocked her, soothed her with gentle words until the tears subsided.

'Did you love him?' her grandmother asked quietly when grief was spent at last.

Severina wiped her nose and nodded.

'Did he love you?'

'Yes.'

'You wanted his child.'

'Yes.'

Neither of the older women chastised her.

Her mother spoke gently. 'I'm sorry, Aloli. Truly, I am sorry.'

'Me, too. Please, I…I need some time alone.'

Severina fled the room without looking backwards.

There was silence. Esho turned a worried gaze towards her daughter. 'She loved him, Nafrit.'

Nafrit turned away, making a harsh sound of pain.

Esho moved to her. When Esho's thin fingers touched her shoulder, Nafrit began to cry. 'I can't do it, Mama. I...just *can't*!'

Her mother took her into her arms. 'You can. You must think of your two daughters. Of Sheriti and her pain that she cannot be wife to Kahotep. Of Aloli, who longs to give a child to her lover. Think of *them*, Nafrit. Give them the love you were denied. Think of them, and I do believe you'll find the strength.'

The following day Nafrit, Esho and Sheriti were invited to luncheon with the wife of the Roman Prefect. Aloli was not invited; she was still confined to the apartment and under guard. Not that she cared to go with the other women. The last thing she wanted was to partake in frivolous conversation or—even worse—be asked to help finalise the plans for her wedding to the Prefect's son.

Once the other women had left, however, she found she wouldn't have long to enjoy the silence. Guards knocked at her door and Kahotep himself was ushered in. Aloli was made breathless by his sudden appearance and by the bold majesty of his commanding presence.

Kahotep wasn't the scrawny boy Severina remembered. As five years had changed her sister from a girl to a woman, so they'd worked a similar magic on the Prefect's son. He was now a man full grown, fine and handsome. His shoulders were wide, his legs long and muscular.

Severina moved forwards and, as protocol demanded, knelt in respectful dignity before Kahotep, looking up into a surprisingly attractive face. His eyes were of deep, shining amber flecked with warm gold and fringed by dark lashes. His brow was high, his jaw firm. There was intelligence in his face.

For the first time, Severina felt admiration for him. Like her, he was caught against his will in this madness of her father's making, asked to sacrifice his wishes for the good of Egypt. He would probably do so. Kahotep had integrity; he was not selfish. Her sister had chosen well.

He touched her shoulder and gently encouraged her to rise. 'Leave us,' he commanded the guards.

'But your father—'

'Leave us!' Kahotep's voice brooked no interference. 'Guard the door from outside if you must, but I will speak with my future bride in private.'

He breathed in stark relief when they closed the door behind them. 'I hope they will not talk,' he said quietly. 'I'd prefer that no one know I came here.'

Severina remembered that her mother had been rather surprised to receive the invitation to luncheon. 'Did you arrange the invitation for the others?'

'Yes. My mother proved most helpful once I told her how urgently I needed to speak with you.'

Severina bowed her head modestly. 'I'm honoured, my lord.'

He studied her a moment. 'You've changed, Aloli. You've grown very beautiful. I used to think when I was a boy that you were the prettiest woman in the world. But you've grown even more lovely with time.'

Severina felt heat rise in her face under his deep scrutiny. 'Thank you. You've also changed for the better, no longer a fledgling boy. No longer skinny with huge ears.'

He laughed, and took her hand. 'Thank you for noticing that I've finally grown into my ears.' He kissed her knuckles politely.

The gentleness behind the action caught Severina by surprise. She'd rather expected the same hostility from him that she'd first received from Sheriti. But Kahotep was proving to be mature and surprisingly kind.

She met his gaze. 'Thank you. Your thoughtfulness amazes me.'

'It does? Why?'

'Because I know you don't truly wish to wed me.'

Pain flickered through his amber gaze, quickly subdued. 'Ah, that,' he said quietly.

'I also know *why*,' Severina ventured, when he offered no denial. 'I know you love Sheriti.'

He closed his eyes. His pulse pounded furiously at the base of his throat.

'I'm sorry,' she said. 'I've racked my brain for some way to extricate us from this.'

'And did you find one?'

'No. But even if I can't prevent this marriage, I won't let it...' She glanced down, feeling awkward by what she must say. 'I won't let it keep you from Sheriti.'

Kahotep's gaze on her sharpened. 'Meaning...what, exactly?'

'Meaning that she'll be invited to live with me in my royal apartments. When you visit me there, it will be Sheriti's bed you enjoy rather than mine.'

Kahotep drew in a hard breath.

'Eventually, she'll bear your child, but with enough care and secrecy, her baby could be presented to the world as mine and so take his place as your rightful heir.'

Kahotep was quiet for a long moment. 'You'd do this for Sheriti?'

'Yes, and for you.'

'Why?'

Severina's eyes abruptly filled with tears. It startled and embarrassed her. 'Because it hurts not to have the love you want.'

Kahotep made a soft sound and stroked her knuckles with his thumb. 'You're a generous woman, Aloli, and you have a virtuous heart.' He lowered his voice. 'I appreciate this gesture, but the prophecy was specific. It's our *union* that brings prosperity to Egypt.'

'We'd be married.'

He looked at her then—directly, assessingly. 'Marriage is not merely a ceremony. It's the physical union of which I speak.'

She looked down at the floor. 'Oh.'

'There would have to be that. At least once.'

'I see.'

'Do you?' He looked away, the muscles in his jaw tensing.

He finally spoke. 'I came to bring you news.' He met her gaze.

'Emperor Trajan has sent a diplomatic envoy from Rome to make an appeal for your release, led by Senator Marcus Flavius Donatus. The terms offered were extraordinarily generous, given that the Emperor could have simply demanded that Egypt comply. Instead, he opted to give gold to the nobles of Egypt in exchange for your immediate return to Rome.'

'And?'

'Anok Khai did not agree.'

'Of course not. He wants immortality for himself.'

Kahotep sighed. 'Yes. And my father wants prosperity for Egypt. So our wishes are to be sacrificed on the altar for Egypt's greater good in a few days' time. Unless…' Kahotep met her gaze, his eyes dark and intense '…unless something happens in the meantime to prevent it.'

'Something like *what*?' Severina shook her head and lifted her hands in mute frustration. 'I'm imprisoned here. Rashui and his palace guards know my every move.'

Kahotep stepped lightly backwards, pulling her with him. 'Come, Aloli, and let me show you the path to freedom.'

He led her into her mother's bedroom and stopped in front of an ornately decorated marble niche set into the wall as an altar to the household gods. 'See this?' he asked. 'If you'll put your index finger here…' he indicated a small indentation carved into the petals of a lotus flower '…and press down firmly, you'll see…'

Severina jumped as a small doorway opened in the wall. It was only knee-high, and barely wide enough for one person to wriggle through.

'That,' Kahotep finished triumphantly.

'A secret passageway?'

He nodded. 'Anok Khai thinks my father an old fool,' he said. 'That he doesn't know about the labyrinth of passages that Anok Khai and his spies have tunnelled beneath the palace in their efforts to gather information. But trust me, Aloli—my father has many resources of his own.'

Severina was almost breathless. 'So I could escape and flee?'

Kahotep smiled. 'Yes. Unless you prefer to stay and marry me.'

'Forgive me, Kahotep, for being less than enthusiastic about wedding you, but…'

He shrugged. 'I know. Livius Lucan's already explained the situation to me.'

Severina gasped. 'Lucan? He's here in Egypt?'

Kahotep's laughter was soft. 'Of course. What did you expect? That he'd vow his love for you one minute and forget you the next?' Kahotep clucked his tongue. 'Fortunately for you, your Roman's love is no slight or fickle thing. He means to rescue you even if he must slay Anok Khai to do it.'

Severina gasped. 'No! Lucan must not face my father. He doesn't understand such evil—'

'Shh.' Kahotep put a finger against her lips. 'I've explained many things to your lover and he knows now that there's a better way.' He gestured towards the small door in the wall. 'There's risk in using these passageways. They're heavily used by the spies of Anok Khai. But they're still the best way for Lucan to get you out of here and to the east gate where your friend Semni will be waiting with an oxcart of grain to smuggle you out of the city.'

'Semni? Oh, no! He betrayed me!'

'He knew you'd think so. But truthfully, he had no choice in that at the time. Your father's men had already prepared their trap for you and he was forced to go along or be killed. Yet nothing forced Semni to find Donatus and Lucan later and tell them all that had happened. Nothing forced him to offer his help—and indeed, he's been spending his own gold to buy the loyalty of servants here in this palace. You'll find yourself surrounded by friends in the hour of your escape. Don't be surprised if some who now seem faithful to Anok Khai prove otherwise in the end.'

Severina dragged in a long, deep breath. 'This almost seems too good to be true.'

Kahotep shook his head. 'Don't be too confident yet, Aloli. The greatest danger has yet to be faced. When Lucan comes for you tonight, you must stay sharply focused. If you're captured this time…'

He didn't have to say what Severina already knew. Failure this time would cost Lucan his life.

'I'll be ready,' she said. 'But please tell Lucan to be careful. I couldn't bear it should anything happen to him.'

Kahotep, seeing that her eyes filled with tears, bowed slightly. 'I must go now, but I must first give you both my heartfelt thanks,' he said quietly. 'I love my father and Egypt, but I love Sheriti more. Your successful escape tonight will make happiness possible for your sister and me, so I'll be praying that the gods might look upon you with favour.'

Severina nodded. As she closed the door behind Kahotep, she whispered a heartfelt prayer of her own that somehow love might prevail over the powerful ambition of Anok Khai.

Chapter Eighteen

Nafrit, Esho and Sheriti returned by mid-afternoon after having shared an enjoyable luncheon with the wife of the Roman Prefect. Severina listened with only half an ear as they told her of the richness of the royal apartments, of the delicacies that had been placed before them and of the lively gossip to which they'd been privy.

She was nervous, filled with anxious questions that she wished she'd asked Kahotep before he left. When would Lucan come? How would he keep from alerting the other women in the apartment?

By the time servants brought in their evening meal, her nerves were so knotted she could scarcely eat. When the young slave girl placed the tray down before her, lifting the lid on the dish so that the fragrance of roasted meat wafted up, Severina swallowed down her nausea.

'For you,' the girl said with a smile. 'The cook said this one's specially prepared just the way you like it.'

'Please give my thanks to the cook. I'm sure it'll be delicious, but…' Severina bit her lip '…I'm not hungry at the moment. Please leave the tray. Perhaps I'll feel more inclined to eat after I've had a hot bath.'

The slave nodded. 'I'll have water brought up.'

'Uh-hmmm.' Sheriti looked up from her food. 'You sure you're not hungry, Aloli? This is really good.'

Nafrit tested her own food and frowned slightly. 'Goodness. A little too much spice for my taste.'

'I like it,' Sheriti said. 'Try yours, Aloli, and tell us what you think.'

Aloli tested a bite. Spicy, Sheriti had said? Hers seemed no more spicy than usual. 'It tastes fine to me,' she said, setting down her spoon. 'Maybe even a little bland.' She added as she excused herself to her bedroom in preparation for bathing.

A knock at the door some time later interrupted her anxious thoughts.

'Hot water for your bath,' a servant called. Severina rose to let the servants bring in the heavy buckets.

'There in the tub,' the head servant directed the slaves. 'And hurry. The mistress wants to enjoy it before the water gets cold.'

One by one, the slaves emptied their buckets and left.

All but one.

Severina gasped when she turned from the window and found him still standing beside the tub, staring at her.

She spoke to him in rapid Egyptian. 'You'd better hurry. The others have left you.'

He answered in broken Egyptian, 'I'm not here for them. I'm here for you.'

The words, the voice, the broken cadence…it took a moment to register. Her gaze flew to the man's face.

Lucan carefully lifted the turban from his golden hair and set it aside.

'Lucan? It's you? It's really, really you?'

He came to her, pulled her hard into his embrace and lowered his head. The scorching kiss told her of his passion, of his pain, of his desire and need for her.

When he finally drew away, she was weak and trembling, scarcely coherent. His golden eyes glittered above her. 'You didn't doubt I'd come for you, did you?' His voice was husky. 'I made you my wife the night I lay with you. I will never allow any other man to take what is mine.'

'You don't understand,' she moaned. 'This is too dangerous, too—'

He laid a finger on her lips. 'Not quite as dangerous as you think. Your Semni's an amazing man, with a vast network of friends, all of them on our side. For now, his gold has bought us some time together. Your mother, sister and grandmother are now sleeping heavily in the outer room, thanks to the draught put into their food. They won't awaken until dawn. By then we should be long gone.'

'Is Semni really to be trusted, Lucan?' She wanted to believe. She'd been hurt by the loss of Semni's friendship.

'We couldn't have got this far without him,' Lucan said. He tucked a stray hair behind her ear. 'You're surrounded by friends. Donatus is here, too, and he leads a whole unit of Trajan's Praetorian Guard. One way or the other, we're going to get you out of here.'

Severina saw the determination in Lucan's eyes. 'I want to believe that,' she said. 'But I fear for you.'

'Show some faith, love.' His hand slipped beneath her hair to capture her. His beautiful lips turned up at the corners as he drew closer. 'I've never disappointed you before, have I?'

She thought of Lucan's love-making, of his large, gentle hands sliding across her skin, of his lips parting to take her breast…and shivered her response. 'No, never.'

And then his lips were upon hers and all thought ceased as the reality overshadowed even her most pleasant memories.

'Semni's friends guard our door tonight. We have a few hours before we're to slip through the tunnels,' he murmured as his lips warmed the curve of her neck. 'It won't be long enough to give you all the love you deserve, but maybe it will be enough to last until we're safely away.'

A savage bitter-sweetness tore through Severina.

Lucan was bold and confident, but he didn't know his adversary. Even with Semni's network of friends and the help of Donatus and the Emperor, Anok Khai would be a formidable foe. Severina wanted to hope, but she had more cause to doubt. She knew Anok Khai.

But if love held its own strong power, then she would give him that, as freely and wildly as she could, pulling energy and heat from the universe for his sake. She who had never submitted to any man now willingly subjugated herself to his need as if she could become his shield, his armour-bearer, the unleashed strength of his sword arm.

Perhaps Lucan sensed the change in her. He let her take possession of his mouth. He let her hands clutch and hold him, allowed her body to make demands of his. It was subtle, this shift in power and purpose, but they both understood it.

Severina drew back to look into his face. There was sharp intelligence within his gaze, as if he knew what she meant to do, and found harsh pleasure in the knowing.

She went to her knees before him, and his long, gold-tipped eyelashes lowered to veil his thoughts. She laid her cheek against his loins, nuzzling his hard ridge through his clothing. 'Severina,' he whispered, 'you don't have to do this.'

'Shh,' she commanded, reaching beneath his rough tunic to unwrap the soft layers of his undergarment. His phallus sprang free of confinement, large and magnificent, and she took him into her hand.

Blood pulsed through the thick muscle. He was fully engorged and aroused; already a drop of moisture glistened at the sleek tip. She touched it lightly with a fingertip before she bent to take it on her tongue. He tasted sweet and hot, fully male, fully hers.

'Sweet gods,' he breathed, sucking in a sharp breath.

She showed him little mercy, knowing instinctively that this gift must be fiercely given. One hand moved to the base of his shaft and held him tightly, pleasuring him until his breathing was ragged and harsh, serving him on her knees like a wanton.

His fingers tangled in her hair and held her. Hungry, begging her for more, he groaned out his need, reduced by awful pleasure to nothing more than the needs of his sex. She looked up; his eyes were closed, the skin over his facial bones tight. Her body clenched hard at the sight. Already her passage was hot and pulsing, awaiting his pleasure.

As if he read her thoughts, he pulled himself from her, tugging at her hair until she let him go, his shaft now a deep, fiery red and rigid down the entire length, stretched and glistening wet.

He pulled her up and lifted her, carrying her across the room to the high bed. He laid her halfway across the edge, jerking her skirts to her waist and her underclothes to the floor. The position arched her body and opened her up, making her the offering she meant herself to be. In this she served him, too, whimpering only in pleasure when he thrust hard into her and used her.

They found glory together, Lucan grinding out her name with a deep, guttural cry as he plunged deep and flooded her womb. Her muscles convulsed all around him and she knew without doubt or shadow of worry that she had possessed him as certainly as he possessed her.

'It's not a public bath, but it's not bad,' Lucan said as he held Severina in his embrace within the large tub of steaming water. 'You're much nicer to bathe with than a group of flabby old men.'

'I would *hope* so,' Severina said, splashing him playfully.

'Your bottom feels wonderful snuggled up against my loins,' he murmured, his lips nuzzling into the fragrant curve of her neck.

'Uhmmm…'

'And your breasts fit nicely into my hands.'

'They're not too small?'

Lucan smiled against her skin. 'No, they're perfect. Perfect shape, perfect size…' He squeezed one nipple playfully. 'Perfect for me.'

'You're just saying that so you can have your way with me,' Severina said in a teasingly sultry voice. And Lucan wondered, not for the first time, exactly what it was about this woman that even her *voice* could arouse him.

'You see?' Severina whispered, wriggling her bottom wickedly across his thickening loins. 'You *do* mean to seduce me. Shameless behaviour, and I do protest it.'

Lucan chuckled. 'Play fair, Severina. A man can't help the response of his body when so sorely tempted.'

She gasped in mock anger. 'Then you'd make *me* out to be the villain?'

'Perhaps my judgement is a bit hasty,' Lucan said, kissing the soft shadow behind her ear. 'Slide against me again so I can make a more informed decision.'

He was ready for her this time, his hands on her hips to steady her, to keep her from moving too quickly, to lift her up and then down again as he impaled her on his shaft.

She shuddered, air hissing through her teeth as she surrendered to the pleasure that speared her.

'You are…' she gasped as he lifted her again, and brought her down '…an utter…reprobate.'

He laughed softly. 'For that saucy attitude, I really must punish you with another sharp bite of pleasure.'

He went into her deeply, finding and touching that feminine place of most delicious sensation that he'd learned about from past lovers. He wasn't proud of how he'd gained the knowledge, but at least he could use it now to gratify his wife.

Severina closed her eyes and moaned, trembling in his arms.

'You like that?' he whispered. 'You want more?'

'Yes,' she panted softly. 'Oh, yes.'

He gave her more, moving her, shifting her so that he could penetrate her deeply, going slowly so she was forced to savour their joining, resisting his own desire for as long as he could. She fought his decision, urging him to move, begging him for harder, deeper, faster.

He gave in only after he'd drawn out the feeling to a taut, thin line ready to snap.

He startled Severina with a sudden reversal of position, intent now on completion; she leaned over the edge of the tub and he took her from behind, increasing the tempo, moving them both towards climax in a steady, driving rhythm.

By now Severina was biting her lip to keep from making noise. Water sloshed and sucked at them, overflowing the tub, running in rivulets down its sides to puddle on the floor. It dripped from her hair; it trickled down his face, a fusion of fire and water, of man and woman, of two creatures desperate to become one.

She forgot herself and screamed his name at the peak. With the hot blood pulsing hard in his ears and his own explosion imminent, he was scarcely aware of her wild abandon.

But later, he recalled it and smiled, tucking her tightly against his body as they nestled together in clean sheets. Whether she realised it or not, Severina belonged to him now. And he would never let another man take her, not even if death was a possible outcome.

They dozed for a while—satiated, filled, content to breathe in the scent and warmth of the other. But soon, too soon, it was nearly dawn and Lucan was shaking her awake, murmuring low-voiced commands as he helped her dress.

It still seemed part of a sweet dream, that he was here with her after these past weeks apart; he dropped light kisses on her brow, her shoulder, her knee as he knelt before her to tie the leather thong on her sandal.

He had just finished securing it when a thunderous knock on the door made her gasp.

Ever the warrior, Lucan acted instinctively, jerking himself upright in one swift movement, snatching up his sword from his leather pack of clothing beside the bed. He stood poised with his *spatha* in his hand, fierce and muscular, balanced with agile grace on the balls of his feet.

'Hide!' Severina hissed. 'You've got to hide!'

She looked wildly around and gestured to the heavy curtains that separated her bedroom from a dressing alcove. 'There,' she gestured. 'Get behind that curtain.'

Lucan nodded; she scarcely breathed until he was hidden from view.

Another knock rattled the hinges before she could shuffle to the door.

Rashui stood outside, his countenance intent. 'I apologise for waking you, but I came to give your mother a message from the

Prefect and…' He glanced over his shoulder towards the dim room behind him where Severina could see the still-sleeping bodies of her mother, grandmother and sister, sprawled in disorderly fashion against the silk pillows of the couches. 'I thought I'd better check on you. Something doesn't feel right here. Your mother won't awaken, and neither will Esho or Sheriti. The food on their trays scarcely looks touched. It almost seems they've been drugged.'

'They were very tired from yesterday's outing,' Severina said, yawning. 'Perhaps they needed sleep more than food.'

His dark eyes scrutinised her. 'You're up early. And already dressed?'

'I normally arise early. And if you recall, I had no outing yesterday to tire me. If you'll give me the message, I'll see that my mother gets it later after she's finished sleeping.'

Severina held out her hand. He ignored it, pushing past her into the bedroom. He glanced around suspiciously, his eyes narrowed. 'There's an odd smell in here. Something strong, something like…sex.'

Severina met his gaze. 'You've a vivid imagination, Rashui. Could I outwit your own guards to take a lover into my prison?'

He eyed her speculatively before turning his attention towards the bed. 'Your bedclothes are badly rumpled. Wild dreams in the night?' He walked forwards and laid his large hand on the mattress, smoothing his palm over a wide area. 'Still warm. On *both* sides.'

Severina shrugged. 'I move around a lot.'

Moments ticked by as Severina waited for Rashui's hawkish stare to travel the room. His gaze touched on the shutters at her window, tightly latched. On the bathing tub, still filled with water for slaves to empty later. On the curtains at each side of her dressing alcove. She prayed Rashui would not move around the bed; Lucan's pack of food and clothing lay on the floor there, and the belt and scabbard for his *spatha*.

She breathed again when the guard turned away, dropping a

thick, tightly wrapped bundle on to a nearby stool. 'Your father's sent these garments for you.'

Severina frowned. 'Since when did Anok Khai concern himself with his daughter's clothing?'

'Since she is to be betrothed to the son of Egypt's ruler. Tomorrow, with all the nobles gathered.'

'Tomorrow?' Severina gasped. 'So soon?'

'He thought to give you a few more days, but something's come up.'

Severina's eyes narrowed. 'What?'

'The Emperor of Rome wants to prevent your betrothal. He's sent a diplomatic envoy to negotiate for your release.'

'And so Anok Khai will flout the will of Emperor Trajan and betroth me immediately.'

'You know your father well. The Roman diplomats will be given front-row seats at the ceremony.'

When she did not answer, Rashui shrugged. 'You're to dress in the clothing Anok Khai has sent and be escorted to the palace tomorrow morning. Be ready. I will come for you myself.'

She nodded. Rashui moved towards the door.

He paused at the threshold to look back at her. 'Your Roman lover is part of the envoy sent from Emperor Trajan. But trust me in this, Aloli…if you care anything at all about him, do not defy your father.'

The door closed with finality behind him. Severina stood motionless, fighting the cold seeping into her soul.

'Severina.'

She turned. Lucan came to her. He took her chilled hands and raised them to his lips, kissing them one by one. 'Do not fear,' he whispered. 'We'll be long gone before then.'

Severina nodded only because his eyes implored her to agree. But in her heart, she knew a strong, powerful fear. Lucan did not know Anok Khai. He had no idea of the evil he'd soon confront.

Chapter Nineteen

'This way,' Lucan whispered, his callused hand tightening around Severina's. He held the torch high in his other hand as they turned into yet another of the large, square-cut doors hewn in the rock beneath the palace fortress.

'You're sure?' Severina asked. 'It feels like we're going the wrong way to me.'

Lucan chuckled. 'Some of these tunnels wind for long distances in what seems the wrong direction before making an abrupt turn towards their destination. You'll have to trust me. Donatus and I have dressed as Egyptians and wandered these tunnels almost constantly for the last five days. Kahotep gave us a rudimentary map of the tunnels, but we thought we should learn them for ourselves. Semni's helped us, too. He measured the traffic in all the main tunnels both by day and by night. It was his decision to bring you out just prior to dawn. It is the quietest time.'

'Amazing,' Severina said, in awe that so much effort had gone into her rescue.

'If you and I become separated, stay in place until I come for you. These tunnels are a confusing labyrinth. We could end up circling one another. That would waste time, and we have little enough of that. Once it's known that you've fled, Anok Khai's spies will be on the alert and these tunnels will be especially unsafe.'

'I understand.'

Lucan nodded and then placed his finger against his lips to urge her into silence. They moved stealthily through the tunnels for what seemed to Severina like a long time. Occasionally they stopped as Lucan listened for approaching footsteps. Once he heard men coming and pulled her into a dark side tunnel, snuffing out their torch before flattening his body alongside the wall. Only a minute later, Severina heard male voices and footsteps moving along the corridor from which they'd come. She watched as light passed by the end of their passageway, illuminating her and Lucan for mere seconds despite their attempts to slink deeper into shadow.

'They weren't moving hurriedly.' Lucan breathed in relief after the men had moved on. 'That's good. They don't know you're gone yet.'

Severina heard him fumble in his pack and then the sharp click of stone against stone echoed down the corridor as he worked for a spark to relight their torch. She held her breath until light flared. Lucan smiled into her anxious face.

'Not afraid of the dark, are you?'

'No. Only rats and snakes. And spiders.'

'Ah.' His laughter was soft. 'The list grows longer with each of our adventures.'

She glared at him. 'This isn't funny, Lucan. Let's hurry and get out of here.'

He gave her a quick, reassuring kiss and they started on their way again.

After they'd moved in silence for what felt like hours to Severina, Lucan touched her sleeve. 'Someone's approaching.' He looked around. 'Damn. No side tunnel for us this time.' He dropped his heavy pack on to the ground and reached into it. 'Follow my lead,' he urged her as he drew out a small skin of wine and proceeded to use its contents to douse his clothing.

He'd barely dropped it back into his bag before Severina saw light coming in their direction. 'Play along,' Lucan reminded her before pushing her back against the wall and lowering his face to hers for a startling kiss. Reflexively she began to protest.

'Look there!' she heard one of the approaching strangers say.

'Hey, you!' the other man said with a note of anger in his voice. 'You're not to use these tunnels for this. Did not Anok Khai forbid it?'

'He's drunk,' the other man said. 'Gods above, he reeks of wine. You can smell him all the way over here.'

Lucan turned and leered at them, looking for all the world like a drunken sot. He took a step forwards towards them and fell over his pack, sprawling on the uneven bricks with a groan.

'Damn fool,' one man said, coming forwards to lift him up again.

Lucan thanked him in the Egyptian tongue, the words heavily slurred.

'Get out of here,' his rescuer commanded. 'And take the woman with you.'

The other man with him held up his torch. 'Wait a minute,' he said musingly. 'She looks familiar. Is she not the daughter of Anok Khai?'

Lucan attacked without warning, throwing his torch aside and knocking his from the hand of the man who held it. Light flickered and died, throwing the passageway into blackness. Strong arms grasped Severina and flung her several feet away. She landed hard on her knees, too stunned to grasp Lucan's effort to protect her from the fight ensuing behind her.

Disoriented by the darkness, she could tell little of what was happening in the struggle behind her. She heard something crack, something like the snap of a tree branch underfoot and then the muffled sound of a man's body falling heavily to the floor. Then there were more sounds of struggle along with much laboured breathing and a low, masculine gurgle before another body fell. She shuddered and prayed it was not Lucan's.

The quiet unnerved her. She stood and waited, afraid to breathe in the unnatural quiet. 'Lucan?' she finally ventured.

'I am here.' And then, he was with her, taking her hand in his. She felt the stickiness of blood on his fingers. 'You're hurt?' she asked.

'No,' he said, and she realised the blood was that of the man he'd slain. It seemed then that the smell of blood was in her nostrils and its coppery taste was in her mouth. Despite that, she could scarcely believe that the gentle hand guiding her through the darkness had just ended two lives.

She wasn't squeamish. Life as a gladiatrix had made death a daily affair. But Severina realised now that she and Lucan had turned a corner, crossed a line. This was no coy game of hide-and-seek here in these cool, dark tunnels. They were fighting for their lives.

Lucan breathed hard in her ear. 'I can't risk lighting the torch again. Others may have heard our struggle. We've got to get out of here. Follow me.'

He grasped her hand and pulled her along. Stifled by the darkness, hardly able to breathe and panicked by the speed with which Lucan moved, she began to lag and stumble. Finally she could not go on and fell hard on to her bruised knees on the cool stone. Lucan's hands found her and lifted her.

'Easy, love,' he whispered. 'We're almost there.'

'Please slow down a little,' she urged him. 'The darkness…I hate it!'

He placed her hand on the wall. 'Feel this wall? It's solid and you can follow it. Soon you'll come to a corner and a sharp turn to the right. A few feet past that, the texture of the stone changes to brick. That means we're almost there.'

His words calmed her, giving her something on which to focus besides her fear.

'Here,' he said at last. 'There's a door here somewhere, but first…' Severina heard his palms slide along the rough brick. 'I must be sure the courtyard's clear and that Semni's cart is in place.'

She watched as a brick moved and sliver of light pierced their dark tunnel from the outside. 'A spy hole,' Lucan whispered, answering her unspoken question. 'They're all over the place. Kahotep's marked most of them on his map. Donatus found two more that Kahotep didn't know about and Semni found a third.' He shrugged. 'Your father clearly wants to know everything that's going on in this palace. He and his men seem especially fond of peeping into the bathing chambers of the women.'

That news didn't surprise Severina. She'd heard rumours of her

father's perversions long before she was even old enough to understand most of them.

'The courtyard's empty,' Lucan said. 'And good old Semni's
placed that oxcart right where it's supposed to be.'

'So what do we do now?'

'We'll leave this tunnel and ease over to the oxcart. There are
two large clay vessels nestled there among bags of grain. We'll get
inside them. Semni will be watching for us, disguised as a peasant
farmer. He'll hurriedly tamp lids on and roll those huge jars into
place, burying them under the grain. Then if all goes as planned,
he'll drive us out of the courtyard, through the east gate and on to
the harbour.'

'We can't leave on one of Semni's ships, Lucan. My father will
expect that. When he discovers I'm gone, that'll be the first place
he'll look.'

Lucan grinned at her. 'I know. That's why we're not going
aboard one of Semni's ships. The jars in which we're hiding will
be strapped on to camels, part of a caravan heading across the
Negev to Terna in Arabia.'

'Arabia!' Severina gasped. 'That's such a long way to be riding
inside a clay pot, Lucan!'

His laughter was soft. 'You won't be in the pot the entire
distance, my sweet. Only until we're safely out of this city. Then
Semni's friend who leads the caravan will help us out of our jars
and we'll ride on the camels like the rest of the traders. Are you
game for that?'

She dragged in a deep breath. 'I'm ready for anything, as long
as I'm with you.'

Lucan captured her face with both hands and kissed her hard and
deep. They were both a little breathless when he pulled away.
'What's that for?' she asked.

'Mostly because I like to kiss you,' he said, smiling down at her.
'But also for good luck, too.'

She found herself hoping they wouldn't need that much good
luck before he turned away from her to slip his index finger into a

worn crevice near the base of the wall. A door sprang open before them, narrow and taller than the one in her mother's apartment.

'And so our adventure begins,' Lucan said in a low voice. 'To the oxcart, my love. Semni's waiting.'

Semni had tried to make the jars in which Severina and Lucan would be hiding as comfortable as possible. The lids he'd used to seal them had been specially made with tiny slots to provide ventilation and light. He'd also folded soft cotton blankets and placed them inside to cushion knees and elbows as they were bumped around, but Severina decided after she'd been jostled for a while that Semni's attempts to give comfort were appallingly meagre, well meaning though they were.

By the time the cart slowed and stopped, and her large clay jar was hefted by strong men on to the back of a camel, Severina was sure she'd be sore and bruised for the rest of her life. She was also tired of the airless gloom and perspired so profusely that rivulets of sweat ran down her back and buttocks and between her breasts; it was nearing mid-morning and the day was already hot. She wondered if Lucan was as miserable as she was, but having him nearby brought her comfort. He was, she knew, strapped to the camel behind her. To relieve her discomfort, she relived her beautiful memories of the night before, thinking only of the pleasure he'd brought her in his arms.

Thinking of Lucan helped her endure this painful, uncomfortable part of her journey. Soon the camels would take her outside the city. Soon they'd stop and she and Lucan would be free of their confinement, the first step towards ultimate freedom in which they'd find a safe haven somewhere and settle down to a happy life together.

She was busy envisioning this pleasant future when she noticed her camel had stopped. She heard men's voices, muffled through the clay walls of her jar, then endured more bumping and tossing as the vessel was lowered to the ground. She looked up, fully expecting the lid to be pried off.

Instead, an iron cudgel smashed into the side of the jar. She screamed and jerked backwards as it shattered into jagged pieces around her.

'Ah, what have we here?'

She was hauled roughly to her feet. Her cramped position in the earthen vessel had hindered blood flow to her limbs, so she had trouble supporting her weight. Her eyes narrowed against the too-bright sunlight; she stumbled as she fought a stranger's tight hold on her upper arm.

'You told me there were dried dates in that jar,' he said.

The trader Eloim snorted. 'Obviously a mistake made at the docks,' he said, spreading his hands wide. 'Would the magnificent trader Eloim give up even one camel in his caravan for a miserable stowaway? Of course not! Eloim must make a profit. He'd never—!'

The smash of a second clay jar made Severina jump and look around. Burly soldiers surrounded Lucan.

Lucan jumped to his feet and launched himself against his attackers even though they outnumbered him. Stunned by his ferocity, they nevertheless recovered quickly and threw themselves upon him with a roar.

Severina, still blinking against the harsh sunlight, tried to make sense of the flailing limbs and grunts and the solid sound of fists meeting flesh.

When at last the chaos settled, Lucan was jerked to his feet, his hands cuffed in iron behind him, his right eye already bruised and swelling. Blood trickled from one side of his mouth, and from a gash on his brow. Yet he lifted his head in defiance, his gaze finding her as she stood in mute dismay beside the officer in charge.

'*Another* stowaway, Master Eloim?' the low voice of the commander chided the trader. 'And you know, it's amazing how strongly these two resemble the runaways who escaped the palace some time in the night, arousing the ire of the High Priest and the Roman Prefect.'

Eloim shook his head, his face carrying stunned disbelief. 'Imagine! For Eloim's caravan to be used in such a way! I'm appalled, yes, and angry, too! For I paid good coin for dried dates and what am I to do now? I cannot even sell these two for slaves if you take them back to the palace. But if there's a reward...' he thumped his chest '...it is owed to Eloim the trader. Do not forget.'

The commander's eyes narrowed. 'No reward, you old swindler! Consider yourself lucky that I don't take you back to Anok Khai, too. You were probably paid well to spirit them away to Arabia.'

The commander ignored Eloim's protest and moved to Lucan. 'Ah, so this is the poor, love-smitten Roman!'

The other soldiers laughed.

The commander raised a hand and they quieted. 'We return to the palace now. The girl will ride with me in my chariot. The Roman will be tied to run along behind it. He won't be nearly so haughty by the time he faces Anok Khai. Zadok, keep your lash handy in case he begins to lag. We can't have him slowing things down, you know.'

The laughter of the men and the sight of Lucan's strongly muscled arms being lashed to the chariot made Severina almost sick with rage.

'I will help you,' she murmured to him as she was pulled up into the conveyance.

The commander overheard her and laughed. 'You'd do better to save your strength, precious Aloli, daughter of the High Priest. Save it for the hard rutting soon to be forced upon you, for I'll be surprised if Anok Khai does not see you wed within the very hour of your return. I've never seen him as furious as he was this morning. You've angered him greatly.' He eyed Lucan almost regretfully. 'For that, you will pay.'

Severina fought against tears, desperate to do something. If only she had a weapon. A *spatha* or a *gladius*. Even a dagger.

As if he read her mind, Lucan caught her eye and dropped his gaze to the short weapon sheathed at the commander's side. *Take it and run*, his eyes seemed to say. *Save yourself.*

No, she answered him wordlessly. *I'll not leave you.*

She ignored his impotent frustration. She concentrated instead on willing Lucan to hold on, on urging him to pray to his god and not lose hope. She willed strength to him every time the burly guard brought the lash down on his back. She willed strength to him when he gasped, chest heaving from the gruelling pace set for him by the chariot driver. And she willed strength to him when he could go no further and was dragged, only half-conscious, through the palace gates.

She leapt from the chariot and startled the guard who'd wielded the lash, striding forwards to jerk the weapon from his hand. Shaking out the cords, she stood over Lucan like an avenging warrior queen, her flaming hair loosened from its braid, her eyes flashing her determination to keep harm from him. He lay on the filthy brick pavers of the palace courtyard, pale and weak and with eyes closed, seemingly unaware of his surroundings.

By the time Anok Khai found Severina, she'd worked herself up into a rage so mighty that none dared come near her or the golden-haired Roman at her feet.

'Aloli,' her father chided, moving heedlessly forwards.

The lash snapped and caught him in the chest. He jerked backwards with a snarl of rage. 'You bitch!' he screamed. 'You vicious, nasty… By the goddess, you'll pay for that!'

Severina's eyes narrowed, but she didn't answer. A crowd was gathering quickly. She saw her mother racing down a flight of stairs towards her, followed by Sheriti and by Esho, moving slowly because of her age. From another building she saw palace guardsmen rushing in her direction. From still another, the startled Prefect and his wife came, accompanied by noblemen, counsellors and servants. A soft but familiar voice spoke from her far right and she turned to see Kahotep, his amber eyes anxious and full of deep compassion.

'Aloli,' he said quietly, 'this is not the way. Let me help you.'

She shook her head. 'Stay out of this, Kahotep. Let my father's anger rest on me alone.'

The Prefect elbowed his way through the crowd to Anok Khai. 'What's going on here?'

'My daughter's been found by the palace guard. But as you can see, she… Her mind's unsettled by her recent misfortune and now, confused as she is, she mistakenly protects the Roman who kidnapped her.' He shook his head in mock concern.

'My mind is fine. I am not confused. And this man did not kidnap me,' Severina said, looking directly at the Prefect and speaking loudly enough that those in the crowd could hear her. 'I went with him willingly.'

'But…why?' The Prefect looked genuinely puzzled. 'Are you not to be betrothed to Kahotep this very morn?'

'I pray not, your Excellency. For it is this man, Livius Lucan of Rome, who holds my heart.'

Anok Khai's howl of rage caused every head to turn in his direction. 'A seduction, then! A wicked, vile seduction, selfishly perpetrated with no care for the desperation of Egypt's people! Need any of you hear more? This Roman must be put to death for obstructing the sacred command of Isis!' He turned to Rashui. 'Throw the Roman dog into the inner prison.'

Rashui started forwards. Severina's whip snapped and caught him on the upper arm, but the huge guard ignored his pain and caught it as it wrapped around his flesh. He yanked it from Severina's grasp with a mighty jerk. Two other guardsmen leapt forwards to capture her, separating her from Lucan, ignoring her screams and kicks and clawing fingernails.

Lucan heard her cries and suddenly roused from his stupor to fight off Rashui's restraint. The big captain of the guards was caught off-guard and howled in pain when Lucan's elbow jabbed hard into his ribcage and Lucan's knee gouged into groin.

Rashui responded reflexively, his fist thudding hard into Lucan's face. The crowd gasped as the Roman's golden head snapped backwards, his eyes rolled towards the sky and he slithered into an unconscious heap on the pavement, iron chains rattling as he went down.

A sob caught in Severina's throat. 'Noooo!' she moaned. 'Oh, no! Lucan!'

The guards held Severina fast as she renewed her struggle, desperate to go to him.

Anok Khai watched as Rashui and his guards hauled Lucan away. Then he stepped forwards to address both the Prefect and the crowd. 'This Roman has bewitched my daughter with his fair looks and smooth lies, but she'll forget him once she is wed to the Prefect's son. It must be done quickly, first thing tomorrow morning, here in this courtyard, so all of Egypt can witness their marriage.'

The crowd roared approval. The Prefect nodded.

'Furthermore, for this Roman's attempts to take what was not his to possess, he should hang on the gallows there, immediately after witnessing their sacred vows.'

The crowd roared approval once more. The Prefect frowned.

Severina's protests were lost in the clamour. With her eyes she appealed to the Prefect. He met her gaze briefly, and she sensed his concern for her. Then he looked towards the cheering crowd and his expression changed. He would do whatever seemed best for Egypt.

Her father's eyes held triumph. 'You thought to outwit me, Aloli,' he growled. 'But you cannot. It is over. Accept your fate.'

He gave low commands to the guards who held her and they took her from the crowd.

But Severina knew her father was wrong. This wasn't over, not as long as breath still remained in her body.

Chapter Twenty

The first sensation to break through Lucan's darkness was the throbbing pain in his head. He tried to move and discovered that he ached everywhere else, too.

Pain everywhere. And the coppery taste of blood in his mouth. And the stench of the floor on which he lay, in moisture whose origins he didn't care to know.

He groaned.

'About time you woke up, Roman. I didn't hit you *that* hard.'

'The hell you didn't.'

Rashui laughed. 'It would have been better for you if you'd not struck me in my family jewels, but even so, I took pains to spare your pretty face.'

Lucan lifted a hand and tested his jaw. 'Too bad your soldiers did not.'

He felt, rather than saw, Rashui's shrug in the dim light. 'I couldn't let them in on your plan, but their ignorance added authenticity.'

'It added *pain*, too.'

'Your lady's worth it, isn't she?'

The words brought an immediate image of Severina, standing like a pale goddess in the sunlit courtyard, her eyes wide, her face anguished. 'Yes,' Lucan sighed. 'She is.'

He struggled to sit, noticing that Rashui had already removed his shackles. 'But our plan's working, isn't it?'

Rashui grunted. 'Hard to say. I wish you two had succeeded in getting away, but since that failed despite my subtle efforts to the contrary, we must simply trust in the backup plan you devised.'

'All is in place?'

'Yes. Nafrit and Esho were visibly shaken by that scene in the courtyard and by the pronouncement of your death sentence. Sheriti wept bitterly all the way home, presumably because Kahotep will be married to Aloli in the morning. So it seems that all is in suitable chaos.'

'Now we simply wait.'

'Yes.'

'What if Anok Khai is too eager to let my blood?'

'He won't do anything tonight. As much as he enjoys torture, he'll be content to wait until the morning. And hopefully he'll be too busy then to do more than taunt and hang you.'

'Wonderful. I'd dearly love to keep my testicles where they are, even as he stretches my neck.'

Rashui didn't laugh. He knew much of Anok Khai's past cruelties. 'Do not jest of such things,' he said. 'Your situation is precarious.'

'That depends on Nafrit.'

'That's what worries me. Your friend the Senator says you know women better than any man alive. He swears your gamble will pay off, that the information Semni got from Aloli's old nurse will ultimately resolve everything, but I confess…I fear for you.'

Lucan shrugged and drew in a deep breath, then was sorry he did. 'Ooh. This cell's the best you could do for me, Rashui? It *reeks*.'

'Prisons aren't normally a delight to the senses.'

'More authenticity?'

'More authenticity.' Rashui stood. 'Do you need something to eat before I go?'

'Uh…no. The stench rather diminishes the appetite.' Lucan was silent for a moment. 'Rashui,' he asked finally, 'can I ask you something…? I'm glad you're helping us, but…*why* did you offer it?'

Rashui crossed his massive arms in front of his chest. 'Anok Khai thinks me loyal to him and I maintain the appearance of that because it allows me to keep a watchful eye on him. But in reality, I serve the Prefect and I always have. The Prefect is no stupid man. He knows of Anok Khai's cruelty and thirst for power. So we watch him very carefully.' Rashui shrugged. 'I've sided with you because you've given us a perfect opportunity to lessen Anok Khai's power, and that will be good for Egypt.'

'I'm grateful for your help.'

'Well, don't be too grateful just yet. My instincts say you could still lose with one quick toss of the knucklebones.'

'A man can't control his fate, Rashui. He can only accept his vulnerability, trust God, and follow his heart.'

'Well said, my Roman friend.'

The iron door made a cold sound as it clanged shut behind the guard. Lucan gingerly touched the floor all around him, found a spot that was reasonably dry, and settled himself to wait.

Anok Khai was tired. The events of the day had taken their toll—first the incident during what should have been Aloli's betrothal ceremony, and then some aggravating mishaps in the priests' quarters. As it was sometimes said, when it rained along the Nile the home of every crocodile would flood.

Except that it hadn't rained along the Nile in so long he could scarcely remember what rain sounded like. And it was all his daughter's fault, damn her wicked heart.

Well, the Roman was his toy to play with now, or he soon would be. In the morning Anok Khai would exact a thorough and humiliating revenge.

Anok Khai smiled as he entered his apartment. The thought of inflicting punishment on Aloli's arrogant lover pleased him. His mood much improved, he considered calling for the slave girl Tameri for his pleasure. But perhaps not—he really was tired.

He started nervously when a figure rose from a bench near the window.

'Nafrit?' He frowned. 'What are you doing here? I told you never to visit my apartment unless I summoned you.'

She lifted an eyebrow. That made him angry. She always had been arrogant.

'I must speak with you. About Aloli.'

He made an exasperated sound. 'What about her?'

Nafrit didn't answer immediately. He moved across to a table that always held a jug of wine. He poured himself a liberal portion.

Nafrit watched him with disgust, but he ignored her. Their marriage had been arranged, and they'd never been fond of one another. He'd suffered through ten long years of physical relations with her until she'd finally borne him a male heir. Anhuri, their third child, who'd fallen from a chariot when he was eight and died.

Nafrit had been beset with grief. She didn't want intimacy afterwards, but no matter. He'd long been weary of her anyway. It was easier to use his slave girls than to endure the capricious moods of his wife. Besides, Nafrit was repulsed by the sexual activities he'd come to enjoy, the ones involving chains and whips and the careful infliction of pain. The things that aroused him most disgusted her, so it had been no great disappointment to him when they'd stopped sharing a bed together.

Eventually, he'd taken his own apartment. It allowed him greater freedom, and kept him from having to deal with whining females. In recent years, he'd sometimes almost forgotten that he had a wife and daughters.

But now Nafrit had ignored his command and come without a summons. Haughty Nafrit, who stood there looking at him with scorn.

'Well?' He gestured impatiently with his goblet. 'Get on with it or leave. I'm tired and would seek my rest.'

Again, that arrogantly lifted eyebrow. Oh, how he hated her.

'Your rest? Or your pleasure with one of those slave girls you abuse so eagerly?'

His eyes narrowed. 'Careful, Nafrit.'

'Never mind. It's Aloli I came here to discuss.'

'So you said.' He took a drink. 'What's the problem with Aloli?'

'It's not a problem. Not exactly.'

'Good. I've had enough problems for one day.'

Nafrit met his gaze. 'Aloli will not be the salvation of Egypt. You must release her and let her go back to Rome with the senator's entourage.'

'Like hell I will. You know the prophecy. She *will* fulfil it. She has no choice in the matter.'

There was a long moment of silence. Tension stretched between them like hemp cords, taut and near to snapping.

'The prophecy said your first-born child must wed the ruler's son. But Aloli is not your daughter.'

Anok Khai heard the words but could scarcely comprehend them. '*What* did you say?'

'You heard me! Aloli's not your daughter. I was already with child when I married you.'

He stepped towards her and wrapped his large hand around her neck, tightening the pressure. She glared at him, but did not show the fear he'd hoped to see. 'You deceitful slut,' he whispered through tight lips. '*Who?* Who fathered her?'

Nafrit smiled at him so beautifully that he was tempted to snap her spine in half. 'Who does she look like?' She laughed softly. 'All these years, and you never noticed. But tell me now, Anok Khai. Who does she look like?'

The truth suddenly slapped him. Aloli had the fire of the sun in her hair, almond-shaped eyes of grey… Oh, gods…

Nafrit laughed when his eyes widened. 'Yes, Anok Khai. Your brother Kemnebi left his seed to grow within my womb. He planned to wed me, for we were truly in love. We would have been happy together, if only he hadn't taken ill and died.'

'You knew. All this time, you knew. And you never told me.'

'There was no need. At first I feared Aloli would suffer if you knew. But as it turned out, you never loved any of your children, so I doubt it would've made a difference either way. Until now.' She met his gaze. '*Now* it makes a difference.'

He sucked in a deep breath, just beginning to consider all the consequences. 'Then Sheriti is my first-born. But if I tell the truth now…'

Nafrit laughed. 'Oh, yes. Ironic, isn't it? The great Anok Khai, cuckolded by his own dead brother, and the whole realm of Egypt will hear the tale and laugh at you.'

Anok Khai's eyes narrowed dangerously. 'Unless you were to die, rather unexpectedly, tonight. Then the truth will die with you.'

She laughed again, which angered him. 'You think I didn't prepare for that? I *know* you, Anok Khai, and what a vicious brute you are. So, no, you're not the first to hear this story.'

'Who?' His voice was coarse with anxiety. 'Who did you tell?'

'Why, the Prefect, of course.'

'You lie. The Prefect would never grant audience to you.'

'Oh, but he did, once I let it be known that I had important information about Aloli.' She lifted her chin. 'Now he knows. He was…oh, how shall I put it? He was most disturbed. Yes, that would be it. Most disturbed.'

Anok Khai jumped to his feet and started towards his wife. 'I should kill you just so that I won't have to look at you any more. You were never a good wife to me!'

'Why? Because I didn't let you beat me with a whip when you came to my bed? Or maybe because I'd already given my heart to your brother? Your *brother*, Anok Khai, the one you always wanted to be—the handsome one, the smart one, the popular one! The one you never could quite measure up to, because he was a good man and a kind man and *you were not*!'

She screamed out the last words as her husband captured her by her long tresses, dragging her backwards with him towards the bed, though she fought him with all her strength.

'I'll teach you, you self-righteous shrew!' he yelled at her, ripping her tunic and tossing it aside. 'I'll show you who's master. You gave yourself to my brother? You preferred Kemnebi to me? Well, now you'll give yourself to me and, yes, you *will* like it!'

'No!' A tremendous, booming voice from the doorway startled both of them. Anok Khai froze, his hands on his already loosened undergarments.

'Get off her, Anok Khai, or I'll see you hang on the gallows before the sun rises in the morning.'

Anok Khai dropped to his knees beside the bed, shaking uncontrollably. 'Your Excellency.'

The Prefect turned to the huge guard who stood at his side. 'Rashui, find shackles. A few days for Anok Khai in the inner prison will allow us time to cool our tempers.'

'But you don't understand,' the High Priest said as Rashui shackled him and pushed him towards the door. 'This woman provoked me. I…I wasn't myself.'

The ruler turned a cool, assessing gaze in his direction. 'I already know what you are, Anok Khai. I know about your cruelties, your perversions. So unless you're a stupid man, you'll submit to Rashui without complaint.' The Prefect's gaze met that of his High Priest. 'Just because you've thought me an old fool doesn't mean I am one.'

Anok Khai whimpered in dismay as he was shoved towards the door, but he knew better than to utter any sound that might be construed as either rebellion or anger.

Chapter Twenty-One

Kahotep's voice was low and urgent in the dim, flickering light of the torch. 'The spring that opens the door is here somewhere,' he said. 'It's not one I've often used myself, so I'm not as certain of it.'

He glanced around as his fingers groped the rough stone. 'Prepare yourself, Aloli. The sights of a prison are not meant for gently bred females like you.'

She waved away his concern, hardly able to explain to him about her past life as a gladiatrix. 'Trust me, Kahotep,' she said, 'I've seen worse. And as long as Lucan lies somewhere on the other side of that wall, I can endure anything for his sake.'

The door sprang open and they were through it. 'You've got the key?' she whispered.

He nodded. 'Let's hope Semni's gold has done its work again and that all the guards are dozing from the sleeping draught in their wine.'

'Your kitchen staff has certainly done their part to help. You'll have to give them all a raise in pay when this is over.' Severina was rewarded with the flash of Kahotep's smile in the dimness.

It didn't take long to locate Lucan's cell, and Severina was pleased to find that he was no longer unconscious. He looked up in amazement when she called his name through the iron bars.

'Severina? Kahotep?' He jumped to his feet and came to her. 'What are you two doing here?'

She took the key from Kahotep and twisted it in the lock, satisfied by the pop and creak of metal as the door swung open for her. 'What does it look like? We're getting you out of here.'

'But you can't,' he stammered. 'Not until Nafrit…' He raked his hand through his hair in agitation.

'My mother? What's she got to do with this?'

Lucan shook his head and slipped through the door, taking her hand. 'Nothing. Don't worry about it.' He looked to Kahotep. 'There's a plan, I suppose?'

Kahotep nodded. 'We go back into the tunnels.'

'And our destination is…?'

'My own apartment.' Kahotep grinned. 'They'd never imagine that a jilted bridegroom might harbour his ex-fiancée and her lover in his personal quarters, so you and Aloli are completely safe there for as long as you want to remain in Egypt. When everything calms down a bit, you can quietly slip away to a life of your own.'

Lucan's battered face showed brief admiration. He held out his hand. 'You're a good man, Kahotep. I'm honoured to call you *friend*.'

Kahotep smiled and took Lucan's hand. He glanced towards Severina. 'Would you two be honoured also to have me among your relations? I intend to wed Sheriti as soon as I can convince my father to allow it.'

Severina smiled. 'Of course. May the gods bless your union. And may they favour you for all you've done for Lucan and me.'

He nodded and gestured towards the small door that remained open, beckoning them into the tunnel. 'We still have to get you to safety.'

'And to a hot bath, I hope.' Lucan sighed. 'I shudder to think of how bad I must smell.'

Kahotep chuckled. 'Well…if the torch goes out, we could still find you in the darkness.'

Lucan grimaced. 'That bad, huh?'

'Oh, yes. But perhaps Aloli will scrub your back if you ask her.'

Lucan grinned roguishly at the other man. 'Then lead on, Kahotep. I grow more eager for that bath with each passing second.'

Kahotep laughed softly. 'I doubt it not, my friend. I doubt it not.'

'I'm sorry, your Excellency, but I don't know where they are.' Donatus frowned as he answered the Prefect's question.

He had been disappointed to hear of Lucan and Severina's capture and of Lucan's subsequent imprisonment the night before, but he hadn't been completely surprised. He and Lucan had accepted the possibility and planned accordingly.

Much later, well past midnight, Rashui had come to him and told him that their backup plan had worked. This time Donatus had been pleased, but again not surprised. Lucan had an uncanny sense of the female mind and he'd believed that Nafrit could be provoked into giving up her secret under the right set of circumstances. The old nurse had made much of Nafrit's basic goodness and stressed how much she loved her children.

But this morning's news, delivered to him just now by the Prefect himself, had startled Donatus into silence.

Anok Khai was dead. Apparently he'd traded a gold ring to a fellow prisoner for a length of rope with which to hang himself, unable to bear the shame of public disgrace. So much for the man's dreams of immortality. In Donatus's opinion, the tragedy wasn't Anok Khai's ignoble death. It was his tragic life so poorly lived.

Before Donatus had time to fully accept that news, the Prefect stunned him with more. Lucan and Severina were gone. Nobody knew how Lucan had escaped his prison cell, or Severina her mother's apartment. Furthermore, nobody knew to where they'd flown.

Donatus didn't, either.

'That's unfortunate,' the Prefect said, scowling darkly. 'I don't like to leave any matter unresolved and this one in particular, as it so strongly concerns my son.'

Donatus glanced towards Kahotep. Did he imagine a flash of triumph in the younger man's eyes?

Donatus considered that for a moment. Kahotep had made himself their willing ally once before because of his secret love for Severina's sister. Nobody stood to gain more from Lucan and Severina's disappearance than Kahotep did. Could he possibly know what Donatus did not?

He turned back to the Prefect. 'What resolution would prove satisfactory, your Excellency?'

The Prefect sat back in his chair and looked thoughtful for a moment, drumming his fingers against his knee. 'In truth, Senator, I am tired of this whole thing. I want Kahotep to wed the first-born of Anok Khai and be done with that.' His gaze found his son's. 'Have you any objection to wedding Sheriti rather than Aloli?'

'No, Father. I do not. I welcome the chance to do whatever is best for Egypt.'

'Good. Then let's call for the holy man and secure that union this morning.' The Prefect sighed. 'If only Aloli hadn't escaped with her Roman lover once again, we could have made this a double ceremony and finished with a happy ending for her as well.'

Donatus turned to Kahotep. The younger man met his gaze. Unspoken communication passed between them before Donatus turned back to the ruler. 'If you'll hold off on the wedding ceremony until this afternoon, your Excellency, I believe that perhaps Lucan and Aloli might yet be found.'

The Prefect lifted an eyebrow. 'Agreed. Only don't take too long, Flavius Donatus. I long for an ending to this matter. I'd like for Kahotep to wed and give me grandchildren before I'm too old and feeble to enjoy them.'

Donatus nodded. 'Give me but two hours, your Excellency, and I'll see what I can do.'

Chapter Twenty-Two

Lucan and Severina hadn't slept much during the night. So even though it was nearly noon, the sudden hammering at their door and the insistent voice that accompanied it woke them both out of a deep, contented slumber.

'Oh, no!' Severina's voice held fear as she scrambled for the bedclothes to cover her nakedness. 'They've found us! My father's men have found us!'

'No. I know that voice.' Lucan jerked himself upright and strode angrily to the door, yanking it open without any attempt to hide either his anger or his nudity. He scowled ferociously at Donatus, who stood grinning at him from the hallway. 'This better be important,' he growled, 'or I swear—!'

Donatus's laughter irritated him all the more, especially when Donatus sauntered past him into Kahotep's small apartment.

Severina gasped and sat up, clutching the sheets to her bosom.

'Well, well.' Donatus's voice held amusement, but little surprise. 'Severina, too. How cozy.'

'It *was*,' Lucan said drily. 'Before you came along.'

Donatus grinned at his friend. 'And here I thought to do you a favour. But if you don't care to know that Nafrit went last night to the Prefect with her secret, which then caused Anok Khai to be put into prison where he later committed suicide, or that you'll be missing your own wedding if you don't get up right now and find some appropriate clothing…well, no harm done. I'll just let you go back to your nap or whatever else you want to do, and see myself out the door.'

Lucan caught the back of Donatus's garment just as he would have crossed the threshold. 'Hold on a minute,' he growled. 'Not so fast.'

Severina brushed her hair out of her eyes. 'My mother had a secret? And my father's dead? By suicide?'

Lucan reached for his clothing. 'Anok Khai's not your father.' He drew his tunic over his head before moving to her side. 'Your mother already carried you in her womb when she wed him. Your father was his elder brother and her one true love, but he died and she was forced to wed Anok Khai.'

Severina's eyes closed briefly. 'He's not my father,' she said when she opened them again. 'Thank the gods. His blood does not run in my veins.'

'No.'

'But if I'm not his child, then…?'

Donatus finished the thought. 'Sheriti is his first-born. This was the secret your mother's carried for long years, the secret she finally told the Prefect last night. Anok Khai was so enraged that he would have killed her for it, but the Prefect arrived in time to protect her. He ordered Anok Khai put into prison, but he hung himself in his cell rather than face the humiliation of his altered circumstances.'

Severina was quiet for a moment. 'I wish I felt grief for him, but truly I cannot.'

'He was a cruel man,' Lucan said quietly, stroking a hand down her hair. 'I doubt any will mourn him.'

Severina looked up at Donatus, who waited quietly near the foot of the bed for her to absorb all the startling information. 'You said there's to be a wedding?' she asked.

'Yes. Kahotep will marry Sheriti. You and Lucan might wed one another as well, if you wish it so.'

Lucan did wish it so. It was the most fervent desire of his heart. He knelt beside Severina and took her hand. Her eyes were wide and dark as he kissed each knuckle and cleared his throat. But Lord, he was nervous. Why should he be so nervous? It wasn't as though she'd refuse him. They'd been lovers already. Even now his child might be growing in her womb. Surely she wouldn't tell him no…

He swallowed hard. 'Do you remember the promise we made before to God and to each other, Severina?' he said in a low voice, staring into her sombre gaze. 'Do you remember all we said…before we…before that first time?'

She nodded.

'I meant it with all my heart. I still do. And if you feel the same…' He sucked in a deep breath, hoping it might calm the fear in his stomach. 'Will you marry me?'

Severina gave a squeal and threw both arms around his neck. 'Yes! Yes! Oh, Lucan! Yes!'

Donatus cleared his throat and Severina hurriedly caught the sheet that was threatening to slip too low for modesty.

'I'll leave you two to get some clothes on,' Donatus said with some amusement in his voice. 'But don't be long. The Prefect is eager to move this marriage business along.'

'He's not the only one,' Lucan said. 'So don't worry, my friend. We'll be there with time to spare.'

Donatus smiled happily as he closed the door behind him, already envisioning a happy life ahead for them.

'Oh, Aloli!' Sheriti's voice held awe. 'You look beautiful.'

Severina smiled. 'I could say the same for you.'

Sheriti laughed softly and hugged herself. 'Being in love does work magic, doesn't it? But I'm so nervous I feel like I might vomit. This is happening too fast!'

'Please don't. It wouldn't make for good memories of your wedding day.'

'Or yours.'

Both girls laughed. Sheriti reached up to adjust the crown adorning her head. 'This thing is really heavy. I suppose it's absolutely necessary that I wear this?'

'Quite. The Prefect's taking no chances. He insists on a wedding immediately, so it's hugely important that everyone understand that you, my dear Sheriti, are the promised one who'll bring prosperity to the land.'

'And with any luck, maybe the promised one won't vomit on her bridegroom.'

Severina chuckled. 'We hope not. But as gentle as Kahotep is, I think he'd take even that in stride.'

'No! Don't even think it! I *couldn't* embarrass him that way!'

A voice from the doorway caused both young women to look around. 'That's a good thing, my daughter, because it's almost time to go out.'

Sheriti paled. 'So many people…'

Her mother embraced her. 'Think of Kahotep, my sweet. He's beside himself with joy at this moment.'

'He is?'

Severina smiled. 'Of course he is! Is he not marrying the woman he truly loves? And saving Egypt at the same time?'

Nafrit turned to Aloli and took her hands. 'And you, Aloli. You look radiant.'

'I'm happy, Mother, and truly thankful for what you did to make this possible.'

'Your Roman… His courage in rescuing you inspired me to show some bravery of my own. I should have told the truth long ago, but then—'

'But then I never would have met Lucan at all,' Severina finished. 'So everything's worked out for the best.'

Nafrit reached up and stroked Severina's hair. 'You'll return to Egypt to visit, won't you?'

'Of course.'

'Write me when you find out you're with child. I'll come to be with you at the birthing.'

Sheriti made a small sound of protest.

Nafrit smiled. 'Unless… Well, maybe you two girls should work out a schedule or something. I simply can't be attending two births at once.'

Sheriti smiled at Severina. 'Perhaps Aloli will want to come *here* as her time draws near. Egyptian doctors are the best in the world.'

Nafrit laughed. 'All this talk of babies. But it does occur to me that perhaps your marriages should come first, if you two are ready?'

Sheriti bit her lip. Severina took her sister's hand and smiled. 'Come, my sister. Kahotep awaits you.'

'Yes,' Sheriti said with a sigh. 'And Lucan the Roman awaits you.'

'We are among the luckiest of women today, aren't we?'

'Yes. We are.'

Soon Severina was more certain than ever of her good fortune. She walked slowly along the portico that surrounded the courtyard, keeping her eyes on the raised platform at the end of it where Lucan stood with Kahotep, both men looking with eager faces towards their brides.

Lucan was handsomely dressed. His tunic was of fine cloth, dazzlingly white, with a hem embroidered with gold. Thrown dashingly over one shoulder was a cloak that shimmered in rich, kingly purple from Phoenicia. But it was Lucan's face that held her attention, for he couldn't keep from smiling and his eyes shone with happiness.

The hush that descended over the crowd as she and Sheriti ascended the steps and took the hands of their lovers was heavy with meaning and expectation.

The Prefect stood and welcomed the crowd to the solemn occasion, leading them himself in the song traditionally sung to bless the union with peace and fertility. Hearing it, Severina's eyes filled with tears.

She had once believed this moment would never come. It seemed beyond belief that she stood here now with Lucan's strong hand clasping her own. Surprisingly, she felt no fear. It seemed that they'd been through too much together for fear to ever have a place between them again.

The priest stood before them now and motioned for the two women to kneel. Severina did so without hesitation.

'I promise you…' she began, reciting the words to Lucan as Sheriti also said them to Kahotep '…to serve you as a virtuous wife, to love you and honour you and give my strength to you. I will hold nothing of myself back from you as long as the gods give breath to my body. This I do solemnly pledge to you.'

And then it was Lucan's turn. His eyes found hers as he knelt before her, squeezing her fingers to emphasise his sincerity as he repeated his own vows. 'I promise you…that I will cherish and honour and love you all the days of my life, that I will serve you and protect you. I will be your shield, bless your womb with children, and give to you abundantly of all my substance as long as the gods give breath to my body. This I do solemnly pledge to you.'

A beautifully attired young woman brought to them a scroll, and in the presence of all the witnesses gathered there, Kahotep and Sheriti signed their names in The Book of Marriage, followed by Lucan and Severina.

Then, as custom demanded, they turned to face the crowd and knelt. The High Priest, newly appointed that very morning, led the chanted benediction that officially sealed the union.

Lucan helped Severina to rise and took her into his arms to kiss her deep and long in front of all the people. Then he turned, a smile on his face, to accept the well wishes of the Prefect, Donatus, Rashui and so many others that Severina couldn't keep up, surrounded as she was by many happy well-wishers of her own.

Chapter Twenty-Three

Lucan sighed with relief as he shut the door. He listened to the raucous sounds of revelry grow dim as the wedding procession made its merry way back down the long portico that led to this luxurious—and private—suite in the Prefect's palace.

He turned to face Severina. She sat in the middle of a massive ebony bed, her long hair loose and curling softly around her beautiful, thinly clad breasts, her hands fisted around the bedclothes.

As before, he knew her well enough to read her emotions. He went to her. 'What's wrong?'

Her tongue flicked out to moisten dry lips. The sight made him dizzy. 'Nothing. I'm simply…overwhelmed. To be your wife is an honour I never thought to have.'

The words humbled him.

He slid his fingers beneath her hair, his palm against the warm curve of her neck, lightly tracing her lips with his thumb. Her pulse pounded furiously against his touch. He touched his lips to her hair.

'I'm your wife,' she whispered. 'I can hardly believe it. Finally, I am your wife.'

'You've been my wife since the night you gave me your virginity.'

He took her lips then, taking care to be gentle. He wanted to move slowly, to make their wedding night a special and loving celebration, to give her sweet memories to last a lifetime.

But she was like dry tinder, and his lips a flame. The gentle kiss deepened, changed tenor, grew fierce and impatient. Her lips parted and drew him in. Her tongue slid against his, mating with him, their breaths mingling and sighing in primitive, erotic rhythm.

Lucan struggled to slow the pace. He gathered her into his arms, aligning their bodies together in one long, body-to-body touch. He wanted Severina to finally see herself as totally, irrevocably, irrefutably *his*.

He wanted her to understand how much she meant to him.

His wife, his woman, his love.

Without lies between them, without veils or screens or any needful pretence.

Without running. Without hiding. Without the taint of guilt or shame or fear.

Man. Woman. Lovers.

He took her lips again, and tasted desire on them. She was, had always been, like liquid flame in his arms, and their mutual desire was a molten river that threatened to sweep him away. Before, he'd kept that fire banked, controlled, contained by the dictates of his faith and conscience.

This night would be a new experience, holding out unique promises and challenges. It would be uncharted territory.

Vows had been spoken, and she was his. He felt the weight of that, the responsibility. Not to take, but to give.

She lifted her face, her lips parted. He read the invitation in her eyes and responded. Carefully, so carefully, he deepened the kiss, ensuring that neither of them would be overwhelmed by need. In every love there was a time to be swept away, seared by desire and consumed by it. But tonight was not that time.

Lucan deliberately let the passion simmer, a steady burn to savour. A fire to warm them both as desire slowly unfurled and settled in deep.

Severina let Lucan lead her. The path was not as familiar to her as to him.

She let Lucan seduce her, let his knowing lips give affection to her and possess her, always tasting of hunger, but never impatient to devour.

Small details became important, caught as she was in this beautiful, ever-changing, constantly moving dream of sensation. His kisses...oh, such kisses. The pressure and the heat of them, their taste of wine and man, their slow and unhurried dance across her skin.

And beneath all that, the unspoken message. That she was cherished. That her worth was enough, would always be enough. That even within marriage she'd have freedom to be herself. How odd it was, that Lucan's kisses could communicate so much.

Her response was willing submission. She let Lucan move her along the path, let his kisses leave her lips and trail their moist heat down her neck, into the sensitive hollows behind her ear and beneath her hair, down to her collarbone and along the upper swell of her breasts. She arched into him and moaned her accord when his hand found her curves, moulding and shaping them through the delicate fabric of her garment.

Let him strip away her clothing, and savoured the coolness of the night air against her skin, the sensation heightened yet more by his hands, his large, warm, callused hands, and their slide of heat down her back and over the smooth skin of her buttocks.

She let him press his lips back to the place they'd left, touching to bare skin now. She let him suckle her and pull at her, tugging hard at the cord of need buried deep until she ached to her core, growing hot and senseless and hungry.

She let Lucan leave her breasts tingling with need, sensitive to his every touch. Let him move lower to lay a fiery trail down her stomach, over the smooth skin of her abdomen and across her hips, finally tasting the soft flesh between her thighs.

Gasping, senses reeling, her skin flushed and damp, she speared her hands into his tousled curls and fisted them there. 'Oh, no!' she protested. 'Lucan, I can't *bear* it!'

His voice was low, hoarse and warm. 'Bear it,' he commanded. 'Let me give you this.'

She acquiesced, rejoicing in submission once again. To think she'd feared the loss of control…

She writhed against the pleasure and let him use sensation—oh, such wicked sensation!—to lift her higher, higher, until his hot tongue moving with firm sureness against her tender flesh drove her up and over that last scintillating, pulsing peak.

Radiance brighter than the Egyptian sun broke over her, washed through her, filled her with fragmenting fire and pleasure pouring through every vein.

She was breathless, gasping, unable to take in air enough to soothe her scorched body. Her legs trembled, she became listless, helpless, weak from the slow return of her senses.

And still Lucan would not release her from his savage-sweet torture. He remained at her core; he continued to love her, gently licking and tasting and savouring.

She had too little strength to protest. She could only endure this vulnerability to the man, allowing this most tender of possessions, yielding herself with jerks and tiny gasps as he drew the pleasure out long and longer, making her yearn anew, making her hurt again, making her want more.

She let him possess her, command her, destroy her and renew her. She gave over all her sovereignty to become one with him, but could not mourn the loss.

'I love you,' she heard him whisper. In one fluid motion, he stood and pulled her unresisting body closer to the edge of the mattress. She watched with vague, dreamy eyes as he stripped himself naked and stood beside the bed, the hard planes of his body washed in a silvery glaze of moonlight, his arousal heavy and full as he parted her thighs and lowered himself to her. She felt the momentary pressure, the thick, blunt head of his erection at her entrance.

His gaze locked with hers. 'I love you,' he said again, his voice thick with emotion. Then with one slow, forceful, unrelenting thrust, he filled her.

Lucan had been nearly desperate to take her. When he could hold back no longer, he joined their bodies, thrust himself into her and...found peace.

All those months, all those years, all the pain and relentless yearning...all were worth this one, glorious moment.

Severina arched beneath him, crying out at the pleasure of his intrusion, welcoming him.

Her passion didn't surprise him; there had always been fire between them. She didn't lie beneath him passively, and this pleased him. She became his beloved wife, his wanton mistress, his divine reward and his most sinful fantasy.

She was the heat he'd searched for, the life-giving sun of his world. He'd always been drawn like a moth to her flame. He would die within it, and be renewed.

He ceased fighting to maintain control. He couldn't hold back now if his life depended on it. Severina drove him past all control, taking him into her heat as deeply as she could, matching her movements to his, kneading the muscles of his back and raking her nails across his skin in a sensual ecstasy of near-pain that pleasured and tortured him.

'Use me,' she urged him, and he went forwards into feral need. Nobody had ever brought him so close to insanity. Nobody had ever made him shake like this, or grind his teeth until his jaw ached. His muscles were on fire. Every part of him cried out for release.

But, oh, she was as mad with feeling as he. She twisted hard beneath him and mewled like a wild thing, eyes closed, panting hard.

They'd be burned to cinders, but they would burn together, two beings fused into one passionate creature, there in the hottest part of the flame. No rational thought was possible, only passion, only pleasure.

There could be no stopping, not until they reached the end or died together in the fierce act of their coupling.

Together they cleared the final hurdle, found the crest, topped the glorious rise to view a breaking dawn. Together they hurtled over the edge of the precipice, fingers locked as they fell together into the void, shattering, fragmenting in pleasure so hot it engulfed them in a conflagration of flame.

They drifted slowly back to reality.

Lucan gradually became aware of his wife's body, delicate and slight beneath him. With a groan he rolled and withdrew, slumping heavily on his back beside her on the bed.

They lay side by side, staring at the ceiling, breathing hard.

He felt her sidelong gaze and wondered if she wanted him to say something, to respond somehow, but he couldn't. He honestly couldn't. He'd never experienced anything like it before. He'd had lovers, hundreds of them. But he'd never felt so lifted out of himself, never been so intimately a part of another person, never become so joined soul to soul.

He could hardly think. He couldn't have forced a coherent sentence.

He was spent, confused, his nerves quivering with sensation. He'd been shaken to the utter depths of his soul.

Severina lifted herself on one elbow and smiled down at him. He could only stare at her, dumbly, stupidly, like a man who'd had his brains pulled out of his head through his nostrils.

'Lucan?'

He swallowed, grunted.

Her laughter was soft. She smiled down at him. Gloated, it almost seemed, her eyes alight with happiness. 'Now I know your God is real,' she said.

He lifted one eyebrow.

'I prayed our joining would be the most marvellous that you've ever experienced. That it would be better than anything you had with any other woman—ever—in your whole life.'

Lucan saw her eyes travel over his body, over his still-heaving chest, his still-quivering legs. 'Yes,' she said, lying back down beside him with a happy sigh. 'I believe your God heard my prayer, don't you think?'

Lucan groaned.

Indeed. His God had heard. And in his generosity, he'd very nearly killed Lucan with the answer.

Chapter Twenty-Four

Exactly one week from the date of their wedding, Lucan and Severina, along with Donatus and Semni and twenty-four soldiers of the Praetorian Guard, departed for Rome aboard the first available grain transport.

Semni pretended to grumble about the number of passengers—non-paying ones at that!—who'd be making use of his vessel, crowding the decks and limiting the amount of room for valuable cargo. But the twinkle in his dark eyes told them that he was merely teasing.

He did, however, earn a squeal and hug from Severina when he announced that he had built on deck, as a favour to the newlyweds, a new addition—private quarters just for them, complete with an oversized mattress of soft, Egyptian cotton and thick, tightly-woven draperies to…ahem…muffle the sound.

Their departure was accompanied, of course, by diplomatic fanfare. The Prefect couldn't be present himself to see them off, but he sent a worthy representative in his stead.

His son Kahotep arrived early, carried to the busy port in a luxurious sedan chair, along with his beautiful wife who looked gloriously happy in her newly wedded state. And indeed, she had reason, for all who watched them noted how gently her husband lifted her down, and with how much courtesy he attended her.

Thankfully, his speech was brief. The awning held over them all wasn't quite spacious enough to provide adequate protection from the inclement weather.

For the rains had begun to wash Egypt on the morning following Kahotep's union with his bride. It had rained at least a portion of every day since, even though such an occurrence was unusual for the season. The people took it as an omen of good things to come.

Severina believed they were right, though perhaps not for the reasons they all believed. Yet however prosperity for Egypt came about, she believed Kahotep would be a wise and generous husband, and that he and Sheriti would enjoy a love that would be, in a word, divine.

The journey to Rome took more than three weeks, nearly twice as long as they'd expected because the winds blew contrary most of the way. Severina was plagued with seasickness so obvious and prolonged that Lucan began to wonder about it.

He hadn't said much. But Severina noticed that he stroked the smooth, flat skin over her stomach often when they lay quietly in bed together, his gaze distant as if he already envisioned the child they might have made. Sometimes he'd rest his head there, and kiss her navel.

It was true that her monthly flow hadn't come, but it was only slightly overdue. Severina couldn't be sure yet, of course. But she wasn't about to dampen Lucan's hopes. It touched her to realise how far he'd come from the hedonistic, self-serving man he'd once been.

And since Lucan's faith had been so important in helping that change along, one of the first things she did upon arrival in Rome was to arrange for a Christian wedding ceremony.

Donatus was both startled and relieved to find that Lelia, Druscilla and Faustina weren't at all upset that they'd missed the first wedding.

'Well, of *course* Lucan and Severina should have married immediately! What *else*?' Lelia had said, rolling her eyes and looking at Donatus as if he were the biggest dunce in the world for having ever thought she'd want it otherwise.

Obviously, there was something in the mysterious realm of female knowledge that he'd missed. Lucan slapped him on the back, chuckling. 'Don't worry about it,' he said. 'You'll never understand them. Don't be foolish enough to even try.'

Donatus was forced to agree.

But still, it pleased Lelia that Severina would now wear the lovely orange embroidered *flammeneum* she'd painstakingly hand-sewn, even if the wedding would be a small one. Ariadne also ful-filled a long-time wish of her own, buying for Severina a beautiful *stola* especially made for the long-awaited day. It was sewn of smooth gold silk and fastened with an ornate *fibula* of sapphire and topaz. Severina cried when Ariadne presented it to her.

This wedding ceremony wouldn't be their first, but it would be special, since it would focus on the vows so sacred to Lucan's Christian brothers and sisters. He'd been restored to their fellow-ship with joy on the part of all, and this time, he'd speak his vows in his native tongue. He'd struggled through the first ceremony with his broken, poorly pronounced Egyptian.

Best of all for Severina, her friends would be there—among them Ariadne, Orthrus and Juvenal, now all freedmen who served in Donatus's household for set wages. Though Severina had earlier been told about Ariadne's escape from the fire, her former slave's rounded belly now brought a gasp of happy surprise. Un-consciously, Severina smoothed her hand over her own abdomen in a quick, scarcely noticeable gesture. But Lelia, always closely attuned to Severina through friendship, did notice.

She didn't say anything at the time. The wedding feast, with all its happy chaos and gaity, wasn't the place for such an intimate secret to be shared. But the following morning she found her friend seated by the fountain in the atrium courtyard, enjoying a cool, fruited drink and a slice of buttered bread.

As soon as she could delicately do so, she asked the question.

'I…I don't know yet,' Severina stuttered. 'I may be. I mean, my flow is a little late.'

'How late?'

'Three weeks.'

Lelia gasped her delight. 'Then it's probably safe enough to say you're with child.'

Severina's face flushed. 'It seems likely.'

Lelia hugged her. 'I take it that you're pleased?'

'Of course.' Severina's expression softened. In that moment, Lelia was struck by her friend's undeniable beauty.

Severina seemed changed in so many ways since she'd returned home. There was a softness that hadn't always been there, a radiant joy. And her voice held something like wonder. 'Lucan will be a good father. He's already become an excellent husband.'

'I can see that, and I'm glad. He's a good man and deserves the happiness you've brought him. And you deserve all he's brought to you.' Lelia sighed happily. 'Just think. Our babies, and Ariadne's, will all grow up together. They can be playmates.'

Severina turned her head abruptly to face her friend. Perhaps she'd misheard, but it seemed that Lelia wasn't talking about the two children she already had. 'You're with child, Lelia? *Again?*'

'Yes. Isn't that amazing?'

'Not really. Passion's a marvellous thing. And obviously, you and Donatus take it rather seriously.'

Lelia laughed. 'As you and Lucan undoubtedly will, also. In fact, I predict that we'll *both* have prodigiously large families.' She rubbed her hand down her belly, which, Severina noticed, did have the slightest little bulge, hardly noticeable on Lelia's trim figure. 'Luckily, I adore children; each stage has its own special joys.'

Lelia's face darkened. 'Well, at least until they become old enough to have their own minds. Then the course becomes more difficult.'

Severina wondered at the sudden change. Lelia seemed worried, and Severina couldn't understand why, since Lelia's children wouldn't be at that difficult stage for a long time yet. 'Certainly you and Donatus will have wisdom enough when the time comes.'

'I hope so. I see Faustina's efforts to coax Druscilla into her proper feminine role and I wonder.'

'What's going on with Druscilla?'

'What *isn't* going on with Druscilla? I swear that headstrong young woman will be the death of her mother. She absolutely refuses to accept her societal role. She won't even consider the possibility of marriage, though several suitors from worthy families have approached Donatus already.'

'And Donatus hasn't forced the issue?'

Lelia looked offended. 'Of course not. He could simply choose a young man and command her to wed, but…'

'But having had a love match himself, he wishes the same for his beloved sister.'

'Exactly. Except that Druscilla isn't co-operating. In fact…' Lelia lowered her voice '…her behaviour's been shockingly scandalous. If word of it gets out, she'll not receive any offers of marriage at all.'

'Scandalous? How so?'

'She's been *acting*. On the *stage*.'

'But she's female.'

'A female who masquerades as an adolescent boy. And does it well, I might add. I saw one of her performances and hadn't the slightest clue it was she. Her talent was that good, Severina.'

'Amazing. But she was, I take it, discovered somehow?'

'Yes. Donatus was livid. He forbade her to continue acting.'

'I hope she obeyed.'

'Yes, as far as we know. But then…' Lelia bit her lip '…I found a manuscript she'd written tucked beneath her mattress when I went to change her bedclothes.'

'A manuscript.'

'Yes. A play, surprisingly good, but full of humour that could only be described as…well…'

'Sexual?'

Lelia exhaled forcefully. 'Yes.'

Severina shrugged. 'Well, Druscilla's not a child any more. She knows of such things—'

'Yes, but, Severina, to *write* of them! And that's not even the worst. That play was actually performed. Donatus took me to the theatre and what should we watch that night but the very work I'd found in Druscilla's bedroom!'

'You didn't tell Donatus, I hope?'

Lelia frowned. 'No, but…whose side are you on, anyway?'

'Druscilla's, I think. I'm rather impressed that she's found such a unique outlet for her sharp intellect.'

Lelia harumphed. 'Well, I didn't tell Donatus, but I did tell Faustina. Faustina did some discreet questioning and found out that Druscilla—or rather, the lad Druscilla's been pretending to be—has been making good money through her acting and writing. This play is the latest of several she's done, it seems. She's invested her earnings and became a *shareholder* in the acting company!'

Severina's eyebrows lifted. 'Wonderful! Druscilla becomes more fascinating with each passing moment. Imagine having enough business acumen to do that. At her age—!'

'Severina! You're not helping. Druscilla's deception will eventually come out and when it does, she'll have no hope of finding a proper husband and marrying into polite society. She'll be a social outcast!'

'But, quite possibly, a wealthy one.'

'You know money alone doesn't bring happiness, nor the deep joy that you and I have found with our husbands. I want better for Druscilla than a life of social ostracism and a cold, lonely future with no man to cherish her, no chubby little babies to smile and give her their sweet, wet, messy kisses.'

Severina wondered if Druscilla wanted a husband or sweet, wet, messy baby kisses, but she let that go without comment.

'What can I do to help?' she asked, knowing it was expected, though she hoped Lelia wouldn't answer.

'Well…there *is* something.'

'I was afraid of that.'

'You know Druscilla thinks highly of you. She admires your independence and the fact that you operated your own business. And Lucan, too. She *adores* Lucan.'

'And?'

'She'll listen to anything you say. You could give her all kinds of sage advice about men and marriage, and she'll hear you. And maybe with Lucan's wealth and social connections...'

Severina laughed. 'Lucan's wealth? Social connections?'

The ironic tone caused Lelia to look at her sharply. 'Yes, Severina.'

'Lucan?'

Lelia's eyes widened. 'You don't know? Oh, my. Perhaps I've let a tiger out of the cage.'

'What wealth? What social connections?'

'I... Maybe you'd better talk to Lucan. I've strayed into territory I shouldn't have ventured, so I...I think I'm needed in the kitchen. Or nursery. Or somewhere...else.'

Severina watched her friend depart in a hurry. While she was relieved not to be tasked with taming Druscilla, she'd suddenly been left with a bag full of questions. And no immediate answers.

Lucan looked up from a tall sheaf of papers when Severina found him alone in Donatus's study. 'There you are, my love,' he said, a smile on his handsome features. 'I was about to come find you. I want to take you out on an excursion. There's something I want to show you. Have you time now?'

'Of course.' Not only did she long to be alone with him, she wanted an opportunity to ask her questions. She'd realised to her consternation that there was much she still didn't know about her husband.

These thoughts plagued her as they were carried in Donatus's comfortable litter through the crowded streets of Rome. Most of the city's inhabitants were busily about their tasks, heading for the baths or the markets or the shops along the narrow streets.

'Where are we going?' Severina couldn't tell because Lucan had ordered all the curtains closed around them.

Lucan's smile was mysterious. 'It's a secret. But we'll be there shortly. It's not far.'

As if the slaves carrying them had heard, they suddenly stopped and lowered the litter to the ground, rapping sharply against its wood frame to notify the occupants of their arrival.

Lucan took her hand. Severina drew in a breath, startled by the jolt of feeling that accompanied the contact.

Lucan felt it, too. 'Ah, love,' he whispered. 'You arouse me with the merest touch.' His eyes glowed with amusement, and his lips curved upwards. Severina's gaze moved to them. His mouth was beautiful, sensual. She was overcome by the sudden, powerful urge to push him back against the pillows and taste him.

His eyes darkened as if he read her thoughts. 'Now is not a good time, but I will make it up to you. Tonight. In the privacy of our chambers.' He reached up and opened the curtains. 'Look,' he said. 'My wedding gift to you.'

Framed like a huge and beautiful canvas before her was a magnificent building, three storeys tall and faced in shining white marble, resplendent with shaded porticoes and arches.

She scrambled from the litter to see it better.

It was still under construction, judging from the scaffolding that surrounded it and from the veritable army of labourers who moved like dark ants all around it.

'What *is* this place?'

Lucan came close behind and placed his large hands on her shoulders. He bent his head and touched warm lips to her neck. 'It's your new inn, built on the very spot of the one you lost to the flames. Onesimus did a miraculous amount of work while we were in Egypt.'

Because she couldn't respond, because she could only stand, gaping in astonishment, Lucan took her hand. 'Come. I'll show you the rest. It's not finished, but it's near enough that you'll get a fair idea.'

'Lucan?'

He turned to her, making a soft sound of distress when he saw that tears coursed down her cheeks, and gathered her into his arms.

'Why?'

He lifted her chin and kissed the salty trail of moisture on her face. 'I know you value your independence. Marrying me should not take that away from you.'

'But I don't really care about it any more. I'm content to be your wife. And anyway, I…' She bit her lip. 'I may not have enough time to run the inn, Lucan, not when the baby comes.' She glanced at his face. 'There *is* a baby coming. I'm almost sure of it.'

Lucan's expression softened. 'So my suspicions are confirmed.' He pulled her deeper into his embrace and sighed contentedly. 'I'm pleased. And I hope our first child will be a girl.'

'Not a son?'

'I know I could use an heir, but I'd really prefer a sweet little daughter, especially if she were as intelligent, as wilful, as impetuous…and as *beautiful* as you.'

'Oh, Lucan.'

He ended the embrace and pulled her forwards. 'But don't worry. You and I won't have to run the inn ourselves. Ariadne and Orthrus have already asked if they might do it. Of course, they'll need plenty of help. This building's much bigger than the last, with more rooms for guests and enough amenities to attract the most elite visitors to the city.'

'Can we afford this?'

'I told you, I've got some money put away.'

'How much money?'

He must have sensed something serious in her manner, because he stopped and looked directly into her face. 'I know I should have told you already. But every time I'm with you, there are other things I'd rather do than talk. Forgive me.' He lifted her hand and kissed her fingertips. 'I am heir to a large fortune. In addition, I've made another of my own by purchasing property and either renting it or selling it at a profit. Neither you nor any children we have will ever lack anything. You're now an incredibly rich woman, Livia Severina.'

He chuckled at the stricken look on her face. 'Don't look so distressed. I'm actually glad you didn't know. I wanted you to love me for myself, not because of my money or because my father's one of Emperor Trajan's most distinguished diplomats.'

'He *is*?'

'He's Governor of Pontus in Asia Minor, but he'll shortly be resigning the post. He and my mother plan to return to Rome by the end of the year. Probably they've been thinking they need to hurry me along, to make sure I get properly wed and started on making their heir. They'll be delighted to hear I've found a wife all on my own.'

He stroked his chin thoughtfully. 'My mother will *definitely* come when she hears you're with child. And so now I wonder…should I write her immediately or keep this secret just between us for a while?'

The mischief in his eyes made Severina laugh. 'Oh, my. Such a difficult choice, dutiful son that you are.'

He flashed her a roguish grin. 'Not difficult at all. I'm selfish and want you all to myself.' He placed a large, warm hand on Severina's abdomen and sighed. 'Until I absolutely must share, that is.'

Severina smiled at his rueful expression. 'How many rooms did you say there were in this new inn of ours?'

The change of topic surprised him. 'I don't know exactly. Around fifty, I think. I'll have to ask Onesimus.'

Severina leaned close, so that her breasts touched his chest. She was pleased with the sudden catch in his breath. 'Well, fifty should be enough,' she said, her eyes meeting his with a hot, seductive intensity.

He swallowed convulsively. 'Enough for what?'

'Enough for us to slip away from parents and baby for some passionate love-making whenever we want. I'm sure Orthrus and Ariadne would never, ever, tell on us.'

Lucan's hand lifted and then clenched as he realised he could hardly fondle his wife while standing beside a busy street. 'Ooh,' he said in a gravelly voice, 'I like this plan of yours. I like it a lot.'

Severina took his hand. 'Then, come, my love. Let's go in and choose our room.'

His laughter was low and masculine. 'Almost any will do. As long as there's a bed. Or a thick rug. Anywhere I can be alone with you.'

The warmth in his eyes touched her. There was more than passion there, more than the sexual excitement that had always existed between them. She saw friendship, tenderness, shared values and memories. Love.

Severina lifted a hand to stroke the firm line of his jaw. 'We must make sure there's a bathing room, too,' she whispered. 'One with couches. *Sturdy* couches that can take a lot of…abuse.'

Lucan lifted an eyebrow. 'Are you envisioning what I'm envisioning?'

'I don't know,' Severina said provocatively. 'Exactly what are you envisioning?'

'You…and me…on a couch together…'

'Yes?'

'…with one very large, very pregnant belly between us.'

Their sudden, shared outburst of laughter was enough to draw the attention of several nearby workers who grinned down at them from atop tall scaffolding.

Lucan took her hand. 'Come along, my sweet. Our inn, our room and our future. All await us.'

Severina sighed happily and let herself be pulled forwards, certain that with this man as her husband for a lifetime of shared dreams, that future would be full of adventure and joy.

* * * * *

HISTORICAL

Novels coming in September 2010

REAWAKENING MISS CALVERLEY
Sylvia Andrew

Lord Aldhurst rescues a cold, dazed lady one stormy night – and now the nameless beauty is residing in his home! Horrified at her growing feelings for her handsome protector, she flees to London, where she regains her status as the *ton*'s most sought-after debutante. Until she sees James's shocked and stormy face across a ballroom…

THE UNMASKING OF A LADY
Emily May

While she dances prettily by day, the *ton* doesn't know that by night Lady Arabella Knightley helps the poor – stealing jewels from those who court her for her money. Upon discovering it's Arabella, Adam St Just should be appalled. Instead, captivated by her beauty, he proposes to unbutton Lady Arabella… or unmask her!

CAPTURED BY THE WARRIOR
Meriel Fuller

With the country on the brink of anarchy, Bastien de la Roche will do what it takes to restore calm. So when he captures the spirited Alice Matravers, a servant to the royal court, he charms her into gaining an audience with the King. Could Alice's courage and kindness begin to mend Bastien's shattered heart…?

MILLS & BOON

HISTORICAL

Another exciting novel available this month:

LORD PORTMAN'S TROUBLESOME WIFE

Mary Nichols

Wanted: Wife and Mother

Homeless and penniless, Rosamund is forced to marry Harry, Lord Portman. In return for a comfortable life, she must produce an heir! But, far from sweeping her into his bed, Harry seems determined to keep her at arm's length!

His attraction to Rosamund unsettles Harry, and threatens the terms of their convenient marriage – and his undercover work bringing criminals to justice! Guilt over his first wife's death tortures Harry. But when Rosamund falls into danger, he has to find the courage to let go of the past and fight for the woman he loves…

The Piccadilly Gentlemen's Club
Seeking justice, finding love

 MILLS & BOON®

HISTORICAL

**Another exciting novel available
this month:**

THE DUKE'S GOVERNESS BRIDE

Miranda Jarrett

Prim governess

Former governess Jane Wood is on borrowed time – and she
doesn't want the fairytale of her Grand Tour to end. She
awaits the arrival of her employer, Richard Farren,
Duke of Aston, with trepidation…

Passionate mistress

To widower Richard, meek and mousy Miss Wood is
unrecognisable as the carefree and passionate Jane. Seeing
Venice through her eyes opens his mind and heart to romance!

Proper wife

Yet a sinister threat hangs over their new-found happiness: to
protect Jane, Richard will have to overcome the demons of his
past and persuade her to become his proper wife…

MILLS & BOON